I made my way around the building to the entrance with the padlock, and I pressed my ear against it. I could hear very faint sounds coming from inside. Voices. From their volume, they were coming from the other side of the building.

I had to shove hard with my shoulder to get the door open, and I moved quickly inside and closed it behind me, leaving myself in inky blackness. Somewhere at the other end of the building there was light, and the voices were louder now. I was evidently in some kind of hallway.

At the end of the corridor I went through an open doorway and found myself in an enormous storeroom. I could hear the voices more plainly. "Easy, man, don't tear the headliner. We wanna be able to sell this car..." I took the pistol out and held it loosely in my hand. There was no sense in not being prepared.

But there's no way to prepare for something crashing across the back of your neck with sickening force. A hot red pain spread across my shoulders and down my spine, and a vivid light engulfed me behind the eyes. I don't even remember hitting the floor....

DEEP SHAKER

DEEP SHAKER

LES ROBERTS

SMP

ST. MARTIN'S PAPERBACKS

This book is a work of fiction. Names, characters, places, and incidents are either the product of the author's imagination or are used fictitiously. Any resemblance to events or persons, living or dead, is purely coincidental.

DEEP SHAKER

Library of Congress Catalog Card Number: 91-7396

ISBN: 0-312-92795-9

Printed in the United States of America

St. Martin's Press hardcover edition/June 1991
St. Martin's Paperbacks edition/July 1992

10 9 8 7 6 5 4 3 2 1

For Jim and Eileen Terry Reed

1

THE sprawling mass that is Cleveland Municipal Stadium can be cold and uncomfortable at the best of times. In the winter —not the best of times—being there constitutes cruel and unusual punishment. On this particular November Sunday a freezing rain was drubbing the faithful football fans of northern Ohio, those small hard drops that sting your face and eyes, falling at a forty-five-degree angle, and most of it was finding its way down my collar. The temperature was about twenty-six above zero, and the wind howling in off Lake Erie sounded like an avenging Mongol horde. The Browns were in the process of blowing out the hated Pittsburgh Steelers, and for all intents and purposes the game had been decided at the end of the first quarter.

Matt Baznik and I had been friends since high school. He'd managed to snag thirty-yard-line tickets, one of the perks of his civil service job at the Department of Public Works, and when he'd called and begged me to join him, I couldn't think of a single reason to say no. So I had dragged myself out of bed—or out of my girlfriend Mary's bed, to be more precise —and met him at his house for the drive to the stadium. Mary's bed had been more fun—and warmer. Mary is the sales manager for Channel Twelve, a local TV station, and someone had offered her tickets to a Willie Nelson concert that Saturday night, but we'd spent the evening watching an old movie on the VCR and cuddling instead. Why should I waste an evening seeing someone who dresses worse than I do?

Like me, Matt Baznik is Slovenian, a big solid guy with a receding hairline, a roll of fat around his middle, and blue eyes that he squints as a result of the myopia that kept him off the school football team and out of the service. He was huddled in frigid misery in his car coat, draining his sixth beer, which undoubtedly added to his chill, cheering listlessly every time the Steelers fumbled or had a kick blocked, which seemed to be every few minutes or so. He didn't appear to be having a very good time.

"You want another beer, Milan?" he said. "Or maybe a sausage sangwidge?"

"I'm okay, Matt," I said. But I wasn't. I wished that pro football teams occasionally conceded games so we could go home, where it was warm and dry. But then the impossible happened—the Browns' offensive line grew suddenly porous and Bernie Kosar got sacked. The capacity crowd let out an outraged roar. In Cleveland it's unforgivable to lay unfriendly hands on our quarterback. Bernie Kosar is more than a popular sports figure or a mere celebrity; he is a local hero, an icon, a shining example of young American manhood. And at home, when Bernie gets sacked, it is simply not tolerated. A yellow penalty flag sailed through the soggy air and landed in the backfield, but none of us had to wait for the crime to be identified. No matter what they called it officially, we all knew it was fifteen yards for roughing the Deity.

While the referee paced off the penalty, Matt said to me, "Milan, I think I'm in trouble."

He was peering through his Coke-bottle-bottom glasses at the nonaction on the field, but from his distracted expression I doubted if he could have told anyone the score. The corners of his mouth were pulled down by invisible five-pound weights.

"What's the matter?"

He shrugged. "I can't talk here."

"Then let's go someplace where we can."

"Naw. You want to watch the game."

"There'll be other games. Come on." The weather had gotten

2

steadily wetter and colder, and I felt as though I'd just been paroled.

We made our way through the crowd, which was screaming in delight at the gift first down, and I was glad when we reached the shelter of the stadium's overhang, out of the pelting rain. The loonies who paint their faces brown and orange and sit bare-chested in defiance of the elements each week in that enclave near the end zone known as "the Dawg Pound" were barking like fox hounds.

We got into Matt's Plymouth after about ten minutes of wet and silent walking. When the engine warmed up, the blast of the car's heater was a benediction. Matt drove out of the jammed parking lot and onto the street.

"You want to go for a beer?" I said.

"Let's just drive around a little, okay?"

He turned east, the lake a roiling gray mud soup on our left, out the Shoreway and then along Lake Shore Boulevard, past the high-rise apartments that now stood on the old site of Euclid Beach Park, that magical place of amusement known to seven decades of Clevelanders as simply "the Beach," where Matt and I and our friends had gone to meet girls and ride the Thriller and Flying Turns and Laff-in-the-Dark, where I had encountered my first real fistfight and copped my first real feel. There isn't much left of the park now—a cement bridge from one of the old thrill rides is now part of the entryway to an apartment building—but it has long been rumored that some optimistic and sentimental citizens bought up the components of the old rides when the park closed in 1969 and stored them somewhere, in the hopes that someday there would be another Euclid Beach Park. The memories got to both Matt and me at the same time, and he turned and gave me one of his few smiles of the day.

Our original plan was to repair back to Matt's house after the game to have dinner with his family. He seemed distracted, a million miles away, but at least he was headed in the right direction. He chewed on his lower lip and peered out at the rain-slick streets through the rhythmic sweep of the wipers, and swung west again. He didn't seem to have a destination.

"What's up, Doc?" I said.

"I don't know what to do anymore. About Paulie."

Matt's son Paul was a year younger than my fifteen-year-old, and they had been playmates, combatants, and friends to one degree or another since before they could walk. At times when they were in grade school, Paulie had been over at our house so much I almost wondered which one was Milan Jacovich, Jr.

"What's the matter with Paulie?"

Matt steered through the madness that passed for a traffic pattern at University Circle, and past the various departments of Case Western Reserve University, past Severance Hall, the Newton E. Baker Memorial, the Art Museum, and the breathtakingly beautiful gothic Church of the Covenant, and headed up Mayfield Road through Little Italy. "He hardly ever comes home anymore, and he never tells us where he's going or who he's with. He's gotten really fresh to his mother, and me he won't talk to at all. He just grunts. He won't come out of his room, and if Rita Marie goes in there to clean he gets like a crazy man. He won't take out the garbage or dry the dishes. He's more like a boarder than our kid. It's real bad, Milan."

"It's just the age," I said. "They all do it. They start getting hair under their arms and think they can walk on the water. He'll grow out of it."

He shook his head forcefully. "It's more than that. Like he don't give a damn for anything anymore. You remember his dog?"

Once you'd seen him, you'd always remember the dog. For Paulie's tenth birthday, Matt had bought him a rottweiler puppy, which they'd named Croat in honor of the centuries-old friction between the Croatians and the Slovenians, with the expectation that he'd grow big and mean and serve as a protector for the boy. Croat had matured into an amiable monster whose most aggressive behavior was slobbering on those unfortunate enough to come within range of his pendulous dewlaps. Boy and dog had forged steel bonds of love on sight.

"Sure," I said. "The sprinkler that walks like a bear."

Matt shook a Winston out of his crumpled pack and ignited it with the dashboard lighter. "Well, Paulie don't even talk to him or play with him anymore. He even shuts him out of his

4

room. The big bastard just lays by Paulie's door and whimpers all night long."

"He's probably in there whacking off. Fourteen-year-olds have different priorities than the rest of us. Don't you remember when you were fourteen?"

"I wasn't like this, that's for sure. My father would've handed me my head."

I lit a cigarette of my own. I didn't really want one, but what with him smoking in the closed car, it was a matter of self-defense. The roaring heater fought to drown out the persistent tattoo of rain on the roof. "How long has this been going on, Matt?"

"Oh, since spring, I guess." He stuck the fingers of one hand under his glasses and rubbed his eyes. "It started getting bad in the spring and summer; now it's like there's a stranger in the house with us. I tried talking to him, I yelled at him—I even knocked him around once or twice. But I just see him slipping away."

"Don't you think you might be overreacting?"

"I don't know," he said. "I just don't know anymore."

"Teenagers are tough," I said, hunching down in my seat in a futile attempt to get warm. "There are times when I think Milan Jr. hates my guts. Other times the decent, funny kid we raised pokes his head through all the garbage and relates to us, and it's almost like old times again. You just have to get through it."

"Yeah, but there's other things. Like Paulie asked for a new stereo for Christmas. Well, he already had a stereo, and I told him that. He said he wanted a good one. Showed me an ad for some damn Japanese thing costs eight hundred dollars. I told him no way, and he went out and bought one for himself."

"For eight hundred dollars?"

"He told me he got it used from some other kid, but I don't believe him."

"I can't see Paulie stealing a stereo."

"Me neither. I think he bought it all right. But where did he get the money?"

"Doesn't he have a job after school and weekends?" It sounded silly even as I said it.

5

"Delivering pizza. Could you save up eight hundred dollars for a stereo you didn't really need delivering pizza?"

"I couldn't save up eight hundred dollars *now*," I said.

"I think Paulie's into something really shitty, and it's scaring hell out of us."

It sounded shitty to me, too, but I didn't want to tell Matt. The sadness in his eyes was leaking out and casting a further pall over a day already daubed in grim shades of gray. I reached over and switched on the radio, which was tuned to Magic 105, but it didn't help any. It certainly didn't do anything to improve my frame of mind.

My heart went out to Matt Baznik. I was a part-time parent these days, trying every other weekend to come up with meaningful and fun activities for two boys who were four years apart in age, making sure I gave each of them a certain amount of private time so they could talk to me of their fears and problems and triumphs and failures and dreams. And with every fortnight that passed, I became just that much more alien to them, a father who lived six miles away. I had watched in helpless anguish this last year as Milan Jr. grew apart from me like a ship pulling away from the dock.

Fatherhood of a boy—which is the only kind I know—is a bear at the best of times. They hand you this little bundle of squalling, peeing humanity and tell you that for the next twenty years it's your job to not only feed and clothe and house it, but to raise it up into adulthood with a sense of responsibility, morality, and decency. You're supposed to teach it to fish and to swing a baseball bat, to impress on it that school is good and necessary, stealing is bad, and hurting other people is wrong, and you try getting it to respect women, its elders, and the dignity of all living things. You point out that some day it will have to leave the nest and it better learn from you the lessons that will enable it to hunt and forage for itself, and through all this you have to somehow convince it that you are all-wise and all-knowing and what you're saying is the True Word.

And then this hunk of protoplasm that sprang from your loins in a moment of careless abandon starts feeling its own hormones expanding and banging against one another like bumper cars. It gets into high school to find its peer group is cutting math class, smoking in the john, and feeling girls up, and all of a sudden the guys in woodshop are the cool, "rad" ones and you're just an aging, stupid asshole who's losing his hair.

"Is there anything I can do, Matt?" I had to make the offer first; Matt would have died before he asked me.

He mumbled his answer in a voice so low I could hardly hear. "Could you maybe try and talk to him tonight? He might open up to you where he won't to me. I mean, you're like family anyway."

This was obviously why he'd invited me to the football game; it would forever remain unspoken, but it was tacitly understood. I traced my finger across the condensation our breath had misted on the car window, feeling the wetness through my knit glove. "I can try. I'm not the number-one father figure in town these days, but I'll give it a shot."

He allowed me a half smile of gratitude. Yugoslavian men are not comfortable showing their emotions, especially to other men, and I knew how hard it was for Matt to ask for help. I hoped that little smile would be the end of it, because neither of us wanted to talk about it any further.

We pulled into the driveway beside the Bazniks' brick house in Euclid. Matt had suspended a basketball hoop over the garage door years ago for Paulie, and knowing what I now knew, it seemed sad and poignant and pointless in the rain. When it comes to our kids, most of us don't believe there will ever be a rainy day.

Croat pounded out from his shelter under the steps and greeted us. The dog was a leaner, pressing his hundred-pound bulk against my legs while I petted him hello, and he shook himself all over, spraying rain and strings of saliva in every direction. I took an extra long time rumpling his soft ears, knowing that he must be aching for the attention he used to get from his young master, which was now being withheld from him. How do you explain to a dog that the human he's idolized since puppyhood has turned into a sullen and silent jerk?

We walked in the kitchen door and were assailed by the unmistakable aroma of *punjena snicla*, Serbian stuffed veal, and I was glad I hadn't eaten much at the ball game. Rita

7

Marie, Matt's wife, looked momentarily confused, glancing from us to the little black-and-white TV set on the counter, where the football game we had left was still in progress.

"It got too cold and wet for us to stay," I explained to forestall any questions, and kissed the rosy cheek she offered me. Rita Marie had gone to school with us too, but Matt had fallen in love with her about seventy pounds ago. She now looked like a cocktail waitress in a neighborhood bowling alley.

She said, "Twenty years ago a little rain wouldn't have made you guys leave a Browns game."

"Twenty years ago we were dumb," I said, peeling off my wet coat and hanging it on the rack by the door. "Is coffee on?" The question was rhetorical. The only time coffee wasn't on in the Baznik kitchen was at four o'clock in the morning. She fixed steaming mugs for both of us; black for me, and loaded with cream and sugar and calories for Matt.

"Where's the kid?" he said.

Rita Marie frowned, vaguely waving a hand. "He said he'd be back for dinner."

He looked pointedly at me, and the two of us repaired to the living room. The furniture had been of good quality when it was new thirty years ago. Most of it I remembered from when Matt and I were kids. The football game was showing in there on a larger color TV. It didn't improve the quality of the play any. Fumbles and stumbles were the name of the game.

"Back for dinner," Matt mumbled. There was a bitterness in his voice that disturbed me. "Where the hell is he on a rainy Sunday like this?"

"He's probably watching the game at a buddy's house."

"Nah. He don't even give a shit about the Browns now." There was a touch of wonder in his voice; disinterest in the Browns was the strongest indictment yet of a kid from the East Side of Cleveland. "I'm telling you, Milan, something bad's going down."

"Let's just wait and see, okay?"

He slurped angrily at his mug as though everything that was askew in his life was the coffee's fault. Sitting in his favorite upholstered chair, big as he was, he seemed somehow diminished, his family problems pressing him down like an anvil.

Then he said, "You never have any problems with your kids, do you?"

"Sure I do. I told you, Milan Jr. can be pretty damn stubborn when he wants to be. Of course, Lila catches most of the crap because she's there with him every day."

Matt said, "How do the boys get along with Joe?"

I stared down at a little amoeba-shaped rainbow of oil floating on top of the black coffee. I put the mug down on the end table. "All right," I said.

"I don't know if I could take that, Milan; another man raising my kids."

"He's not raising my kids!" I answered with some heat. "He's living with their mother. My kids are *my* kids, and I'm the only father they've got!"

"I'm sorry, I didn't mean to piss you off."

"You didn't piss me off," I said, pissed off.

I slumped back against the sofa cushions and watched as the two-minute warning sounded at the Stadium, but the crudely-played game didn't hold my attention. It kills me that wimpy Joe Bradac is living in my house and watching my sons grow up while I'm halfway across town in a rented apartment. The boys, Milan Jr. and Stephen, have been what's kept me going since they were born, and not having them with me hurts so bad that most of the time I just sweep the ache under my emotional rug so I won't have to deal with it. I'm not mad at Joe Bradac for being there, although he's never going to be my best friend; I just hate it that I don't have more time to spend with my sons. They grow up so damn *fast*.

The fact that Joe is openly cohabiting with my ex-wife, Lila, doesn't annoy me at all any longer. I care deeply for Lila as a person, and I probably always will, but whatever romantic love we shared when we were young sputtered and turned cold a few years after I got back from Vietnam, and all that's left is the caring friendship of two people who have shared most of their adult lives together. Whomever she might be sleeping with, it hardly bothered me a bit. Mainly because I had a new someone in my own life, a golden angel named Mary Soderberg, who has blue eyes and Swedish cheekbones and is ten years too young and ten times too pretty for me, and who'd made the

9

last nineteen months of my life seem like only nineteen minutes, the most joyful nineteen minutes I'd ever known.

The front door opened, admitting a blast of cold, damp air, and then slammed shut again, hard, and Paulie started up the stairs two at a time, dark hair rain-plastered to his skull.

"Hey!" Matt barked, an uncharacteristic meanness in his tone. Paulie took another double step up, then thought better of it and stopped.

"Where you been?"

Paulie shoved his hands into the back pockets of his jeans. "With the guys," he said, barely audible.

"Don't you say hello to Mr. Jacovich?" I would have preferred him to call me by my first name—Jacovich is a mouthful for anyone, even another Slovenian—but his father insisted on the formality.

Paulie looked at me for the first time, and there was a softening of the sullen cast of his features, so slight as to be nearly unnoticeable. We'd always been pals. "Hiya," he said.

"Whaddaya say, Paul?"

Apparently not much, because he tossed his head and continued up the stairs. I noticed as his top half disappeared that the cuffs of his jeans were sopping wet.

"See what I mean?" Matt said.

"Frankly, no. He's fourteen years old; you expect him to run in and give Daddy a big kiss, for God's sake?"

Matt put his face in his hands. "Jesus, Milan, go talk to him, will you? He's always respected you. Talk to him. I don't know what to do anymore."

I went back out into the kitchen and lifted the lid of the simmering pot on the stove to take a sniff. In the neighborhood, Rita Marie Baznik's punjena snicla was almost a legend.

"Get away from there," she warned, waving a cooking spoon at me. "Don't go sticking your dirty fingers in there."

"Mmmm. I've been looking forward to this all day, Rita Marie. I hope you made a lot."

"Don't I always?"

I refilled my coffee cup and began ascending the narrow stairway to Paulie's room. It was a long damn trip.

THERE wasn't much to the second floor of the house. As in most houses of that era, circa 1937, a miniscule central hallway upstairs opened onto three bedrooms. Matt and Rita Marie occupied the largest one, Paulie another, and the room in the middle was a catchall for storage and the rare house guest. Although the layout of the house was similar to the one in which I grew up, and not all that different from the house I had lived in during my marriage, standing in that minihallway still made me a bit claustrophobic. Maybe it was because I was so uncomfortable with the role that had been thrust on me all of a sudden by one of my oldest friends. It was tough enough having man-to-man talks with my own kids; playing Judge Hardy with someone else's was going to be no picnic.

I stood outside Paulie's room for far longer than was really necessary. Then I took a gulp of my warmed-up coffee and knocked. Through the door I could hear sudden frenzied activity, the scuffle of sneaker-clad feet on the wood floor, and the slamming of a drawer.

"Yuh?" I heard him say from inside, his voice muffled as if he was talking into a pillow.

"It's Milan, Paul. Can I come in?"

There was a long pause, and then he unbolted his door and opened it with an abruptness that almost made me spill my

11

coffee. Paulie was a skinny malink, fair-complected and dark-haired, wiry under his high school sweatshirt. He still wore his damp Levi's, but he had dried his hair with a towel, leaving it uncombed and wildly tangled. His face seemed flushed, almost feverish, and his nose was red and running slightly.

I went past him into the room, noting that he was about three inches taller than I'd remembered him. Sometimes it seems as if kids that age just go into the other room and grow. "I wanted to visit a little bit, Paul. I haven't seen you for a long time. You grew up on me while I wasn't looking."

He didn't say anything, but my remark didn't seem to call for a response; it was one of those dumb things adults say to kids, and I silently cursed the banality of it. I looked around the room. The single bed Paul had slept in since he was five had been ineptly made and covered with a spread of vaguely Navajo design, and there were lots of clothes on the floor. Posters of heavy-metal rock groups with names like Anthrax and Slayer adorned the walls, and a student desk was piled high with indeterminate cloth objects I assumed were more clothes, T-shirts and underwear, blocking the screen of the portable TV set. In one corner was the new sound equipment, almost glowing with its own importance, flanked by two enormous Dolby speakers, with a CD player and tape decks and equalizers and a remote control unit and lights that danced to the music, looking as though a bachelor's degree in audio engineering might be the minimum requirement for operating it. It was a powerful sound system more appropriate for a big, sprawling family den than a tiny second-floor bedroom, and I imagined that if the slight Paulie ever turned it on full volume it would blast him through the wall.

I sat down on the edge of the bed. The boy stood with his back against the door, his arms folded across his bony chest, but he was far from immobile. His whole body seemed to vibrate to a frequency no one else could hear, and his jaws worked on a piece of gum he didn't have in his mouth. The body language told me I wasn't particularly welcome there in his sanctuary, but he didn't possess enough maturity to do anything about it.

"Lousy weather to be out in," I observed. "Did you watch any of the game?"

"Nah," he said with a vehement shake of his head, as if football was for little kids.

"Boy, the Steelers really stink this year. Their special teams killed them today."

His feet didn't move, but his eyes flickered around the room looking for either a hidden escape hatch or a saviour. He wasn't going to make this comfortable for me.

"So what are you up to these days, Paul? Just hanging out with the guys?"

"Sometimes."

"You see Milan much?"

"Around, at lunch." He sniffled.

"God, I remember when you and Milan were little. You used to come over almost every day after school, and the three of us would sit around on the living room floor playing the Uncle Wiggily game. Remember that?"

He didn't answer, but hugged himself tighter. Most kids hate anecdotal reminiscences of their younger days, as though having been little and cute and cuddly and loving is something never to be talked about and better left forgotten.

"Nice stereo," I said, nodding at the electronic monster in the corner. I had the feeling it was looking back at me. "New?"

"Yuh," he said. A spasm jerked his shoulders, and he began moving around in hopes I hadn't noticed. His eyes glittered with an unnatural brightness, the pupils big and dark. They ceaselessly investigated the room in erratic flickers, looking first at the door, then at the desk drawer, but never at me.

I said, "How are you doing in school? Everything all right?"

He shrugged. "Yuh."

"Even math?"

His head bobbed as if it were attached to the rest of his body by a rubber band, and he crossed his arms again, rubbing his biceps with his hands.

"You didn't go out for football this year."

"Nah."

"How come?"

He hunched his shoulders, which I suppose meant that there was no particular reason, or the reason was none of my business. Either way, no answer was forthcoming.

13

"I guess your job at the pizza place keeps you pretty busy during your spare time, huh?" The strain of my near monologue was beginning to tell on me.

"Yuh."

"It's good to have a job, though. Gives you enough bread to buy the things you want, and keeps a guy out of trouble, right?"

Paulie suddenly crossed the room in three long steps—everything he did seemed to be sudden, as though he had just thought of it and it was of the utmost urgency. He rummaged through the pile of clothes on the desk until he found what he was looking for. He held up a school textbook wrapped in one of those brown paper covers with the high school's name printed on it in the varsity colors. "I gotta study," he said.

"Right. Listen, Paul, I'll have the boys with me next weekend. We usually manage to have some fun. Maybe you could come with us, huh? The four of us do something?"

"I dunno."

"I promise we won't play Uncle Wiggily." I held for the laugh. I should have brought something to read while I waited.

From his blank expression I wasn't even sure he heard me. "The Cavs are at home Saturday. Or maybe a movie. And we can go to the video arcade afterwards and play some games. How's that sound?"

"I dunno. I might have to work," he said. It was his longest speech of the afternoon.

I got to my feet, awkward as a dancing bear. "Well, let me know so I can get Cavs tickets, all right?"

He bobbed his head again and filled his chest with air and then expelled it loudly, an obvious sigh of relief. I said, "Everything's okay with you, isn't it, Paul? I mean, you got anything you need to rap about?"

"Nuh-uh."

What a surprise. "I know it's hard to talk to your parents sometimes, so if you want to bounce anything off me, just give me a call, okay?" I tried to smile. "I only yell at my own kids."

"Yuh," he said.

He seemed so anxious for me to leave that it would have been the worst kind of cruelty not to. Heading down the stairs, balancing my coffee mug so I didn't spill any on the dusty rose carpeting, I heard him shoot the bolt on his bedroom door behind me, a prisoner locking down his own cell.

Matt looked a question at me when I came back into the living room, but I shook my head, letting my eyes move toward the kitchen, where Rita Marie was putting the finishing touches on our meal. I wanted to talk to Matt alone first. I was feeling a little queasy, and not even the aroma of stuffed veal wafting through the house was going to help my appetite. It's tough to give your friends bad news.

* * *

Paulie decided not to join the family for dinner, even though Rita Marie went up and tried to convince him through the closed door. She used all the time-tested arguments, from "It's your favorite" to "You're going to get sick if you don't eat," but she didn't get very far. I suppose she'd known ahead of time she wouldn't change his mind, but the motherhood manual mandates such exercises in futility. From the living room Matt and I could hear her entreaties and Paulie's muffled responses. Finally he shouted, "Get outta my face, okay?" and Matt started to rise from his chair, an angry flush suffusing his usually pale skin.

I reached out and laid a restraining hand on his arm. "Let it go, Matt. You'll only make it worse."

He took a second to make the decision and then deflated into his chair, but the flush didn't go away. For the rest of the evening it stayed on his face like a port wine stain. The knots of muscle where his jaws hinged together jumped and pulsated, which happens when you grind your back teeth. A bomb was ticking away somewhere in the Baznik household, and no one knew what specific act might unexpectedly set off the charge.

Rita Marie came downstairs, her face screwed up in that particular way mothers have when they're trying not to cry. "I guess it's just three for dinner," she said too brightly. "More for us, right?" Her hands twisted her flowered apron in a gallant effort to keep control. "Matt, come help me set the table."

Left alone in the homey clutter of the living room, I watched the network NFL wrap-up without really seeing it. I was thinking of Paulie upstairs, and of my own sons, and frustration

15

rose in my gut and formed a ridge against my Adam's apple, that helplessness so familiar to those of us who have children and realize that the world is moving so much faster than we'd like it to, and not always in the right direction. And fear, too, that my friend's boy was into something he might not be able to handle.

Growing up has been tough enough at any time in recorded history. But add to the usual problems the easy availability of drugs and of casual sex that is there for the taking but not the understanding, and the marauding gangs of thugs who would just as soon kill as not to protect their real or imagined turf, and being a teenager in urban America is no barefoot idyll anymore. Father no longer knows best, because he's having an affair with his secretary and smacks Margaret around at home on Saturday night; Bud is the warlord of a street gang, Princess has a fifty-dollar-a-day crack habit, and Kitten drops her panties for every guy in biology class.

Dinner would have been a quiet affair if not for Rita Marie's hyperkinetic chatter. Like a radio disk jockey who can't stand a moment of silence, she felt obliged as hostess to fill in any conversational gaps with trivial reports about her church group, her recent rare foray to the West Side, and the rising prices in the supermarket. Since she was not blessed with a melodious voice in the first place, her running commentary had all the charm of fingernails on a blackboard, made bearable only by her generous pourings of *slivovitz*. It might have been my imagination, but the colorless brandy tasted a bit more bitter than usual. Matt ate in vulturine fashion, his head down and his shoulders hunched, the color rising and fading in quarter-size spots on his cheeks. I tried to give the impression that I wasn't picking at my food. It was a waste of a great *punjena snicla*.

Just as coffee and dessert was being served, the whole house rocked with a blast of sound: Paulie had turned on his new sound system. The heavy-metal beat made the wineglasses in the cupboard vibrate and the brown family daguerreotypes that Matt's grandparents had brought from Ljubljana dance in their frames on the wall. It also made further conversation impossible.

Matt's flush turned from red to purple, and he lunged from his seat and thundered up the stairs to pound a heavy fist on Paulie's door. "Turn that down!" he bellowed. "I'll bust the door in and throw the damn thing out the window. Turn it down *now*!" On the last few words his voice became a croak as he ran out of breath, unable to sustain such a long, loud roar.

The music, if you could call it that, was cut off in mid note, and we could hear Paulie yell, "Lemme alone!" Then there was more shouting as Matt demanded entry, the sound of the door opening and slamming, male voices raised overlapping one another in anger, and finally a retort as sharp as a pistol shot, the sound made by a good hard slap in the face.

Rita Marie stared into her coffee for whatever auguries she might find there, worrying the pink lipstick off her mouth. We didn't look at each other. Finally Matt stomped back down the stairs into the dining room and sat at his place, his large hands two rocks on either side of his dessert plate. It would have taken a stronger man than I to pry those fists apart, and I used to be a defensive lineman at Kent State.

"Jesus," he whispered, his simple mind filled with confusion.

"More pie, Milan?" The question was too loud, too bright.

"Thanks, Rita Marie, I couldn't eat another bite." I pushed my plate a few inches toward the center of the table.

"I'm afraid we're pretty crappy hosts tonight," she said.

I tried to make it easier for her. "We've known each other twenty-five years or so. I guess the friendship can stand up under a little family squabble."

"Squabble my ass!" Matt growled. "This is like a goddamn war—Adolf Hitler alive and living upstairs!"

"Matthew!" Rita Marie said.

"It is, and you know it. The little rat never has a word for anyone, stays out all the time, spends money like it was going out of style while I work my ass off all week long for—"

"Matt, come on," I said, touching his arm. The muscles were taut and quivered beneath my fingers. I squeezed.

"Who the hell made him king?" he bleated. "Goddamn punk, I'll knock some of that meanness right the hell out of him."

"That's no answer," I said. "Look, I'm just in the way here. Let me call a cab—"

"I'll drive you home."

"That's okay. I—"

"That was the deal!" Matt said with finality. "I drive you home. It stopped raining, so don't make a big thing out of it."

I thanked Rita Marie and said good night, kissing her soft plump cheek and giving her an extra hug that was probably no reassurance whatever, and struggled into my coat. It was giving off the not unpleasant smell of damp wool, but the collar felt clammy against the back of my neck. We went out through the kitchen door into the darkness of the driveway, the yellow light from the window giving only the illusion of warmth. Croat squirmed out from his nest under the steps and galloped toward us, thrilled at the prospect of human contact.

"Get away!" Matt growled. "You're all wet and muddy! Go on, beat it!"

The rottweiler screeched to a halt like a dog in an animated cartoon, blinking his big eyes. Then, cowed and hurt, he lowered his head and put his belly as close to the cement as he could to slither back to his sleeping place. Matt watched him go. "Poor bastard," he said. "Nobody gives a shit if he lives or dies. Poor big bastard." I figured he wasn't really talking about Croat.

I put my gloves on as Matt backed the Plymouth slowly down the narrow driveway, but they didn't help much. I hadn't really felt warm since I'd left my own house that morning, the downside of living in the Midwest. He headed toward Cleveland Heights, his jaws clamped together, the car a deadly missile with Matt guiding it. He said, "So?"

"I don't know, Matt, I'm no psychologist."

"Don't bullshit me, okay? We've been friends too long for you to give me bullshit. Now, you talked to him. Whaddaya think?"

"I can't be sure . . ."

"You're sure, and so am I. And we both know it. It's drugs, isn't it? Am I right or what?"

During winter storms, the cold air collects under the many bridges of Cleveland, making the surfaces icy and slick, but

Matt was in no mood to make adjustments. The little Plymouth fishtailed and skidded, but he wrestled it straight again the way a horse trainer would a spirited stallion. I guess he felt that his automobile was the only thing in his life he still had control over. It was better than nothing.

I said, "That'd be my guess. But that's all it is—a guess."

"Right," he said bitterly. "A guess. God, I'd like to kill the little son of a bitch!"

He coasted to a stop where Cedar Road meets Fairmount Boulevard in a lopsided triangle in front of my apartment building. I opened the passenger door, and when the dome light went on he leaned his forehead against his gloved hands on the steering wheel. "What am I supposed to do now?"

"I know what you shouldn't do, and that's go home and punch Paulie around. Hang on for a little bit, and let me see what I can figure out."

"What the hell can *you* do?"

"I don't know. But you stay cool and don't get stupid. Be kind to Rita Marie, too; she needs your support and you need hers. And Paulie needs the both of you. That's what families are, Matt."

He attempted a smile but managed only a pathetic imitation. "Families," he said. "I used to have one of those."

"You still have one of those, schmuck, and don't start thinking otherwise. Just give me a day or two, all right?"

He shook his head. "Like I've got a choice."

"We've always got choices, Matt." I got out of the car, then turned back and leaned in. "Thanks for dinner. And for the tickets."

"Lousy game," he mused. "The Browns weren't really that sharp today. It's like Pittsburgh beat themselves. Funny, isn't it, Milan, but that's what it always boils down to. No one else can ever really get us down; we always beat ourselves."

I watched as the Plymouth went racketing up Cedar and took the curve at the top of the hill, disappearing from sight. I ached for Matt at the thought of the perceived paternal failure that tortured him, the phantoms that were nibbling at his viscera, and what I hadn't bothered to tell him, which he'd probably figure out for himself pretty soon: Paulie was not only using drugs, but the fact that he had so much ready cash to spend on a stereo and whatever else was a fair indication that he was dealing them, too.

Little Paulie, who had practically grown up playing Uncle Wiggily in my living room, was in drug trouble. Somewhere along the line he had taken a bad turn on his journey down the Bunny Trail and had gotten too close to the lair of the Bad Pipsissewah.

3

MONDAY morning was a study in November gray, and it was sad to think that the sun had probably kissed Cleveland goodbye for the winter. I made myself a pot of coffee and read the paper before I phoned Lila. It's a sorry admission, but talking to my ex-wife usually calls for some sort of fortification beforehand. In the mornings, it's strong coffee. The older Lila gets, the feistier she becomes, living up to the reputation Serbs have of being warlike. Every one of our conversations lately, no matter how mundane, always ends up in a slightly confrontational mode. Usually it has to do with the boys, but sometimes not. Lila is on the defensive, probably for installing Joe Bradac in the household as her live-in consort, and I can't even mention his name without setting off one of Lila's near legendary temper tantrums, not even to say, "How's Joe?"

There is some justification in that, I suppose, because I don't care how Joe is, ever, and Lila knows it.

So I drank three cups of coffee and read the account of the game I'd suffered through the day before, eating several handfuls of cornflakes dry out of the package because I'd forgotten to buy milk, and when it got to be nine o'clock and I was sure Joe had left for work, I dialed the phone number that used to be mine and was still listed in the directory under my name.

After we'd gone through the hellos and how are yous that

21

sound so damn empty when you are talking to someone to whom you've been married half your life, I said, "Lila, I'd like to take Milan Jr. tonight."

"It's Monday," she said. Lila is always full of informational nuggets like that.

"I know."

"It's a school night."

"I know. He can do his homework this afternoon, and I'll drive him to school in the morning."

"I don't like him to be away from the house on school nights."

"Lila, he's not going to some biker bar, he'll be with me. At my place. We'll get a pizza and watch the Monday night game and I'll see he goes straight to bed after."

"What about Stephen?"

"This is just me and Milan," I said.

"Stephen's going to be very hurt."

That probably wasn't true. It would have been, a year ago, but now my younger son was growing up and finding his own identity and didn't need his father's attention the way he used to. I said, "I'll take Stephen alone some other night."

She paused for a moment, and I could hear her going through the cigarette-lighting ritual that was so familiar to me after so many years of listening to it. When she spoke, I could imagine the smoke issuing from her mouth with her words. Talking on the phone and smoking was one of Lila's less endearing habits. "I don't like this, Milan, breaking the routine this way. It upsets the whole household."

I didn't say anything. Her oblique reference to Joe Bradac as "the whole household" was designed to get under my skin. For a change, it didn't. Besides, I've known Lila long enough to realize she wasn't quite finished.

"And it upsets the boys."

"You think eating a pizza with his father is going to traumatize him?"

"That's easy for you to say; you aren't here for the day-to-day like I am. Children need a pattern, they need consistency."

I settled back and waited for Lila's litany of the problems of raising two sons alone, which I'd just about committed to memory and which she trots out at the least provocation. She didn't

22

disappoint me. I checked the other football scores in the paper, noting with satisfaction that Cincinnati had lost. When she was finished, I said, "Lila, I wouldn't ask if it weren't important."

Her tone changed, her maternal antenna alert. "Why? Is anything wrong?"

"Nothing's wrong with Milan Jr. I just need a little teenage input about something, and since I have my own teenager, I thought maybe we could spend a few hours together. Why must you make such a big deal out of everything?"

I immediately wished I could have snatched the words back, because it set her off on another lecture about parenting and responsibility. I tuned it out because I'd heard it all before. When the word storm finally settled, we agreed that I would pick my son up at six thirty, thus giving him plenty of time to do his homework, and we hung up on a more or less amicable note. I admit to feeling a little drained after it was all over, but Lila has that effect on me.

I cleared up a few odds and ends of paperwork lying around on the desktop, sent out some statements, paid a few bills. I'm not the most organized guy in the world when it comes to things of that nature and have long considered hiring a part-time secretary-bookkeeper to help me stay caught up. But I don't like the idea of a stranger poking around in my private life, knowing my business and tracking my comings and goings, so I've never made the move. Since I make my living poking around in the private lives of other people, I suppose I'm a bit sensitive on the subject. Also, I work at home, and if I had an assistant I'd have to keep the joint picked up for company seven days a week.

I put on a clean shirt, a plaid sports jacket, cord slacks, and one of my too-wide ties that Mary always kids me about, shrugged into my car coat, and drove west toward downtown. I was still getting used to the feel of my new Pontiac Sunbird —my old gray Chevy Caprice station wagon, which I had accepted from a client in lieu of payment, had been totaled in an accident the summer before.

It had rained itself out overnight, and although the sky was still gray and foreboding, the streets were cleaner because of the storm and the temperature was somewhere in the middle thirties. On the front lawns of Cleveland Heights, fallen leaves chased each other around in the wind, playful kittens of winter.

I stopped at a mailbox and deposited my morning's work, and then headed for the high school, where I'd spent three years of my adolescence tracking the changes happening in my body and the often frightening changes going on in my head. They were years of sometimes rude awakening, of triumph and angst, years spent agonizing over the random pimple, and in mute and unrequited lust for the pretty blonde who sat across from me in biology class, spent exulting in the adrenaline-pumping false power that being a star football player can bring. The old Beach Boys' entreaty to "Be True to your School" had been my rallying cry then, when idealism mixed smoothly with platitudes to form the soup in which our unformed psyches stewed.

My old high school nestles in a neighborhood of two-story frame houses painted a variety of winter grays and blues. The school is constructed of yellowish brick that has faded to drab after some seventy Ohio winters, with gray concrete around the windows and doors. A medieval arch frames the main entrance, and the school's name is carved across the top in Roman-looking letters. A big circular red brick smokestack towers high above the two-story building at the side.

Bleak hedges, denuded by the cold, separate the hibernating lawn from the sidewalk. The athletic practice field, surrounded by a four-foot-high chain link fence that would serve neither to keep the inmates in nor intruders out, looked barren and forlorn after the previous day's rain. Bare scrub oaks, almost black with wetness, watched over the wire batting cage and the rusted trash bin half open behind it. The school had been old when I attended, and now my own son and Paulie Baznik were sneaking cigarettes in the same washroom where Matt and I had puffed them twenty-five years before, and there was something about the symmetry of it that appealed to me. I felt a twinge of pity for those of my generation who had become creatures of the corporate, transferring halfway across the country to another milieu to keep their jobs, leaving their roots and their memories behind them.

My wristwatch told me it was eleven fourteen, one minute before the start of "early lunch," a peculiarly subtle torture for those unlucky enough to be assigned to it, who would then have another three hours to go before the school's prison doors swung open. Milan Jr. had complained bitterly of being stuck with the early break period this year, and Paulie had mentioned to me in his monosyllabic conversation of the night before that he saw Milan at lunch, so I knew I was at the right place at the right time. I parked across the street from the practice field and shifted in the seat so I could see out the side window, lighting a Winston. I could hear the muffled jangle of the school bell from inside the building, and within a few minutes the student body, or that portion of it cursed with early lunch, poured out through the doors in a boisterous, chattering stream, liberated, at least for forty minutes.

The fashions were a bit different than in my day; the girls wore more extreme makeup, the boys' hair was shorter than it had been in the sixties, and about a third of the young faces were black or brown, where years ago there had been fewer than twenty in the whole school, but the scene was comfortably familiar to me, and I had an urge to get out of the car and join them, to complain of the rigors of algebra and the unreasoning stupidity of my English teacher, Mrs. Croton, to my pals Marko Meglich and Sonja Kokol and Alex Cerne. And Matt.

The kids broke up into almost entirely racially and sexually segregated groups of five or six, the occasional male-female couple strolling together, the boy's hand invariably on the back of the girl's neck in a public declaration of possession more effective than a PRIVATE PROPERTY sign. Most of them broke open lunch boxes or brown paper bags stuffed with sandwiches and chips and ate standing up or leaning against the fence. Almost all of them were talking too loudly and making animated gestures; all teenagers are attention pigs, especially when among their peers, vying to see who can make the most noise and attract the most notice. The males strutted and bopped in the way of adolescent boys everywhere; females giggled and chattered among themselves, either boy-watching or making a big show of ignoring their opposite numbers. They weren't fooling anyone. Their new awareness of their bodies and their denim-clad or black-stockinged legs and fresh, laughing faces could make a dirty old man of a celibate saint.

25

My son came out the door in the center of a flying wedge of boy-humanity. He was the tallest in his group, the dark Serbian good looks he'd inherited from his mother's side of the gene pool and his broad shoulders and impossibly small ass drawing the eyes of every girl on the field. He had made the frosh football team as a wide receiver, he had a B-minus average, and from the way the kids around him looked up at him and hung on his every word, he was obviously their leader. Despite his practice of speaking to adults only when absolutely necessary, he was a good kid, and I felt a surge of parental pride in spite of myself.

But I hadn't come here to see Milan Jr.

It took me a few moments to spot Paulie, because he wasn't anywhere I expected him to be. He was standing close to a knot of older, taller kids. They were all black, dressed a bit flashier than the other students, in clothes that might have been featured in a bad-taste edition of *Rolling Stone*—fringed fake-leather jackets and gang-banger caps with pompons, black and purple nylon shirts with gold threads running through them and high-topped sneakers with the last three eyelets ignored. They walked with the supreme confidence of a well-organized hunting pack on their own turf. Paulie kind of moped around on their periphery as if waiting for one of them to talk to him, but except for an occasional disdainful look they pretty much ignored him. His eagerness for acceptance was almost painful to watch.

I was trying to figure out what he was doing with this group in the first place. Integration between the races was a fact of life, even in schools on the east side of Cleveland, but for some reason this particular tableau was striking me wrong. I watched for a few minutes until Paulie said something to one of the other boys, a gangling youth with an earring and black leather pants. The kid turned, grabbed Paulie by the front of his jacket and pulled him close, snarled something, and tossed him away as he might a too eager puppy. There was no menace in the gesture—it was more like contempt. Paulie seemed almost ready to cry, but he bit the emotion back and tried to look nonchalant, as if nothing had happened. He continued to hang around on the fringe of the pack, for some reason preferring

26

his status here as an outsider to seeking recognition with the kids he knew, like Milan Jr. and his crowd.

All at once an expanse of brown corduroy car coat blocked my view through the window, and I hunched down and peered up to see a black man around my age standing in the street by my car. He wore a brown tweed suit, a tan shirt, and a brown and green tie under the open coat, and a pair of horn-rimmed glasses sat on the bridge of his wide freckled nose. He rapped sharply on the window with the kind of authority that led me to think I'd better open it.

"Help you?" he said, but his tone wasn't friendly.

"With what?"

"May I ask you what you're doing here?"

"That all depends on why you want to know."

"My name is Reggie Parker," he told me. Each word came out of his mouth in little puffs of vapor. "I'm the principal here."

I opened the door and got out of the car. When the principal speaks, you're supposed to stand up and be respectful.

"I'm Milan Jacovich. My son is one of your students."

He looked at me for a moment, and then he stuck out his hand. "I know your boy. Football player, weren't you?"

"I'm flattered you remember, Mr. Parker."

"I've watched your kid play. He does okay. We're hoping for big things from him the next few years."

"That's good to hear," I said, meaning it. These were perilous times for parents.

"I didn't mean to startle you," he said, "but when adults hang around outside a high school, it makes me nervous." He darted a look over his shoulder across the street. "Did you want to talk to your son?"

"No. We've got a pizza date tonight."

He gave me a questioning smile, sort of. I said, "Mr. Parker, did you know that I used to be with the police? And that I'm now a private investigator?"

A deep crease appeared between Mr. Parker's eyes. "Are you here officially, then?"

I said, "No, not officially, but on behalf of a friend. And I'm not sure why I'm here—but it isn't to ogle the young girls or to sell heroin out of my pocket, so you can rest easy about that." I tried to be offhand about it and failed. "Do you have much of a drug problem here at the school, sir?"

His laugh was like a file on a steel pipe. "Is the pope Catholic? Don't you read the papers? There's a drug problem in every school in the country—Public school, private school, rich, poor, urban, rural. It crosses all the boundaries, Mr. Jacovich. The only difference between being rich or poor is how many times the drug's been stepped on before it gets to you. We're raising a generation who won't be able to wake up and smell the coffee because all their nasal passages will be shot. Now, when I catch a kid smoking pot I have to discipline him, but what I really want to do is congratulate him that he only does pot, that he hasn't graduated to coke and crack yet, and hope that he stays just as pure as he is. What happened to that Supreme Court nominee who admitted to a little youthful grass smoking won't happen again, because there won't be anybody in this entire country twenty years from now who can cast the first stone. Or whose head is on straight enough to cast a ballot, for that matter." He took a wadded-up yellow tissue from the pocket of his coat and wiped his nose. "Yes sir, to answer your question, there is a bit of a drug problem at the school. It's the U.S. version of the fall of the Roman Empire."

"Where do they get it?"

"That's the worst part: they get it from one another. Where it comes from prior to that is anybody's guess."

"And there's nothing you can do to stop it?"

"Sure—we could search every locker every day of the week. We could search their pockets and purses and book bags. But that's an invasion of privacy, an infringement on the civil rights of the drug pushers, and we can't have that." His lips got so thin they almost disappeared. "I'm not knocking civil rights; too many people fought too long and hard to get them, including my father. But some of those liberal laws and leanings tie our hands when it comes to drugs. So just like every other school administrator in the country, the best I can hope to achieve is a holding pattern." He shook his head sadly. "And they want to know why Johnny can't read. It's because Johnny is coked to the gills!"

I heard a familiar voice behind me and turned around. Milan Jr. was at the fence, peering through the mesh, a troubled frown on his face. His buddies were standing a discreet fifteen feet behind him trying not to listen. "Dad," he said.

I excused myself to Mr. Parker and walked across the street. "Hi," I said. "How're you doing?"

His eyes flicked toward his principal, then back to me. A parent making an unexpected school visit just couldn't be good news. "Is everything okay?"

"Yeah, sure," I said. "I was passing by and I got to talking with Mr. Parker. No big deal." He still seemed uncertain, so I added, "If I'd wanted to see him seriously, Milan, I would've made an appointment, and we'd've talked in his office."

"Okay."

"I asked your mom if we could have dinner tonight and watch the game. It's the Cowboys and the Niners."

"I hate the Cowboys," he said.

I smiled. It was nice to know he shared my prejudices. America's team, indeed. "We'll watch 'em get their butts kicked, then. I figured we'd grab a sausage pizza or something."

"Okay," he said. He seemed to want to look over his shoulder at his buddies, and I realized this was awkward for him.

"I'll see you tonight, then, huh?" I said.

He nodded, gave a small wave, and went back to where his pals waited for him. I noticed his walk become arrogant as he moved, for the benefit of his adoring public. I turned and crossed the street again.

"I hope I didn't embarrass him," I said to Parker.

"You probably did, but don't worry. These kids want their pals to believe they don't have parents, they came from cabbages."

"You mean they didn't?"

We both gave polite, insincere chuckles, and then he said, "You still haven't told me what you're doing here, Mr. Jacovich. Of course, you don't have to; this is a public street and I'm just a working stiff. But I get the feeling this isn't a random visit, and that these questions about drugs aren't just idle talk. If your son is having a problem at my school, I think I ought to know about it. Maybe I can be of some help."

"It's got nothing at all to do with Milan, thank God. But I'll be straight with you, Mr. Parker. I don't know if there's a problem here or not; that's what I'm trying to find out. When I do, I might very well need your help—and you might need mine."

"I'll be glad to help if I can," Parker said. "But sometimes I feel like I'm pissing into a strong wind."

The school bell rang again, signaling the end of the early lunch period, and the kids in the yard began a reluctant shuffle toward the doors at a much slower pace than they'd come out. Parker excused himself and we shook hands again, and I watched him walk back toward the school he tried so valiantly to run. Being a principal in the time of the drug plague is no easy task.

Almost as tough, sometimes, as being a friend.

4

THE Top of the Town restaurant is well-named, perching as it does at the pinnacle of the Erieview Plaza, atop the new Cleveland Galleria on Ninth Street and St. Clair. The Galleria is supposed to be the very latest thing in downtown shopping malls, and I guess it is pretty impressive, with its green-tinted curved glass and salmon-colored facings, behind which are some of the most exclusive shops in town. But as attractive as it is, I've never gotten over the feeling that architecturally it belongs in another city, that it was picked up from someplace like downtown Houston or Phoenix and dropped into the middle of Cleveland. It certainly clashes with the gothic grandeur of the gray arches and heaven-reaching green spire of the Cathedral of St. John a block away on Superior.

I had a lunch date with Ed Stahl, my pal at the *Plain Dealer*, and he had arrived at the restaurant early and laid claim to a window table with a panoramic view of Lake Erie, which was beautiful even in the somber dreariness of the day. To no one's surprise a half empty glass of neat bourbon stood at Ed's elbow, and there were already two piles of pipe ashes in the ashtray. The pipe jutted out from between his teeth á la General MacArthur. Ed is close to fifty, ropy-looking like a college athlete gone to seed. His black curly hair is graying at an alarming rate, and there isn't quite as much of it as there had been a year ago. He wears horn-rimmed Clark Kent spectacles, and he is the only guy in Cleveland whose ties are uglier than mine. To say he's rumpled would be to describe him on one of his rare good days. But Ed doesn't need the trendy wardrobe of an anchorman; he is the best investigative reporter in the business and has a Pulitzer Prize to prove it. He declines to discuss the Pulitzer the way a man might refuse to talk about the time in junior high school when he was voted King of the Holly Hop. He likes talking about anything else, though, especially that which relates to his favorite city in the world, and I've asked for his help more than once since the days when I was a rookie cop and he was a junior reporter on the dayside city desk.

"Nice jacket," he said, dismissing my outfit with a gimlet eye as I sat down opposite him. "Somewhere in Slavic Town there must be a 1959 Chevy without any seat covers."

I ordered a Stroh's and Ed raised his own glass and said, "When are you going to stop guzzling that crap and discover the true joys of drinking?" I think he likes living up to the stereotype of the hard-drinking reporter, but whether for pleasure or for the image, Ed does have a strong affinity for Jim Beam.

"Ed," I said, "what do you know about the drug scene?"

"Personally? Bayer aspirin for headaches, Sudafed for a stuffy nose, and Kaopectate for the runs. But you don't mean that." He bit at his drink and looked wistfully out across the lake. "Time was, drugs weren't much of a problem in Cleveburg. Oh, back in the sixties the kids were smoking weed just like anywhere else, and there's always been a certain amount of horse in the ghetto, but this was one of the few big cities in the world where you could be pretty sure the guy next to you on the Rapid wasn't high on something and ready to rip you off to feed his habit."

"Time was?"

"The world is changing too damn fast for me, Milan. What happened to band concerts in the park and fireworks on the Fourth of July, ice cream sodas and taking a walk after dinner?"

"And nobody runs into the city room yelling 'Stop the presses!' anymore either, do they?"

He rubbed his bulbous nose hard enough to erase it. "They never did. What crap! I lay the promulgation of that base canard directly at the feet of the Warner brothers. Pat O'Brien wouldn't have lasted ten minutes in a city room."

The waitress brought my beer and we ordered lunch. Ed chose some sort of broiled fish. Because of a chronic ulcer, he's always careful about what he eats, which probably doesn't make up for his drinking more than a pint of bourbon every day.

Ed said, "The reason this town was clean vis-à-vis drugs for so long was, believe it or not, your old buddy Giancarlo D'Allessandro."

Giancarlo D'Allessandro is the patriarch of the Cleveland mob, and I've had less than pleasant dealings with him in the past. I had defied them; on one occasion I'd taken a beating from them; my last run-in with them had ended up with guns going off, and I counted myself lucky to be alive. Since then we've maintained an uneasy coexistence made possible by my staying the hell out of their way. But I'm definitely not on their Christmas card list.

"If there's a crooked buck to be made, D'Allessandro will make it," I said.

"Not this time. Hear me out, now. Twenty-five years ago when the world discovered mind-altering substances in a big way, no one was very surprised when the wise guys moved in and made it a Cosa Nostra subsidiary. Every place but in Cleveland."

"Why is that?"

"Because old Giancarlo thinks it's immoral. This from a guy who runs whores and numbers, smuggles illegal whiskey and contraband cigarettes, and has most of the unions in the state by the nuts. But he thought there was something intrinsically horrible about getting little kids hooked on shit that would eventually rot their brains. And as a result, Cleveland was a drug-free paradise for about ten years."

"What happened? He change his mind?"

"It got changed for him. The story is that the wise-guy ex-

33

ecutive committee, or whatever the hell they call themselves, saw this town as a wide-open market, and they wanted their piece. So they told D'Allessandro he'd better get with the program fast or he was going to be right at the top of their fecal scroll."

"Did he?"

"Sort of. He still couldn't see soiling his gnarly old hands with drug money, so he turned the whole operation over to Victor Gaimari."

"Oh, shit," I said. Victor Gaimari is D'Allessandro's nephew by marriage, a button-down Ohio State alumnus who fronts for the mob as a stockbroker just down the street in fancy offices in Terminal Tower. He's one of Ohio's most eligible bachelors, seen at all the best society parties, is unfailingly courtly and never raises his voice. But he's a snake all the same, and for the past few years he and I have been smiling through our teeth and politely tearing at each other whenever we have occasion to meet, like two pit bulls at a Junior League cotillion.

The perky little dark-haired waitress brought the food and set it before us. "My name's Angie if you need anything," she said, making me wonder what her name was if we didn't need anything.

Ed slashed his fish into bite-size hunks with a knife and fork, which wouldn't have scored any Amy Vanderbilt points at the dinner parties Victor Gaimari graces, which tend to be hosted by Cleveland's moneyed gentry. But Ed rarely dines at their tables, and when he does he is looked upon fondly as eccentric and quaint. It doesn't happen often, because Ed's favorite pastime is pricking hot air balloons. As a result, those who are full of hot air make it a point to give him a wide berth.

"Remember," he said around a mouthful of food, "Victor was a kid barely out of college then, and his whole education, formal or otherwise, was geared toward making the dirtbags he works for look respectable. And what he didn't know about setting up a drug operation would fill a branch library. It's a bit like trying to start your own country. Oh, he gave it the old college try, but it was amateur night in Dixie, compared to the drug machines in places like New York and L.A. He didn't know how to take control. His mules were setting up their own

34

stores on the side with Victor's stuff, his suppliers were screaming that they weren't doing enough business to make the risk worthwhile, and pretty soon the whole operation fell in on him like a postwar prefab ranch house. The federal boys got wind that there was trouble in River City and came crawling out of cracks in the plaster, and within six months the illicit drug traffic in Cleveland shut down like a mom-and-pop grocery when a Safeway moves in across the street."

He grazed thoughtfully, looking rather pleased with himself, and I wondered if he was finished with his story. He waved to Angie-if-we-needed-anything and pointed to his empty glass. She hustled toward the service bar. They knew Ed pretty well at the Top of the Town.

"I didn't think Gaimari had ever failed at anything."

"Bear in mind I said he was young," Ed reminded me. "If he were to try it again today, you could take it to the bank that it would be the smoothest operation in the Midwest."

"Why doesn't he?"

"Somebody beat him to it."

Before I could ask who, Angie brought him his drink. He held it up to the light, judged it acceptable, and took a big pull. "Ahhh," he said, meaning it. He set the glass down. "You ever hear of the Jamaican connection?"

"A movie with Gene Hackman and a steel drum band?"

He looked at me very seriously, his face flushed from the fresh infusion of bourbon. "You're the kind of guy," he said in measured tones, "who would make jokes at an orphanage fire."

I pushed my plate away. I was finished with my lunch.

* * *

It might sound downright subversive, but I've never been a pizza lover. Perhaps it's some primordial racial memory, but I've always been more partial to the smoked pork loin, the *gibanica* and *cevapcici* of my Yugoslavian upbringing. And on those occasions when most people might order a pizza, I always opt for good thick Yugoslavian sausage, the kind my mother made by hand in our kitchen on East Sixty-seventh Street.

But my sons, one more generation removed from the old

country, were as hooked on the tomato and cheese pies as any other American kid, and as a nod to Milan Jr.'s sensibilities —this was to be a special night, after all—I had ordered a large pizza with sausage, pepperoni, onions, and green pepper; Milan would never put up with anything as arcane as mushrooms or anchovies. However, I refuse to patronize one of those pizza chains where the sauce tastes like Campbell's soup and the crust resembles shirt cardboard that has been left out in the rain. I had phoned my favorite Italian deli with the order.

When I arrived Lila gave me a fifteen-minute concert of chin music about how she didn't think the kid should stay up late enough to watch the whole football game. I didn't even mind that she was keeping me from my evening because I knew that Joe Bradac was lurking out of sight in the bedroom upstairs, and it gave me perverse pleasure that he felt it necessary to hide from me even in the place where he lived. Joe always makes himself scarce when I come around. We've known each other twenty years or more, but we've never been friends, and now that he's living with my ex-wife and helping my kids with their homework, my guess is we never will be.

So I did a little rough-and-tumble on the living room floor with my younger son Stephen, who is almost eleven and not quite as cuddly as he used to be. He was getting strong and wiry, and when I tickled him he didn't giggle anymore but struggled back with the fierceness of a freedom fighter. I promised that just the two of us would have a special evening together sometime soon. Milan Jr. carried his books and a gym bag stuffed with tomorrow's school clothes out to my car and we picked up the pizza and went back to my apartment, the square box leaking grease onto the back seat.

I reheated the pizza, opened a Pepsi for him and a Stroh's for myself, and we sat in my den, me in my chair and Milan cross-legged on the floor. The football game wouldn't start for about an hour, so I decided to leave the TV off while we ate, and switched the radio to a rock station I figured he would approve of. The heavy dose of fennel in the sausage was almost making my eyes tear.

"So how's tricks, kid?" I said. Not exactly a dazzling opening gambit, but fifteen-year-olds don't expect Oscar Wilde.

Milan shrugged. "Okay, I guess."

"That doesn't sound encouraging."

He took a deep breath, deciding whether or not to open up. Finally he said cautiously, "I fight with Mom a lot."

"How come?"

"I dunno. She's always in my face."

I didn't think he meant it in the basketball sense. "That's what moms do."

"She treats me like I'm some sort of baby, though. She's all, 'Even if you're only going to be ten minutes late, call so I don't worry.'"

She's all. The new English for "she said."

"You're her baby, and you might as well face it. Your mom and I have our problems, but she's the best mother in the whole world, and she loves you and Stephen like crazy. You know that."

"Yeah," he said, struggling with a stringy glop of cheese. "But she was never a guy; she doesn't understand stuff."

"What stuff?"

"Guy stuff. You know. Football, girls."

I ruminated on a piece of pepperoni. "She didn't understand that stuff when we were married, either. I know it's tough for you sometimes, but you can't blame it all on her. It'd probably be just as bad if I was around. You know, you and I aren't together that often, so I try to make sure we always have a good time when we are. And that leaves her to do all the heavy parent numbers, like curfews and getting you to do your homework and making you pick up your room. If I lived there I'd do them too."

He looked at me, not believing, and I added, "Except for the football. I'm really proud that you're playing. Mr. Parker says you're doing well with it."

He ducked his head, accepting the accolade that he felt was his due. Then he said between bites, "Dad."

"Yo."

"What was it like being on the line?"

"What line?"

"The defensive line. I'm a receiver, I run and catch passes and make touchdowns and stuff like that. Guys on the line, they never even get to touch the ball."

"That's why they call it a team, Milan. Everybody's got a particular job to do. Yours is to catch the ball and run like hell. The offensive line is to help you do it, and the defense is to see that the other guys don't. It's all part of the game, and no one man is more important than the others."

"Yeah, but don't the linemen feel bad sometimes?"

I grinned, remembering the aches and pains. "Only the day after the game." I separated another slice from the remaining half of the pizza, deftly cutting through the cheese so that it didn't go all over the place in long viscous strings. "The main thing is being involved—being in the game and not just watching." I looked at him. "You've got to stay in the game. That's all anybody can ask."

He ate thoughtfully.

"And you've gotta play teamwork, look out for your buddies just like they look out for you."

"Uh-huh."

"You know, some of the guys I played football with in high school are still my friends, after all these years. Lieutenant Meglich, Dr. Cerne—"

"My dentist?" Milan said, unable to conceive of a man who treated puffy gums ever running pass patterns.

"Sure; he had great hands even then. And your friends will be around when you're a grown man, too, Milan. Like Paulie."

He looked off somewhere over my shoulder. "Paulie don't play football."

"Doesn't," I corrected. "So what? You've been friends since you were babies." I waited for him to say something, but this time he wasn't going to come through. "You and Paulie are still friends, aren't you?"

My son stuffed the entire wide end of a slice of pizza into his mouth to avoid answering.

I waited until he had disposed of it. "Aren't you, Milan?"

"I guess. Paulie gets on my nerves."

"Why?"

"Just does."

I slid my butt off the edge of the chair and onto the floor to be on eye level with Milan. It wasn't comfortable; I've never been a floor sitter. It comes from being large-boned.

"In what way?"

He stretched his shoulders, his elbows cocked, and I could see the muscles rippling under his sweatshirt. "I don't know. He hangs around with a bunch of dorks."

"What kind of dorks?"

"Black ones."

"Hey, I don't like that kind of talk. We didn't raise you like that."

"It's not 'cause they're black, Dad. Jeez, half the football team is black, that don't mean anything."

"Doesn't."

"Doesn't. But these guys Paulie runs with are creepy. They're scary."

"Why?"

"Could I have another Pepsi?"

"It's bad for your teeth. Why are they scary?"

"They just are. Not just tough. They're mean."

"And Paulie's mean too?"

He shook his head. "He's scared shitless of 'em."

"How come he runs with them, then?"

He looked down and shook his head.

"Come on, Milan. Paulie's your friend; you've gotta look out for his ass, just the way the linemen look out for yours. Is he in trouble?"

He didn't answer for a minute. Then he said, "Not yet."

"What do you mean by that?"

"Jeez, c'mon, will ya? I feel like I'm talking to a narc!"

I shifted my position on the floor. My left buttock was going to sleep. "A narc? Is Paulie into drugs?"

"Dad, don't ask me to rat, okay? Just don't make me rat."

"Milan," I said as gently as I could, "I'm not out to get Paulie. I want to help him."

He put down the slice of pizza he'd been staring at and clambered to his feet, a lot more gracefully than I could have. "I got to go to the john," he said, and disappeared.

I got us fresh drinks and plopped into my chair, then thought better of it and sat on the floor and waited for him to come back.

He returned to the den and sat down cross-legged on the other side of the depleted pizza box. "I've been a cop of one sort or another all my life," I said. "I left the force to work private because I can do things uniforms can't do, without having to ask anyone's permission. And I help people when they need it. It's possible I can help Paulie without his name ever appearing on a police blotter. But if you don't give me a break, kid, there's a good chance your buddy is going to wind up in a cell someplace. Or in a detox ward—or worse. You're old enough I don't have to spell it out to you. And if that happens, I'd hate like hell to be you and have to live with knowing you could have helped him and didn't. I'm asking you to trust me, Milan, and I've never lied to you yet. What do you say?"

He ripped the tab off the Pepsi can as though he were dismembering it and drank angrily, getting red in the face. Finally he slammed it down, gasping. He stared at me, his chest heaving, flame flickering deep inside his dark Serbian eyes. "Those guys—they're from Jamaica. They're dealing crack," he said. "It's no secret. Everybody in the school knows it."

"Is Paulie dealing too?"

He shook his head. "I don't know that for sure. But he hangs out with them, runs their errands, licks their asses—" He stopped, still breathing hard, and looked at the watch I'd bought him for junior high graduation. "Let's turn on the game."

"In a minute," I said. "Where do these kids get the stuff?"

"Huh?"

"Come on, Milan, they're fifteen years old; they don't run their own pipeline to South America. Where do they get it? Who's their supplier?"

"I don't know, Dad. Honest to God, I don't. I don't have anything to do with drugs. I'm not gonna fu—screw up my body with stuff like that."

It sounded good, like he was telling me the truth. I hoped he was, anyway. I waited, not saying anything. I lit a cigarette,

40

took a swallow of beer, and waited some more. Being a father teaches patience. Finally Milan said, "There's this guy comes around school all the time. An older guy."

"As old as me?"

He screwed up his face as if no one could be *that* old. "A guy about twenty, I guess. His name's funny. Deshon, I think."

"That's his last name?"

"I don't know," he said. "Everybody calls him Deshon. Listen, Dad, if it gets out that I said anything—"

"Nothing's going to get out," I said. "And your name won't be mentioned. Neither will Paulie's. Okay?"

He didn't answer me, but his look entreated me to stop, and I knew he'd had enough. So had I. I don't like using people, although in my business it's sometimes unavoidable. I certainly didn't like using my own son, and I felt pretty lousy about it. Kids that age weigh every little misstep their parents make, and I knew I had chipped away some of the glue that holds a fragile father-son relationship together. It had to be done, another kid's future was at stake, but that didn't make me any happier about it. I supposed there would be time to make amends, especially if things turned out all right, but I'd pushed him hard and he was feeling used and a little resentful. I didn't blame him. I was never able to talk to my father much. He wasn't a bad father, but he worked too hard and drank too much and was always tired or irritable, and I learned early that if you can't count on your old man, there's not many other places to turn. There were times I wished I hadn't become a cop and had opened a Slovenian restaurant like Sterle's Country House instead. This was one of them.

So I did the only thing I could do. I said, "Let's not miss the kickoff," and switched on the TV.

The Cowboys, formerly America's team and now not even Tom Landry's, got clobbered, and there was a certain satisfaction in that. But I can't say that my son and I went to sleep happy.

5

WHEN I drove Milan Jr. to school the next morning I told him
that I might be around at the closing bell, and that if he saw
me he was to ignore me. There were misgivings in those grave
dark eyes, and I could tell there was mistrust. It wrenched my
guts, but I had to sing myself the mantra that every parent
knows by heart: "Some day when they're older, they'll understand." I hoped it, but I didn't really believe it; I'm forty years
old and I still don't understand a lot of the things my parents
said and did when I was Milan's age.

I watched him lope off across the school grounds. He seemed
to move more easily, more freely, now that he was out from
under the yoke of parental supervision. I understood that; I've
been there. We all have. Everybody starts out as a kid, does
kid things, makes kid mistakes. The people who forget are the
ones that have trouble with their own kids.

Feeling hungry, I drove over to Corky and Lenny's Delica-
tessen, located in one of the two strip malls that line either side
of Cedar Avenue. The neighborhood is the hub of orthodox
Jewry on the East Side; there are so many kosher markets on
the street catering to the mostly elderly area residents that it
has been dubbed "the Gaza Strip." It's one of those ethnic
enclaves, along with Little Italy and Slavic Town and the Irish
and German and black neighborhoods, that gives Cleveland its

42

particular flavor and character and makes it such a fascinating place to live. For the most part everyone gets along with everyone else in Cleveland, or at least they used to. The recent appearance of drugs on the street has tended to polarize people, though, as it has in every major city in the country. The peace marches and love-ins of the sixties brought a lot of people together; the crack trade and the gang wars of the eighties drove them apart again. It's not what I'd call progress, but then nobody asked me.

There is a sign on a metal stand inside the entrance to Corky and Lenny's that says PLEASE WAIT FOR THE HOSTESS TO BE SEATED, but since the hostess showed no signs of being ready to sit down, I found myself a table and ordered an onion bagel with belly lox and cream cheese and a couple of scrambled eggs. Mary had recently become a charter member of the omelette police and would have rightly chided me about what such a breakfast would do to my cholesterol count—but she wasn't there. I drank my coffee and gave the *Plain Dealer* the once-over, stopping to read Ed Stahl's column. It was about city-awarded garbage collection contracts and it didn't interest me very much. Neither did the sports page. I was too concerned about Paulie to pay much attention to anything.

After breakfast I headed downtown to police headquarters at East Twenty-first and Payne. I knew the big sandstone building well, had worked there for quite a few years in the shadow of the big black tower behind it that had once been the Criminal Courts Building and then the home of a printing company and was now more than half empty. It was oppressive-looking in the overcast of the morning, its exterior a sooty black from the industrial pollutants that had been cleaned up a few years ago but too late to save the gray sandstone. But then what's the good of a police station that looks like a luxury condominium complex? The business of enforcing the law is serious, and it is somehow right to conduct it in a no-frills atmosphere. The whole idea is to make people not want to have to go there.

Lieutenant Mark Meglich of homicide, however, is not a no-frills kind of guy. Not recently, anyway. We'd grown up together; his house had been right across the street from mine, back when he went by his given first name, Marko. He'd been a receiver in high school and was switched to linebacker when we both got to Kent State. Then he entered police training while I shipped out to Cam Ranh Bay with an M.P. unit. Tough, savvy, and political, Marko had already made sergeant by the time I got back to Cleveland, and he volunteered to be my rabbi when I became a cop too. But where he thrived on regimentation and order, paperwork, court appearances, and figuring the shortcuts to the top of the departmental heap, I had chafed at it. Marko considers my defection from the uniformed ranks one of his own personal failures. He doesn't admit to many.

His marriage was another one; it had unraveled at the same time as mine. I had dealt with the divorce trauma by holing up for over a year until I met Mary. But Marko jumped into singlehood with both feet, growing a dashing Tom Selleck mustache, getting his hair styled every two weeks, and dating a bevy of twenty-year-old women who were largely indistinguishable from one another except for their hair color. In the past few years he's taken to wearing expensively tailored three-piece suits, with a gold chain for the old railroad pocket watch his father had worn for forty years as a conductor on the Baltimore and Ohio. To most of us, the B&O is a desirable property on a Monopoly board; to Marko Meglich it was what paid the rent during his childhood years.

When I walked into his office he was drinking coffee from a mug with his name, rank, shield, and the emblem of the Cleveland Police Department emblazoned on its side. He had gotten it into his head that plastic or foam cups cause cancer and had gone to considerable expense to have his own coffee mug custom made. It was the kind of thing that normally inspires theft, hiding, and practical jokes, but you don't play fast and loose with the personalized mug of the number-two man in the homicide division. So somebody washed it each night and made sure it was on Marko's desk every morning, clean, dry, and upside down on a paper towel. Such were the perks of a gold shield.

"Milan!" he said. "Come to help the poor bumbling police solve another case? Or you just want a free cuppa?"

"I'm all coffeed out, and I have no case. I just want to pick your brain for a minute."

44

"That's slim pickin's," he said, smiling. Marko doesn't much approve of me since I left the department, but thirty years of friendship is hard to flush away. "How's Mary? Gorgeous as ever?"

"Yes, and she'll be flattered you said so. Marko, I need a little boost."

"Tell me about it," he said, settling back in his chair and crossing his hands over his vest.

"What do you know about the Jamaican connection?"

Marko didn't move, but the blue of his eyes muddied, and his interlaced fingers turned the slightest bit white. He looked at me for about five seconds and then expelled a breath. "Why don't you ask me a tough one?" he said.

"Why is that tough?"

"Because," he said, "it's not something that's in the papers every morning. And I don't want it to be, understand? I don't want you running to Ed Stahl the minute you leave here."

"Ed Stahl is the one who told me about it. I'd like you to fill in the details."

Marko sat up. "I don't think so," he said. "Not this time. This is departmental business, kid, and you turned in your badge with an instruction sheet. Whatever your case is, you send your client to the department."

"I don't have a client exactly."

"Then what are you jerking my chain for?"

"It's about Matt Baznik's kid."

His face tightened as though someone behind him had grabbed both ears and yanked them backward. "Little Paulie?"

I nodded and told him what the situation was in the Baznik household. His face turned the color of dead ashes as I talked. In school he'd been as close to Matt as I was.

When I finished, he rubbed his hand over his face, mussing his mustache. "That sucks," he said.

"I agree."

"What do you think you can do about it, though?"

"I don't know, Marko. But I wouldn't count myself much of a friend if I didn't try."

He flushed at that one, moving around in his chair as if his shorts were too tight. "Low blow."

"I didn't mean it like that. I just wanted you to know how important it is."

He nodded his head a few seconds too long. "You're asking me to put my dick in a vise on this. First of all, it's not my table. I got enough problems here in homicide, and I don't want to wind up on the carpet in some pencil-pusher's office because I did a friend a favor. I don't really know what I can tell you and what I can't. It's a highly sensitive area."

"Sensitive?"

"Public image and all that." He waved his hand at me, which I took as a signal to shut up, and I waited while he mulled over whatever was bouncing around in his head. Finally he sucked in air, his chest expanding, and put his hands flat on the desk in front of him. He expelled the breath in a soft sigh. "I'd better let you talk to Ding."

"Who?"

"Carl Ingeldinger. Lieutenant, narco squad. He's the head of the Jamaican Task Force."

"Task force? Jesus, Marko, what's—"

"Crack on the streets is out of hand, my man, and it has been for a few years now. We haven't been able to make a dent in the bastards, but that doesn't mean we're so stupid we don't know about them."

"I didn't mean—"

"Save it." He picked up the telephone and punched three numbers. "Let me see if he's in."

* * *

Lieutenant Ingeldinger was almost as tall as I was, but he must have weighed fifty pounds less. He wore a dark blue corduroy suit, a blue plaid shirt, and a black knit tie with the knot pulled down past the second button. A pair of plastic-rimmed glasses spanned his sad, tapering face, and the only hair on his head was a sparse fringe that ran around in back from temple to temple. He looked like a light bulb.

Marko introduced us, told him what I wanted, and left to catch up on some paperwork. Ingeldinger offered me a butter rum Life Saver and popped one into his own mouth. I noticed

46

he didn't chew it. He looked at me curiously, as if he didn't much understand cops who chose not to be cops anymore.

"Do you know what crack cocaine is, exactly? What they do is, they mix powdered cocaine with baking soda and water and then boil it down until all that's left are little crystalline pellets. When they're dried out and smoked in a pipe, you get a high that's infinitely more potent than what you get from ordinary coke. I know; I tried it once, just to see what all the fuss is about. That surprise you?"

"I'm not going to tell on you, if that's what you mean."

Ding let out a laugh like a basset hound's yelp. "Well, here's the thing, then. The stuff is brutally addictive, and they deal it right out in the open, like hot dogs at a ball game. It's pretty hard to nail them because they move around so frequently that you can't ever pinpoint them. Figure, though, that they set up temporarily in empty or abandoned houses, or over in the projects on the East Side. You can just about imagine what a crack house does to an inner-city community: it destroys it in a matter of a couple of weeks, eats it away from the inside out, like a cancer. Wham! there goes the neighborhood. It's a war. A shooting war, make no mistake about it." He leaned forward in his chair, making it squeak. "I was born here, just like you. I love this town, the Browns and the Indians and the Cavs. I loved the Cavs even when they stunk. I love the museums and the symphony and the old buildings, and the energy and honesty of the people who live here. Cleveland's done a hell of a job in the past ten years in coming back from being a national joke. It used to kill me when people called us the Mistake on the Lake. They don't anymore, because this's turned into a pretty good place to live. But if we're ever gonna come back all the way and realize our potential—well, the law better damn well win."

"What happened, Ding? And why?"

"Why is easy. Before the summer of 1987, crack was no problem here in town. Scum bags can't stand a vacuum, so when the Cleveland mob's cocaine apparatus fell apart, the Jamaican gangs moved in to take over the operation, only they call themselves 'posses' instead of gangs. They run things like a paramilitary group. They're organized, they're vicious, and they're deadly. They make D'Allessandro and his boys look like schoolyard bullies. They don't warn, they don't threaten, they don't talk things over with you, and they don't break kneecaps. Mess with these guys and you aren't even a historical footnote—you're toast. Baseball bats with ten penny nails sticking out of them, machetes, chain saws—and an arsenal of sophisticated assault weapons that would turn the PLO green with envy, most of 'em smuggled in here from some Chiquita Banana country down south who got 'em as a gift from the U.S. government in the first place."

"And D'Allessandro just sits around watching them do it? That's not the old Giancarlo I know and love."

Ding sucked on his candy. "It's the image thing," he said almost sadly. "You believe it? The wise guys are worried about their image. They think a shooting war on the East Side would be bad for public relations. So they've just shrugged it off and left drugs to the Jamaicans."

"How come I never heard about this before?" I said.

"City Hall has kept the lid on pretty tight. There've been a few stories—Ed Stahl wrote one last summer—and we've made a few busts. We came down on a West Indian market on East 116th Street that was Crack Central for a while. But mostly it's swept under the rug."

"I don't understand that."

"It's politics. Until they figure out how to fix it, they're happier if no one knows it's broken." He dug a finger into his ear unenthusiastically. "And here's the most insidious thing of all: you know who they use for their mules? Kids."

I shook my head. Poor Paulie. Why was nothing ever easy?

"Young kids, as young as nine or ten. They got the idea from the Detroit mob; they've been doing that for years. That way, when the kids get busted for possession with intent to sell, they're treated as juvie offenders and get off with a rap on the knuckles. And the scumbolinas who make the millions don't even get touched. It was ever thus, no?" He popped another Life Saver, this time not offering me one. "Stay out of it is my advice. It isn't worth it."

"A kid's life isn't worth it?"

He held the fresh Life Saver between his front teeth and carefully put his tongue through the hole, then neatly flipped it back into the further reaches of his mouth. "You want to change the world, don't you? Run around being Wyatt Earp. Let me tell you a little story, cowboy. A bedtime story to help you sleep. A year ago there was a street kid making a lot of noise, a punk by the name of Randolph Jones, with gold bracelets and earrings and enough slick on his hair to oil a battleship. What they call a real heavy dude, ran with an East 114th Street gang called the Kools."

"I've heard of them," I said, "but Randolph Jones doesn't ring any bells."

"He was what they used to call a comer," Ding said. "About twenty-three years old, built like a linebacker, and as twisted as a licorice whip. A sheet for armed robbery, rape, assault— and that was when he was still underage. Spent his wonder years in reform school." He snickered. "Remember when they used to call it that? Now it's the 'juvenile facility.' " He examined the jagged edge of a fingernail and bit it smooth. "Probably a better name, anyway; no one I know of ever got reformed in reform school. Anyway, when they finally unleashed Randolph Jones onto a waiting world, he decided he was going to make a big name for himself with the Kools. And for a while he did. Big, good-looking bad-ass. The whole town was talking about the Jones boy. But our Randolph was something of an overreacher. He figured he'd cut himself a little slice of the happy-rocks pie and make himself King Shit of the Kools. All by himself, he roughed up a couple kids from one of the Jamaican posses, hijacked their deliveries, and scored himself enough crack to start his own store. It was a modest little operation at first, but he just knew he had the smarts and the pizzazz to go big in no time." He paused for dramatic effect. "They found him in a vacant lot on Chester."

I nodded.

"And in an alley behind 112th Street. And in a men's room in Forest Hills Park. And a few other places I forget. There are some parts of him they haven't found yet—like his schlong. Are you still with me?"

The smell of the butterscotch made me sick, or maybe it was

something else. I sat back in my chair, but he leaned close, and I recognized the hard-guy expression that appeared on his long, sad face. I had worn it often enough myself.

"Jacovich, I know you were a pretty good cop in your day," Ingeldinger said.

"As good as most, better than some," I said.

"But you turned in your badge and you're not a cop and it's not your day anymore. Professional courtesy and your friendship with Meglich bought you this conversation, but that's all it bought you. The brass has gone to great lengths to keep this Jamaican connection business muffled up, and I want it to stay that way. You understand what I'm saying to you?"

"I speak the language, Ding."

"I hope so. This is an open case, an important case, and it's *my* case. I don't want to trip over you one of these days."

"Okay."

"Because if I do, I'm going to land on you with both feet. That's if there's enough of you left to land on after the posses get ahold of you."

"I won't get in your way."

"Damn tootin' you won't. You don't have a client, you don't have a case. Why don't you go home and watch a ball game and forget about it?"

"I'm not sure I can do that."

He crunched what was left of the Life Saver between his horsey teeth. "*Get* sure," he said.

6

IT was two twenty by the time I reached the high school, and this time I wasn't quite as conspicuous, because there were several other parents or guardians waiting in their cars for the final bell of the day, picking up their kids to take them shopping, or to the dentist, or just to take them home before they could get into any trouble. It's that kind of world these days. I had called Principal Parker out of courtesy and told him I'd be outside the school again so he wouldn't call out the militia. After my talk with Carl Ingeldinger that morning I didn't want to have to explain to the police what I was doing there.

At two thirty school was out, and I recognized some of the kids who came tumbling through the doors, celebrating their daily parole, from the previous afternoon. I watched as they polarized into their own little groups, chattering with great animation about the trials, triumphs, and tribulations of surviving another day of high school. After a few minutes my son came out, once more surrounded by his coterie of admirers, and he frowned across the street at me and ducked his head in quick acknowledgment and then moved out across the athletic field, taking the shortcut home. I guessed there was no football practice, and I was glad to see he wasn't in one of the packs that hung around the area after school.

Paulie emerged from the big double doors. He wasn't carrying any books, as if he were the only kid in the school who didn't have homework. He looked around until he found the gang I had seen him with the day before and trotted up to them as eager as a colt. They acknowledged him, barely, and then began leaving the school grounds, moving like a pack of soldier ants. They crossed the street, Paulie with his too bright eyes tagging along behind. They didn't disperse right away but hung out on the corner as if staking it out smoking cigarettes and being rad and buff, making remarks to any girls who had to run their gauntlet. Their collective attitude was the arrogant confidence of every gang of teenage boys since the beginning of history, and if one didn't suffer from the racial paranoia that seems to affect urbanites all over the country, they seemed harmless enough.

I observed for a while, not noticing anything sinister or unusual, other than the fact they still didn't talk much to Paulie. There's certainly nothing illegal about kids congregating on a street corner. If there were, all of us would have gone to jail at one time or another in our adolescence. The social reformers bemoan the lack of places for kids to gather and stay out of trouble, but in truth, it's not nearly as much fun going to the Y or the neighborhood community house as it is to hang out on the corner, torment the girls, smoke, and act unbearably cool.

After about ten minutes a big gold Cadillac Seville rolled around the corner. Its chrome sparkled, and a high-tech antenna had been affixed to the trunk lid as a further badge of affluence and importance. A car like that was out of place on this street, shaming the humble houses and modest front yards and the old, tired high school itself. It glided to a stop in front of the group of dark youths, and its arrival seemed to galvanize them into action. They gathered around the car, composing themselves into attitudes, flashing smiles, and waited for the driver to emerge.

He finally did, and I was able to get a good look at him as several of the boys gave him high fives or clapped him on the back, but along with the camaraderie I couldn't miss the respect, almost awe, with which they approached him. He was very tall and thin, his skin the color of rich black coffee, and he wore a funny goatee and a mustache in the fashion of a bebop musician of the fifties. It was his hair that shattered that image; it was styled in dreadlocks that spilled out from a center part, with little silver ornaments at the end of each rope of hair. His pants and jacket were black leather and clearly expensive, and from what I could see he wasn't wearing a shirt, which might have been cool but on a day like this one had to be cold, too. Around his neck on a thick chain, glittering against his smooth chest, hung a shiny gold cross only marginally smaller than the original one.

Paulie looked frail and pale, the only white face among the dark ones, and when the visitor reached over and squeezed his cheek he fairly lit up with pleasure, even though the pinch was hard enough that it must have hurt—it left a red mark. The gesture was so patronizing it made me sad, and angry.

I reached into the glove compartment and pulled out my camera. It's nothing fancy—a little Kodak 35-millimeter with automatic rewind, not much more than a snapshot camera. But for someone in my profession it comes in handy sometimes, and I usually have it in my car should the need for it arise. Trying to be inconspicuous, I aimed it at the young man with the Cadillac and squeezed off several shots.

Finally he turned around and opened the passenger door of the Seville, reaching down and picking up several small packages off the floor. They were neatly wrapped in white butchers paper, but I got the idea they weren't lamb chops. The nonchalance of the whole operation chilled me. It was so open, so naked, and the young man didn't seem to give a damn if anyone saw him or not. Moving with the assurance of a guy who knows the fix is in, he distributed the parcels to each of the boys present, a dark and benevolent visiting uncle, even giving one to Paulie. The kids jammed them into the waistbands of their pants or stuck them inside their jackets, and their visitor gave them a stern lecture about something, gesturing with his long, slim hands, his dreadlocks swinging, his fingers almost balletic, flying, assigning, admonishing.

Apparently his last words were an order to disperse, because the group quickly broke up into pairs and went off in various directions. Paulie headed back across the athletic field by himself, in the direction of his house. The young man lounged against the side of his Cadillac, watching them out of sight, seemingly relishing not having to be anywhere or do anything for a while. He fired up a long cigarette, possibly a Virginia Slim, filled his lungs, and then examined and admired the smoke he exhaled as though it were an accomplishment, luxuriating in his own celebrity, whatever it was. He didn't miss the opportunity to say something to two young white girls who had to walk past him. It seemed to amuse him, but the girls scurried off as though they'd just encountered a werewolf. High-school girls learn fast.

He tossed his cigarette away half smoked and no longer worthy of his attention and folded his long legs back into the Cadillac. The car meandered down the street, as if its driver was checking out the turf, which was fine with me. If the man with the dreadlocks was admiring the passing scenery, chances were he wouldn't notice me. It was easy to follow him; in his arrogance he must have believed himself invincible.

I trailed him up to Superior, where he veered east, through Rockefeller Park, past the once-elegant high-rise apartment building where the members of the old Cleveland Indians used to stash their mistresses, and then swung up toward the lake on 105th Street, finally turning off onto Merle Avenue, a crumbling side street. This is a part of the city that hasn't experienced the gentrification and rebirth that more fortunate neighborhoods have enjoyed, and the neglect of half a century showed in every falling-down house, pothole, and busted sidewalk.

The Seville stopped in front of a squat red brick two-story with boarded-up windows and a sloping front lawn that hadn't benefited from the ministrations of a gardener or a concerned owner in thirty years. Barren gray clods of soil proliferated where grass had once grown, stamped down by careless feet and uncaring winter, and weeds asserted their ugliness from between giant crevasses in the walkway. The cement slabs of the walk heaved like the floor in a fun house, and the three concrete steps leading up to the covered porch were sway-backed. A sign on a metal pole driven crookedly into the dirt read FOR SALE—CHRISTMAS AMBOY REALTY, with a picture of

Santa Claus and a phone number. The driver got out, fussing with his dreadlocks, and lit up again, as though being out of his car and in the open without a cigarette was unthinkable. Then he sauntered up the broken walkway, but he didn't climb the steps to the porch. Instead he went to the side of the house and disappeared around the back.

My first impulse was to park halfway up the block and stroll casually down the street to the house, but in this neighborhood my white face would render me conspicuous no matter what I did. So I waited at the corner for a minute or two and then pulled in right behind the Seville. I went up the walkway and up the front steps and I pushed the doorbell, but I didn't hear any sound from inside. The bell probably hadn't worked in twenty years. I rapped loudly on the cracked, painted-over window that comprised the top half of the front door. It was a thick pane of cut glass, and when the house was new it had probably been elegant. I could hear movement inside, but no one seemed disposed to answer my summons. I knocked again, and waited again, listening for more sounds, but only silence rewarded me.

I decided to go around to the back, but when I turned the tall young man was standing at the foot of the steps grinning at me. At his side was a big rangy dog, probably German shepherd several generations back, now just shaggy and hungry-looking, with the yellow eyes of a wolf. A few feet behind him stood a light-skinned black girl. She wore a vinyl jacket over a faded pink sweater and a denim miniskirt, and her orange hair was pulled through a bright pink turban, which added eight inches to her height, and fell in a luxurious fuzzy ponytail from the side of her head. At any moment I expected her to break into "Ay, ay, ay, a-chicka-chicka boom-chick." She was probably sixteen, and at around five foot seven she couldn't have weighed a hundred ten pounds. Her body was present and accounted for, but the vacant look behind her light brown eyes proclaimed the rest of her to be off somewhere in a galaxy far away.

"Dey be no one to home, mon," the man said, in the almost dreamy cadence of the Caribbean islands. The silver ornaments on the ends of his dreadlocks tinkled happily.

55

"You're home," I said, smiling back at him.

"Dat be truth. But dey be no one to home for *you*."

"How do you know who I am?"

"Right dere dat be de problem. Don' know you, dey be nobody to home."

The dog made a deep humming sound far back in its throat, a great bass viol of a growl. The man put a hand on its rising hackles, which didn't stop the hum but turned down its volume.

I said, "I'm looking for Deshon."

"I don' know him." He gave an exaggerated shrug, showing me both pink palms.

I came down the steps. Up close he was a handsome devil, despite his extreme hairdo and clothes, and his eyes sparkled with deviltry and something else I couldn't identify. I must have had eighty pounds on him. But I figured we were more than even, because the dog weighed more than eighty pounds, and looked meaner than I could ever think about being.

"You're Deshon, aren't you?"

"Dat depend on who I talk to," he sang. "If it be a fren, or someone owes dis Deshon feller some money, den maybe I be him. But if it be an enemy—or a policeman—den dat be a differen' story."

"I'm not a policeman," I said. I didn't bother refuting the enemy part of it. He wouldn't have believed me anyway. "I'd like to talk to you for a minute. Privately."

His eyes moved over his shoulder but he didn't really look at the girl. "Pay no attention to her, mon. She just a strawberry."

"A what?"

"A coke whore, mon. She fuck guys for drugs."

The girl's shoulders drooped in humiliation. I suppose she knew what she was, but hearing it like that had to hurt anyway. Deshon waved her away imperiously and she slunk around the side of the house, in no hurry and without another word.

"So," he said, "what you be wantin' wit dis Deshon?"

"I hear that you sometimes sell things to people. Things I might be interested in."

"T'ings you mi' be innerested in," he echoed. His mouth twisted. Then he gave in to the impulse and threw back his head, laughing heartily. Laughter is contagious, and his went on so long I found myself chuckling too. But unlike Deshon, I didn't know what was so funny, which made me feel a little silly. The dog growled louder, evidently not amused.

"Mon, mon," he chortled, "you mus' t'ink me pretty dumb. You be one mos' outrageous pisser!"

Being unfamiliar with the patois, I didn't know if a most outrageous pisser was a good or bad thing to be, so I kept quiet and waited until whatever was tickling him went away. It took a while, and then his eyes slitted and his smile withered, replaced by something not exactly hostile, but alert and suspicious.

"How you come here to dis place?"

"I told you. I heard about you—about Deshon."

"Where?" He said it in a musical glissando, sliding up the scale to a D flat.

"I get around."

"Ho ho. Maybe you get around out of here, mon. Dis not be a good place for you."

"You live here?"

"Where I live be my business," he said, once again turning playful. "Why, you want to come my house for dinner? Aki rice an' beef wit' coconut?"

"Are you inviting me?"

"I invite you to fly away, mon," he said "Dis be heavy shit for you, fuckin' wit' me." He was still smiling easy, but there was a machete edge to his voice that hadn't been there before, and the tone made the ruff around the dog's neck stand out like an Elizabethan collar.

I handed him one of my phony business cards, the ones that said I worked for an insurance company. "Give me a call sometime," I said. "I'd really like to talk to you."

Deshon took the card and tore it in half without looking at it. The two pieces fluttered past the dog's nose, and its wolf eyes crossed as he followed them down to the cracked cement.

"Stick your card in your ass, mon," Deshon said.

His eyes flickered to his right as two young black men came around the side of the house and stood several feet behind him to stare holes through me. One wore a pair of camouflage pants and a black windbreaker, and his hair was almost as long as Deshon's, parted in the middle and falling in two kinky waves on either side of his head. The other wore jeans and a Browns sweatshirt, and his hair was cut geometrically, short on the sides with a big crestlike wedge on top like a hunk of pumpkin pie in a roadside diner. They were both in their early twenties, only bigger and huskier than Deshon, and there was no glint of mischief in their eyes. What lurked there was more intimidating than the baseball bats they both carried. I supposed that being new to the area from an island where summer never went away, they didn't know baseball bats were inappropriate in Cleveland in November.

"Come on, Deshon," I said, "you don't need backup. We're all friends here, right?"

"Not all of us, mon," he said, and gracefully stepped aside so I could get down the walkway to where my car was parked without having to go around him. His dog was not quite so polite, and stayed in the middle of the cement. "Right now I don' t'ink you got a fren' in de whole world."

The two batsmen moved apart so that one stood on either side of the walk. The one with the funny haircut was on my left, his bat on his shoulder like he was taking the first pitch no matter what, breathing heavily through his open mouth in anticipation. His companion, who was having trouble keeping his long hair out of his face, held the bat in front of him with both hands as though he'd been ordered to bunt. It seemed I was to run their gauntlet. I looked at them carefully as I approached. They were around Deshon's age, perhaps a few years younger, but there was nothing of the scared kid in either of their faces.

Funny Haircut raised the bat up off his shoulder and took a step forward like Jose Canselo digging in at the plate. When I arrived at a point equidistant between them I slowed my pace just a shade and let my unbuttoned coat fall open enough to let them see the butt of the gun in my shoulder holster, and I said in a voice that couldn't have been heard more than three feet in either direction, "I'm carrying, fellows. And that means the first guy that swings one of those things, I'm going to shoot right in the face, so there won't be enough left of it for his

58

mother to recognize. And then I'll take the bat away from the other one and ram it so far up his ass it'll take a team of surgeons six weeks to even find it."

"Ooh, you be one tough fucker," Deshon said behind me. He had remained by the porch to observe the festivities, a season ticket holder, but his voice gave the two batsmen new confidence. "He bluffing, Javier. He jus' one outrageous loud bullshitter."

Javier, the funny haircut, cocked his elbow to swing. I reached out with both hands, grabbed that elbow, and bent it the wrong way so that it was almost touching the back of his head. He sucked in his breath, his face contorting with pain. I yanked the bat out of his hands and moved around behind him, bringing the bat across the front of his neck and pulling back hard. Gagging and spluttering, he clawed at the wood pressing against his Adam's apple.

The other one moved forward, brandishing his weapon, and I pulled back harder on the bat. "Try me," I said. "Javier takes the first swing in the face. And I guarantee, you won't live long enough for a second one."

He looked at me, then at Deshon, who had his hand on the dog's bristling neck hairs. Deshon just grinned. He didn't seem too upset about the way things were going—it wasn't his windpipe getting crushed. "I t'ink you better drop de bat," he said. "De mon mean what he say."

"Don't drop it," I said. I felt Javier's struggles growing weaker, and I hoped his buddy had the good sense Deshon did, because I didn't really want to hurt anyone. "Throw it. Clear across the yard."

I watched uncertainty and fear replace the dead-calm arrogance in the eyes of the long-haired kid. He lowered the bat onto his shoulder and took one giant step backward. Then he tossed the bat from him in the disgusted manner of a home run hitter who's just received an intentional walk. I released the pressure on Javier's neck, and he fell to his knees in front of me, gasping to draw air in through his bruised throat.

"Wasn't that easier?" I said, and I tossed my bat in the same direction. I looked up at Deshon. "I might be seeing you again," I said.

That didn't seem to bother him much, either. "Dat may be," he said. "But next time it be different, mon."

I walked down the path slowly, my hand ready to draw the gun in case he sicced his snarling pet at me. But he didn't, and I was glad. It would really bother me to have to kill a dog.

* * *

It was a storefront on Eddy Road, just the right size to have been a haberdasher's shop thirty years ago. There were venetian blinds, the slats wide open to admit the light, in the window, which was half obscured by a large tempera painting of Santa Claus. It was still a month early, but Santa stayed there spreading cheer all year round, because this was the real estate office of Christmas Amboy. It must have given unsuspecting passersby on Eddy Road a real start in the middle of August.

I went in. There was a small reception area, but no one was at the secretary's desk, and from the unused look of it no one had been for a long time. An electric heater on the floor merrily toasted the room, empty except for the desk and some old filing cabinets. On the cheap wallboard panels that had been erected to create another, larger room toward the rear of the building hung a framed real estate license, a photograph of the old Thriller ride at Euclid Beach Park, and an autographed picture, yellowed with age, of the young Bill Veeck at the time he had owned the Cleveland Indians and taken them to the World Series. From the inner room I heard a hearty hello and an invitation to come on back.

Christmas Amboy got up from behind his desk to shake my hand. He was red-faced and jowly, with long curly brown hair combed across his balding pate, and a potbelly that had lost its fight with gravity and hung over his belt. His shirt was short-sleeved despite the weather, off-white with vertical gray pinstripes, and several ballpoint pens were tucked into a plastic shield in the pocket. His tie was of the clip-on variety, and of a color I couldn't have described while looking at it. His brown eyes sparkled behind thick rimless bifocals, and his face glistened with a sheen of perspiration.

"Welcome," he said, a gracious host in his own home. "I'm glad to see you. Christmas Amboy."

60

"Milan Jacovich," I said.

"Jacovich. That's what makes Cleveland a great city, the ethnics. Always good to greet one of our Polish friends." I didn't correct him. "Sit down, sit down, make yourself comfortable. How about some coffee? Or a Coke? It's diet, caffeine free." His corn pone accent bespoke the southern part of Ohio or possibly Kentucky, and he seemed to use it deliberately, to cultivate it. I supposed it was his idea of a warm, folksy touch.

"Nothing, thank you."

He sat down and crossed his hands over his stomach, grinning with a delight I found it hard to believe I'd caused just by walking in the door. "Hey!" he said sharply, though my attention had not strayed. "I'll bet you can't guess when my birthday is."

"Your birthday?"

"Go ahead, guess." It was a game he obviously loved and had played many times before.

"December twenty-fifth?"

He beamed his approval, as though I'd just solved a problem in quantum physics. "That's it. Right on the nose." He crinkled his own, archly, "How'd you guess?"

"A shot in the dark," I told him.

"Yessir, I was a Christmas baby, and my mother just fixated on the name. Lucky for me I wasn't born on Groundhog Day, wasn't it?"

A little of Christmas Amboy was going to go a long way.

"Well now, Milan, is it? What can I do for you? Looking for a new home?"

I was deliberately vague. "I'm interested in a property you represent. I saw your sign." I gave him the address on Merle Avenue to which I'd followed Deshon.

His smile dimmed by about two watts. "Aw. Yeah, I represent that proppity. But I'm going to tell you frankly, I don't see you in that house."

"Why is that, Mr. Amboy?"

"Christmas. Call me Christmas, most everyone does. It's such a funny name, most people like to use it." He picked up a yellow pencil from his desk and began rolling it around between his fingers the way he might a fine cigar.

"What's the matter with the Merle Avenue house?"

He crinkled his nose again, this time in distaste. "It's not the best neighborhood in the world. Used to be, back in the old days, but no more. I think I liked the old days better, you know? Life was simpler then, without microwave ovens and computers and civil rights legislation, when Cleveland Ohio was a good place to live, a good place to bring up kids, take 'em to Euclid Beach in the summertime and didn't have to drive all the way to Cedar Point in Sandusky. I loved this town the way it used to be. I guess I'm what you might call an old-fashioned Christmas." He guffawed at his own joke. I was willing to bet he had fifteen minutes of Christmas shtick all ready to trot out for my amusement. "You look like a family man, am I right?"

I nodded. It was an easy lie.

"You don't want your family living on Merle, then."

"Why not?"

"It's the boogies," he said, hitting a rim shot on the desk with the pencil for emphasis. "For blocks around, nothing but boogies. You don't want to bring your kids up around those people, don't want 'em making filthy remarks to your wife."

It was my turn to crinkle my nose in distaste.

"Now I've got several nice homes I could show you, places where your kids could grow up safe and your wife wouldn't have to look behind her every time she went marketing." He started rummaging through a card file on his rather cluttered desk. "What were you looking to spend? Somewhere in the low sixties, maybe? Working man, are you?"

"Most people who want to buy a house work for a living."

A scatological Mel Brooks sight gag couldn't have broken him up more. He wheezed when he laughed, and his jowls shook like Cuddles Sakall's in the old Warner Brothers movies. The spasm finally passed, and he extracted a card from the little tin box. "Here's a nice proppity, f'rinstance, and the seller is motivated. You know what that means?" He didn't wait to find out whether I did or not. "Means he's anxious to sell. Twenty-six years old but in cherry condition, over on Kelton near the park."

"I'm really interested in the Merle Avenue house," I said. "It is for sale, isn't it?"

He breathed loudly. "Yes, sir, it surely is. But let me be honest with you, Milan, because I don't know any other way to do bidness. A man with a name like Christmas, born on the same day as our Saviour, why he's got an obligation toward honesty and morality and ethics in bidness, don't you agree? So let me be real honest with you. I don't recommend that proppity at all. I couldn't close my eyes in sleep nights if I didn't tell you the truth. It's way overpriced. *Way* overpriced. I tried to tell the seller that, but sometimes people just don't listen to the voice of experience."

"Maybe I could talk to the owner. Negotiate a little."

He sat up a little straighter in his swivel chair. "Well, but that's my job, don't you see? If buyers talked to sellers direct, why then there wouldn't be much need for a Realtor." Then he smiled again, broadly, to take the sting out. "You wouldn't want me to go out of bidness, would you?"

"Certainly not, Christmas," I said. "Well then, maybe you can call the owner for me and see what can be arranged?"

"You're not listenin' to the voice of experience either," he said, and shook his jowls. It seemed to sadden him beyond words. "That neighborhood is just awful, and it won't be gettin' any better in our lifetime, I'll tell you that."

"Why don't you call him now?" I said.

Christmas Amboy made a big show of searching through his card file again. When he found the one he was looking for, he didn't take it out of the box but looked at it through the bottoms of his bifocals. Then he frowned.

"Doggone it! There's no way I can call him during the day. After seven P.M., at home, it says. You know, a lot of sellers don't want to be bothered about their proppity at work. It don't make sense to me, someone wants to sell their proppity he should be available during the day. Being a Realtor is an all-day and all-night job sometimes. Tell you what. If you're bound and determined on that Merle Avenue house, I'll call him tonight and then give you a jingle. How would that be?"

"That'd be fine," I said.

The smile came back. "You got a card, a bidness card where I could call you?"

I gave him my phony insurance card. I didn't feel like giving him one that read MILAN SECURITY; DISCREET INVESTIGATIONS. It's always at least a conversation starter, and Christmas Amboy was enough of a talker to kill the rest of the afternoon over it. He pumped my hand again and promised he'd call me that evening as soon as he'd tried to talk some sense into the seller.

I hoped he'd get around to making the call before his birthday.

MY friend Renee, the guardian of the gate down at the Hall of Records, loves to take pictures of her grandson. It's her only hobby, as far as I can tell, and he is her only grandchild. Now almost three, when the little guy is grown he'll have a photographic record of his life rivaling that of the Prince of Wales, and I have seen, it seems, every bloody picture. This new batch, over which I dutifully exclaimed as Renee laid them out on the counter that separates the public from the vital records of the city of Cleveland, had been taken earlier in the fall at the Cedar Point amusement park, and featured the boy waving from several kiddie rides, eating cotton candy, smearing mustard across his mouth, and wearing a Browns football helmet that completely obscured his face. Since Renee had two more envelopes of pictures in her purse, I asked her to look up the information I needed while I perused the snapshots. That isn't the way Renee normally likes to do it; each picture has a story behind it that must be told. But it was pretty close to quitting time, and we both realized that speedier measures had to be adopted.

She brought the huge ledger I had requested back to the counter, and perched on her stool turning the giant pages, she reminded me of Bob Cratchit going over Scrooge's aged receivables in the counting house.

Finally her face brightened in a smile and she turned the

book around so it was facing me. "Here it is, Milan. Tract four-six-seven-one, lot fourteen."

I pulled the book closer. As big as the pages were, the writing was small and hard to read. When you get to be forty, the eyes aren't what they used to be. Tract 4671, lot 14 was the house on Merle Avenue where I'd encountered Deshon, and I wanted to know who owned it. According to the ledger, the owner of record was one Barrie Anne Tremont, with an address just a few blocks from University Circle. I jotted it down in my notebook and then listened to the rest of Renee's running commentary on the pictures.

"How are your boys?" she asked when she was able to catch a breath. "Getting big, I'll bet."

"Bigger every day, Renee. Enjoy your grandson while he's still little and doesn't have problems. They grow up fast."

"Too fast," she said, shaking her head sadly. "It seems like just yesterday my daughter was that age, and now she has one of her own. What do you think, Milan. Are we getting old?"

"Beats me," I said, "but considering the alternative . . ."

She took a playful swat at me, and I watched as she wrestled the unwieldy book back into the stacks. I made a note to pick something up for her grandson, a little toy or a stuffed bear. In an age in which most civil servants usually are neither servants nor civil, little Grandma Renee, with her brassy red hair and bifocals and eagerness to be of service, is one of the wonders of the world. That's just the kind of place Cleveland is, though.

I checked my watch and saw that it was almost five o'clock. I was supposed to be at Mary's at seven, so I decided to drop in at Vuk's and have a beer or two.

Vuk's Tavern has been there on St. Clair Avenue near Fifty-fifth Street ever since I can remember. I had my first legal drink of alcohol at Vuk's bar, and when I'd shipped back from Southeast Asia it was the first place I headed for, even before seeing my parents or Lila. Ever since I moved out of the neighborhood after my divorce, I've stopped hanging out there—too many memories, I guess. But every once in a while I drop in and shoot the breeze with Vuk—Louis Vukovich to his mother but Vuk to just about everyone else in the world—and catch up on the news of Slavic Town. Five o'clock in the afternoon is one of the busy times at Vuk's, when the guys from the mills and factories use it as a buffer zone between work and their evenings at home with their wives or girlfriends, and there were no seats at the bar. I elbowed my way between two checkered wool jackets and caught Vuk's attention. I wasn't sure if he winked at me or if smoke from the cigarette he always had in his mouth had drifted into his eye. Unasked, he placed an opened bottle of Stroh's on the bar in front of me and grunted, "Whaddaya say, Milan?"

Apparently he didn't care what I said, because he moved on toward the end of the bar to serve another customer before I could answer. Over his head Vivian Truscott of the Channel 12 news team was droning on about a zoning hearing in Bratenahl, but the decibel level in the room was so high that no one could hear her anyway. I pulled at the beer and drifted down to where Vuk was working.

"Got a minute, Vuk?"

He glanced down the length of the crowded bar. "Does it look like I got a minute? I'm waiting for a relief guy now. My kid's wrestling tonight at Immaculata—I don't miss it when he wrestles. He's only lost two matches all year, you know?"

"That's great."

"And he goes on Saturday at Holy Name. That's the semifinals. He gets through that, he's at Queen of Angels next Friday night for all-city. Hey, if the relief guy doesn't show up you wanna ride the bar for a while?"

"I can't, Vuk. Any other time."

He nodded, not having held out much hope in the first place. "So what's up?"

"One question."

"Lay it on me."

"Not here."

He looked exasperated for a second, but he knew I wouldn't be asking if it weren't important, so he finished serving the two guys sitting just under the TV set, wiped his hands on a bar towel, came around to my side of the bar, and walked me back toward his postage stamp–size office near the rear door.

"Whyn't you pick a time when I'm not busy? Like during the Super Bowl."

"Vuk, who do you know around here that deals crack?"

His face tightened up the way it does when a stranger wanders into the tavern by accident. "How long you know me, Milan? Twenny-five years? You know how I am about drugs. Anybody tries that shit in my place, they get carried out in a small paper bag."

"Hell, I know that. I just thought you might've heard something."

"I hear a lot of stuff, but not about guys who come in here. You talk about drugs on the East Side you're talkin' about our Jamaican brothers. Look down the bar. See any black faces?"

"Nobody thinks you're dealing, for God's sake."

He gave a self-righteous sniff. "I hope to kiss a pig."

"But see if you can ask around, okay?"

"You want me to go out there and make an announcement? Jeez, you been outta the neighborhood too long. These are good Yugoslavian people like us, like our parents an' the people we grew up with. They don't know from cocaine and shit like that, wouldn't recognize it if it bit 'em on the ass. They go to work, they come in here for a beer, they go home and have dinner in front of the tube, and they're asleep at ten thirty, eleven. Friday nights they bowl, Saturdays they slip the old lady a quick one, Sunday they go to church and then go home to watch the football. Whaddaya, shittin' me about cocaine? You work your ass off for fourteen bucks an hour to raise three, four kids, you don't have much left over to spend on crap like that—and these guys in here are smart enough to know they don't need it."

"Vuk, you better wake up and smell the coffee," I said. "I'm willing to bet you could score some dope within two blocks of here if you knew who to ask. And I'd double that bet that some of the guys who drop in here on occasion are just the people that could tell you. Not dealers—users. It's not pretty, but it's the way things are now."

He didn't answer me, occupied as he was with tucking his shirt into his belt. Vuk was in his middle fifties, and I knew I was talking to him about something as foreign to him as high tea, but from what Ed Stahl and Carl Ingeldinger told me, there was a serious drug problem on the East Side, and bartenders hear things.

"It's kids," I said. "Kids we know."

His heavy brows almost engulfed his eyes. "Not your boys?"

"No, thank God. But kids we know."

"What kids?"

"I'm not going to play twenty questions. Just keep your ears open for me is all I'm saying."

He thought it over for a while. "So if I hear anything I'm s'posed to call you."

"If you would."

"I ain't gonna hear anything in here."

"If you do—"

"Yeah. Right. But I ain't gonna hear anything."

I knew when I was licked. "Hey, tell Petey good luck tonight, huh?"

"Right," he said, mad at me. He'd been mad at me before and he always got over it. That was the nice thing about friends.

We went back out into the main room and Vuk resumed his position behind the beer cooler. I noticed him scrutinizing each of the faces along the bar, as if he could tell which of them used crack by looking. I finished my beer, left three dollars on the bar, and headed out onto St. Clair Avenue. The temperature hovered somewhere in the low thirties and the wind was blowing, but in Cleveland that doesn't even make us fasten our top buttons. I drove down Fifty-fifth to Woodlawn and then headed east on Woodlawn to Buckeye and Shaker Boulevard. From there it was more or less a straight shot to Mary's place just off Shaker Square.

* * *

Mary opened the door wearing a skin-tight pair of jeans and a blue silk blouse that I particularly liked. Her long blonde hair was pulled back at the sides and held by two blue barrettes, and when I took her in my arms to kiss her the perfume she was wearing didn't quite mask the natural sweet smell of her. Over her shoulder I could see the table in the dining area set for two, complete with candles and wineglasses. Easy listening music was playing at background level.

"It's been a long three days," I said when I finally came up for air.

"Did you pine away?"

"Knotty pine."

"Did you ache for me with every breath? Get all sad when you heard a song or passed a place that reminded me of you?"

"All of that."

"Toss and turn at night wishing I was there beside you in your cold, lonely bed?"

"I set a world's record for tossing and turning."

"Good," she said. "Come open the wine."

Mary makes me feel good, and I suppose I do the same for her. Since we'd been together had been a good time for me, one in which I finally came to realize that there is life after divorce, and that just because a guy's single and pushing forty it doesn't have to mean a ratty bathrobe and slippers with the heels run down and TV dinners alone. After being married for most of my adult life I'm not sure what love is anymore, but I thought I was in love with Mary. Whatever I was with her, I liked, and that's the bottom line.

There were two salmon steaks sitting on a piece of aluminum foil on the counter, dusted lightly with black pepper and garlic powder and sprinkled with fresh dill. Mary's a bug about cholesterol, and since the only vegetable I like is lima beans and fruits are sprayed with poison pesticides and everything else you eat either makes you fat or causes cancer, Mary tends to serve a lot of fish when I have dinner at her place. I was raised on meat and potatoes, the rich Yugoslavian dishes that came over from Ljubljana and Belgrade after the Second World War, but nobody much cooks them these days, so when I'm on my own I stick with steaks and chops and let my arteries take their chances. Whenever Mary can, she tries to keep me healthy.

I opened a bottle of 1983 Napa Valley Cabernet, but of course we couldn't drink it just yet. I guess one of the things that has kept me drinking beer all these years is that you don't have to let it breathe.

I went out onto the small balcony that overlooks the courtyard of Mary's apartment building and squirted charcoal starter on the briquets she had neatly piled under the grill of her hibachi. We like the taste of char-broiled fish and unless it's in the teeth of a northern Ohio blizzard, always cook it on the outside grill. I counted to sixty to let the liquid sink in and then set the coals afire, and when they were blazing to my satisfaction I went back in and sat down on the sofa beside her. Mary, rather than tucking her feet beneath her, usually sits with her knees splayed out Indian-fashion, as though she's next in line to smoke the pipe of peace. I put one hand easily on the inside of her thigh, feeling the sleek muscles through the rough denim.

"I missed you."

"I've missed you too," she said. "Did you have a good time with Matt Sunday?"

"Calling it a good time hardly does it justice," I said, and she was unaware of the irony. "And did you enjoy the symphony?"

"I'm not really sure I like classical music. I enjoy going to Severance Hall, though, the whole gestalt of it. And it's always good to see Diana." Her friend Diana was Mary's usual companion on cultural excursions like trips to the symphony or the ballet. She had another girlfriend, Pat, with whom she went horseback riding whenever weather permitted. The rest of her spare time she spent alone, or with me. We had decided at the beginning that our relationship would be mutually exclusive, but we made sure to leave lots of room for each other, to avoid the ever-present danger of smothering. She glanced out through the closed glass door at the coals. "That fire should be ready in a jiffy," she said. "Want a beer while you're waiting?"

"No," I said, "I want to neck."

"Sorry," she said, heading for the kitchen, "but I've got to toss the salad."

I followed her. "You're no fun."

"That's not what you said Sunday morning. Was it the first time Sunday morning, or the second one that I wasn't any fun?" She took a head of romaine out of the refrigerator and began tearing the leaves into a large bowl. That's another thing I learned from her—tearing the lettuce instead of cutting it. I put my arms around her waist from behind and nuzzled her hair. She had soft fine hair that felt like gossamer to the touch.

71

"I'm not terribly hungry," she said. "I had a late lunch at the Hollanden House."

The Hollanden House was the home of Cleveland's power lunch crowd and not really Mary's style. "How come?" I said.

"My boss. He wanted to talk about a new sales push for the station."

"Steve Stunning," I mumbled, meaning Steve Cirini, the young, good-looking bachelor who was general manager of Channel 12, where Mary worked as head of advertising sales. "Did he ask you out again?"

She shook up a cruet of one of the strange mixtures she concocts for salad dressing. "He always asks me out, Milan, I don't even pay any attention anymore."

"He'll just break your heart."

She laughed. "You're the heartbreaker. I called you at home this afternoon but I got your machine. Do you have a new client?"

"Not exactly," I said. "I'm doing some work for a friend."

"Anyone I know?"

"Matt Baznik." I sighed. "His kid is into drugs."

She waved a hand in front of her face. "They all are these days, there's no getting away from it. It's nothing to get excited about, though. They grow out of it."

I pulled back and looked at her. "Not get excited? Are you kidding?"

She shook her head. "Kids have to experiment, to try things. It's like sticking your fingers in the mashed potatoes just to see what it feels like. Drugs are a phase. Part of growing up in the twentieth century. But it works itself out naturally. Look how wonderfully I turned out."

The hair on my neck prickled. "What do you mean?"

"Well, I did a lot of drugs when I was a kid, and it didn't seem to hurt me any."

I guess I couldn't disguise my shock. I felt my mouth hanging open. She looked at me gravely and all at once started to laugh. "Come on, Milan," she said, "I was raised in Boston. Drugs were as available as chewing gum. Of course I did them."

"I didn't know," I managed to croak out.

"It wasn't important enough to talk about. It's like necking in the movies or cutting algebra class, something everybody has to do. Don't tell me you never smoked grass?"

"Once," I said. "I got the giggles and then I got sleepy."

She sprinkled the vinaigrette from the cruet over the romaine. "You were at Kent State in the late sixties and then in Vietnam, and you *never* did coke or pills or acid?"

I shook my head.

She sighed. "You must have been some straight arrow."

"I was," I said. "And I still am. Drugs suck. And so do the people who sell them."

She stopped tossing the salad and looked at me, then went to the balcony door and checked the fire. When she spoke it was out into the night. "And the people who use them, too?"

"I didn't say that."

"You didn't have to, chum."

"Mary, I don't want to start a hassle."

"What's to hassle about? Christ!" She turned so quickly her hair swung around later than the rest of her did. "Another unwritten rule in the Milan Jacovich code of acceptable conduct that I've broken? Do you always see everything in black and white?"

"When it comes to kids and drugs I do. There was a lot of it in Vietnam. A bunch of young kids, away from home for the first time, not knowing whether they'd ever see another sunset, so they smoked and snorted and popped pills. There was a kid in my platoon, name of Tommy Yancey, from somewhere around Cincinnati, I think, on the Ohio side. He was stoned around the clock, grass, pills, peppers, acid, whatever he could get his hands on. We were in a firefight one night, an ambush, and Yancey was so far into La-La Land he didn't have the sense to keep his head down. He stood up, screaming like an entire Comanche war party, and went charging into the enemy. The blast of rifle fire literally blew off his head."

"Well, excuse me for living! I wasn't in combat, unfortunately. I was a seventeen-year-old kid who wanted to be accepted and liked, and I did what everyone else in my school was doing, which was pot and ludes and a little coke! It didn't harm anyone."

"Not directly," I said.

Her eyes took on that dangerous look. "Meaning?"

"For every dollar you smoked or sucked up your nose, ninety-five cents of it went into the pockets of slimeball gangsters who hook kids on heroin."

"Lighten up, will you!"

"It's true," I said, "and you know it. You aren't going to give me the old J. Edgar Hoover party line that there's no such thing as organized crime, are you?"

Her tone flattened out, always a bad sign. "I'm not going to give you anything."

Somewhere in any disagreement there is a line between a difference of opinion and a serious argument, and we'd crossed it without either of us noticing. I tried to laugh. "Why are we fighting about something that happened ten years ago?"

"Probably because you won't ever be able to forgive me for—"

"Mary," I said, getting up and going to her, "nobody is blaming you for anything. There's nothing to forgive."

"Thanks for the presidential pardon," she said in a voice as dry as a pile of fall leaves. She went back into the kitchen to pour us two glasses of wine, even though it hadn't breathed enough. She said over her shoulder, "Am I forgiven my former lovers, too?"

That hurt a lot, so I didn't answer her. I went back out to the living room and sat down.

"Am I?" she asked, coming in and handing me a glass. "I wasn't a virgin when you met me. And as you know, I once had an affair with a married man. Is there a big scarlet letter on my chest that only you can see? You're so damn judgmental! Well, everybody doesn't live up to your standards. But it doesn't mean we aren't nice people living decent, productive lives. Everyone in the world has boosted a candy bar from the drugstore—everyone but you. You're such a goody-two-shoes I'll bet you never did."

"No, I didn't."

"And when you were a cop you probably never even took a free cup of coffee, did you?"

"Coffee, sure. Nothing else though."

Her eyes widened, mocking. "Milan Jacovich accepting a caffeine bribe! Film at eleven!"

"Mary, quit it."

"No," she said. "Let's explore all the wonderful things about you that make you better than the rest of us."

"Not better. Just . . . that's just not what I do."

"It's not what most of us do—but we've all done *something* we're ashamed of, that we wouldn't want on the front page of the *Plain Dealer*. I feel sorry for you that you haven't. What a boring life you must have led." Her beautiful mouth was a slash in her face. "If you're forty years old and you never used drugs, then you're the oddball, not everybody else."

I tried to smile, but my mouth was stiff. "I never needed them," I said. "I'm high on life." It was a weak, inane retort, but I couldn't think of anything else to say.

"Oh, bullshit. You're high on yourself, Milan, up on some mountaintop where the rest of us mere mortals can never climb."

"Mary, the boy is dealing!"

The color left her cheeks, and she looked away. Then she took a quick sip of wine and sat down next to me. "I'm sorry," she said quietly.

"That's the trouble. One thing frequently leads to another."

"Oh, so now I'm a drug kingpin?"

I slumped wearily against the cushions. "That's not fair."

"Well, Christ knows, we always have to be fair. If it isn't fair we just can't have it in our life, can we?"

There wasn't much more in the way of conversation after that. I overcooked the fish, too. At about ten o'clock, when the wine was gone, along with the better part of the evening, and I realized we hadn't exchanged more than ten words, I said, "I think I'd better head on home."

"Why?" she said sadly. "Was the dinner that bad? Or was it just that you had to eat it with a reformed junkie slut?"

"Mary, damn it."

"Can't you forgive me my youthful indiscretions, Milan? Now every time you look at me do you see some crazed hophead with a belt tied around her arm cooking heroin in a bent teaspoon? Don't you ever cut people any slack? Does everyone have to be spotless and immaculate in order to share your world?"

"Of course not. It's a part of life, I guess. I know. Maybe I am too much of a straight arrow. I'm not angry and I'm not judging you. It doesn't matter; it was a long time ago. Everyone has to do what they have to do."

She put her hand on my face, her eyes as sad as a Pierrette puppet. "And you do, too, don't you, Milan?"

"Yeah," I said, "I guess I do."

UNIVERSITY Circle takes its name from Case Western Reserve University, which surrounds it, and is close to much of the cultural life of the East Side, including the Art Museum, Severance Hall, and the Cleveland Play House just a few blocks away. There are hospitals and libraries and museums all within its boundaries, and in recent years it has been invaded by upscale professionals who have renovated and moved into the old character-drenched buildings to create one of the city's most sought-after residential neighborhoods. Being within walking distance of some of the most attractive places in town intensifies the desirability of the area, and its proximity to downtown and to the Flats, another revitalized area of nightclubs and singles bars on the east bank of the Cuyahoga, helps to keep the real estate costs high, too. In University Circle, Perrier and Calistoga water are the beverages of choice, and the cars parked on the street rarely come from Detroit—most young Cleveland lawyers drive four-door Saabs these days. It has always been a curiosity to me that as soon as people make enough money to live any way they want to, they all choose to be just like everyone else in their bracket—the same clothes, the same cars, the same pricey mineral waters.

Barrie Tremont's address was a yellow brick building with a rear view of the Art Museum. The facade had been recently sandblasted, bringing out the intricate workmanship in the masonry, a throwback to the days when even warehouses and industrial structures were designed to enhance their surroundings. Urns of flowers and leaves were carved into the stone, with vines curling down on either side of the doorway, which had been painted bright turquoise in its newest incarnation as fashionable housing.

There were two doorbells mounted in the entryway under a metallic speaker. One read TREMONT and the other SINGER. I pushed the one I wanted and was startled when there was an answering buzz. I went in, wondering why I was admitted without anyone asking who I was, and went up a flight of stairs which were obviously a recent addition; they were more modernistic than the rest of the building and didn't fit their surroundings. At the top of the steps a door opened and a very attractive young woman stood framed in the light from inside. Her dark brown hair was feather cut, and she was wearing a pair of those form-fitting white leggings that look like long underwear. Her silk shirt was the color magenta that you only get when you buy the giant box of sixty-four Crayolas.

"Miss Tremont?"

"Hi, come on up," she said. She was in her late twenties, with a trim, compact body. I walked past her through the door. It isn't often that beautiful women invite me into their apartments, and when they do, they usually turn out to be Amway dealers.

It was one enormous room with high ceilings. Wallboards of the type used in art galleries had been strategically positioned to partition off the sleeping area and were hung with David Hockney and Frank Stella prints and a couple of framed art deco posters. A large neon sculpture stood free in the center of the room, but it was turned off so as not to compete with the morning light that streamed through the industrial windows. One blind wall had been made into a kitchen, and the appliances looked shiny and new. Near them was a blond wood Danish modern dining room set with six chairs upholstered in a discreet charcoal gray around an oval table. Shag rugs in beige and champagne tones were scattered across the hardwood floor and picked up the similar colors in the furniture.

Barrie Tremont said, "Over here," and led me to the dining room set. She squatted down beside the table and jiggled one of its legs. "See, it's ready to fall apart."

"I'm sorry . . . ?"

"Do you think you can fix it here or will you have to take it in to the shop?" she said.

I looked at the loose table leg. "I could probably fix it here," I said, "but that's not what I came for."

She straightened up. "You aren't from Janssen's?"

"I'm afraid not."

She laughed nervously and shook her head. "Jesus, I've got to be more careful. I shouldn't have let you in. You could be just anybody."

"Sorry. My name is Jacovich." I gave her a business card, one of the real ones, and she read it with just a small frown.

"Milan Security? I don't understand. Are you trying to sell me an alarm system or something?"

"No," I said, "but if you're going to let strangers walk in here without finding out who they are, you could probably use one. I'm here on another matter."

She tucked the card in the pocket of her shirt. "You don't look dangerous, big as you are." I wasn't sure I liked that. "Well, as long as you're already in, make yourself comfortable," she said, pointing at the sofa. "What can I do for you?" She sank down onto a low beige chair on the other side of a glass-topped coffee table with a monolithic ceramic base. Back issues of *Vogue* and a current *Cleveland Magazine* all but obscured the glass.

"I wanted to ask you about your Merle Avenue property."

She looked blank, as though she'd heard a vaguely familiar foreign tongue and was trying to translate it in her own mind before answering. Then she said, "Yes?"

"You do own a house on Merle Avenue in East Cleveland, don't you?"

She nodded, still a bit tentative.

"Is it currently occupied?"

"Um, I think so."

"Don't you know?"

She put both hands up to her temples. "I'm not sure. I own

a lot of property, and I can't keep track of all of it. I have people to do that for me."

"You mean like Christmas Amboy?"

"Who?"

"Christmas Amboy. Your real estate broker."

"Oh," she said. "Oh, sure. Yes, he takes care of my . . . holdings."

"I spoke with him yesterday about the Merle house."

"You did?" she said, opening her eyes wide.

"Would you be willing to sell it?"

"Um, no, I don't think so. I'll have to check."

"With whom?"

She looked around, as if hoping the answer was written on the wall somewhere. "I have to talk to my attorney, of course."

"I understand."

"I mean, this is rather sudden . . ."

"But you do have the property listed with Amboy Realty?"

"Y-yes. But I wasn't really thinking about—selling it."

"You listed it but you don't want to sell it."

"Well," she said lamely, "you never know."

"And so you want to check with your attorney?"

"There are a lot of factors. . . ."

I stood up. "Would you do that for me, Miss Tremont? Talk to your attorney? And give me a call when you decide?"

"Yes. Sure. I mean, I guess I can. I have your card and everything."

"That's right," I said. "You do."

* * *

I waited in my car, parked down the block and across the street and positioned so that I could see the entrance to Barrie Tremont's building in my rearview mirror. The morning was just cold enough to make the waiting unpleasant, and I slipped on my gloves after I finished my first cigarette. Even though I was only a short distance from University Circle, there was little traffic, automotive or pedestrian, and I prepared myself for a long wait. After about twenty minutes, a panel truck bearing the legend JANSSEN FURNITURE rolled to a stop, and a burly man in green coveralls got out, carrying a toolbox. He

80

rang the bell, said something into the speaker, and was admitted. I figured that the conference over the table leg would take a while, so I drove to the nearest fast-food joint, used their john, got myself two tacos and a Coke to go, and went back to my post. I had just finished the first taco when the furniture man came out, got into his truck, and drove away. It looked like he'd been able to repeg the table leg without taking it into the shop.

The rest of the day moved like a sloth with a double hernia. Stakeouts are like that, long stretches of pure boredom. I was even glad to see the wino who had evidently wandered over from Euclid Avenue and lost his way. He stopped near me, fumbled in the pocket of his tattered, too large overcoat and extracted a paper bag. He took a long and apparently satisfying draft from the bottle inside, screwed the top back on, returned it to his pocket, and moved on. At least his stumbling passage provided a break in the monotony. But I had to hang around and see exactly what Barrie Tremont was up to; I wanted to find out why she'd lied to me.

I knew there was something funny going on because she'd been hesitant when I asked her about Christmas Amboy. We meet so many different people in the course of our daily lives, it's almost impossible to remember them all, by name or by face, so when you walk down the street and run into the supermarket cashier who checks out your groceries three times a week, you might not recognize her because she's out of her usual context. And you might not register the name of the guy you met at a bar and argued with over the relative merits of Bernie Kosar and Boomer Esiason, even though you might remember he drank Heineken. But you'd recall the names of people you met called Elmer Studmuffin or Ophelia Rass. Or Carl Ingeldinger, for that matter.

Or Christmas Amboy.

At about a quarter to six a well-dressed young man stepped smartly up to the door of Tremont's building, dug into a cute little leather purse he carried on a thong around his wrist, and pulled out a key, which he began to insert into the lock. He had a little trouble with it because of the fading light, which gave me time to get out of my car and across the street.

"Excuse me, sir," I said, and he turned around. He was taken aback by my size, but he didn't look particularly frightened, although he held his attaché case in front of him like a shield. I noticed it was eelskin. His close-shaven face gleamed with a health club suntan, and his alert brown eyes peered out from behind a pair of Sally Jessie Raphael glasses. Above the open collar of his coat I saw a bright red tie peppered with little yellow squiggles with dark blue nuclei, the mandatory neckwear for the young executive on the way up. Red tie at morning, businessman's warning.

"Are you Mr. Singer?"

"Why do you ask?"

I consulted a piece of paper I had in my pocket. It had Barrie Tremont's name and address on it, but he didn't know that. "I'm looking for a Mr. William Singer."

He relaxed a bit. "My name is Jeff Singer," he said.

I'd guessed correctly. No one of his age and social status was named Bill anymore. And if they were, they changed it. Today thirty-something stockbrokers were named Jeff or Jason or Randy. All brittle efficiency, at home or at work. He looked like the kind of guy who'd go out of his way to use *impact* as a verb.

"I'm with Farmer's Insurance, and Mr. William Singer was a witness to an auto accident involving one of our policy holders."

"Can't help you," he said. "I have a cousin Bill, but he lives in Detroit. Well, Bloomfield Hills, really."

God forbid his cousin should live in Detroit proper. Jeff could never show his face at the health club again. I said, "I'm awfully sorry to have bothered you."

"Hey, no problem, guy." I hate being called "guy." The magnanimous little snotnose dismissed me with a wave and went back to the knotty problem of opening his door.

As he discovered the secret to inserting his key and went inside, I crossed the street and got back into my car. Now that I knew who belonged in the building, it wouldn't take much imagination to figure out that anyone else who showed up did not.

Stiff as hell from sitting all day, I wriggled my butt against the seat. I watched the lights go on in the downstairs apartment and figured Jeff Singer was hanging up his Aquascutum coat, loosening his red power tie, switching on the latest Springsteen CD at full volume, and pouring a nice cold Perrier into a Waterford goblet and garnishing it with fresh lime.

At seven ten a brand new top-of-the-line Asian sedan with dealer plates cruised up to the building and stopped. A tall good-looking man in his late forties uncoiled himself from the seat, snakeskin cowboy boots first. He was dressed expensively but with flash, with a camel hair overcoat and headgear that wasn't quite a Stetson but close enough not to be worth quibbling about. He locked his car, looked around casually, and went to the turquoise door, which he opened with a key.

I scrunched down in the seat to look up at the second-floor windows. From my low angle I couldn't see in, but after a few seconds I saw two shadows moving on the ceiling. The visitor was in Barrie Tremont's apartment.

I went over to the import and shone my penlight inside. There were only two hundred seventy-one miles on the odometer. A leather ID case was clipped to the sun visor, and I was able to make out the registration: Henry Morgan of Boyce Road, in the most expensive area of Shaker Heights. Deep Shaker.

9

I SWUNG by the house on Merle Avenue on my way home, but there was no activity visible from the street, and I decided not to look any closer. I didn't want to run into Deshon and his designated hitters. But I had to wonder why a Jamaican crack dealer was operating out of a house owned by a classy lady like Barrie Tremont, and whether or not she knew it. And I wondered too why she happened to own property in one of Cleveland's worst sections. Ordinary slumlords invest in tenement apartment buildings with greater income potential than a single home, and although the Merle Avenue place could certainly have housed several families, albeit in extreme discomfort, there was no sign of any occupants other than Deshon and his buddies.

It took me about fifteen minutes to get back to Cleveland Heights. I parked in my assigned space behind my building and walked across the street to the food mart, where I bought myself a huge link of spicy sausage, some German potato salad, and a six-pack. I carried my dinner home, the prospect of a solitary late meal and an early bedtime stretching before me like the Death Valley landscape. I'd had the whole day to sit in my car and brood, thinking about Mary, and I was no more certain of my feelings than I had been the night before, or of the rightness of them. And that bothered me. Mary was right: I do tend to see things as being either from column A or column B.

Irrational as it seems, it disturbed me to know that the woman I loved had done a lot of drugs when she was younger. Illegal drug use is a subject on which I'm pretty rigid. I've seen too many burn-outs and Jello-heads, too many young lives ruined by substance abuse, too many kids so screwed up by the crap they put into their systems that they either get sidetracked for years or derailed altogether. And those are the lucky ones, the ones that don't wind up in jail or selling themselves on the street or in a sliding drawer in a refrigerated room downtown. Most people delude themselves into thinking drugs are recreational; so are group orgies, but that doesn't make them the all-American Sunday afternoon pastime. Or smart, either. With all the antidrug information available to kids these days, it amazes me that anyone in their right mind would even experiment.

Mary is thirteen years younger than I, and her generation grew up by a different set of rules and values. The Asian war that had been days and nights of endless rain and heat and muck and kids going home in body bags to me was to Mary just something on TV to get through before the good programs came on. I didn't have the right to judge her. But my reaction, while perhaps excessive, was at least honest, and I've learned not to apologize for my gut feelings; I respond to certain things in very specific ways because of who and what I am, and there isn't a whole lot I can do about it. That's just me, and expecting me to be something else is like asking me to be five foot six or have brown eyes. Like Popeye, I yam what I yam.

I took down a fry pan, splashed in some cooking sherry and olive oil. I noticed that it was extra virgin olive oil, something Mary had probably picked up on some long-ago shopping expedition. I'm no gourmet cook—I was never a cook at all until Mary told me she thought men in the kitchen were sexy—so I've never understood about "extra virgin" olive oil. Maybe that's cultural conditioning, too: where I come from, either you are or you aren't.

I put a splatter-screen over the pan of frying sausage,

spooned the potato salad out of its cardboard carton and onto a plate, and popped a Stroh's. When the sausage was done I took the food over to my desk and sat down, opening a fresh pack of three-by-five index cards. I always transfer my case notes to cards, because then I can lay them all out and move them around until they start making sense.

I only had a few cards so far. One was headed DESHON, one BARRIE TREMONT, and another HENRY MORGAN. Not much to shuffle unless you were into three-card monte.

Then I got thinking about Paulie Baznik, and about the hopelessness that seemed to hover around his father like an aura. I thought about it so long that the sausage was cold by the time I got around to eating it. I wound up throwing half of it into the trash.

* * *

In parts of Shaker Heights the houses resemble baronial estates more than Midwestern residences. The feeling on some of the streets is of Europe, but Europe in an older and more graceful time.

Henry Morgan's house was about a five-iron from the Shaker Heights Country Club, a two-story, pristine white with black trim Cape Cod like so many of the houses in the area, except bigger and more majestic-looking. This section in the depths of Shaker Heights, called Deep Shaker either because it's right in the middle of the community or because the residents have deeper pockets than most, is where many of Greater Cleveland's truly rich reside, the kind of neighborhood in which householders give out full-size Milky Way bars to the trick-or-treaters on Halloween night instead of the miniature ones that come twenty to a package. Behind every door lives a patron of the symphony, a VIP box owner at the Stadium, an endower of libraries and scholarships, or a collector of something rare and expensive. Five-dollar cigars complement forty-year-old Armagnac in the library after dinner, and the paintings on the walls are not reproductions. The folks who live here are the giants whose footsteps make the city's financial mountains tremble.

A precise row of tall poplars stood like a close-order drill team, screening the front of the property from prying eyes, and there were so many trees on the rolling front lawn that the house seemed to be sequestered in the middle of a forest. The crushed-oyster-shell driveway meandered like an equestrian trail up a rise, passing beneath a natural archway of over-hanging oak and catalpa branches bowed low by November rains, then sweeping to a magnificent colonnaded entry which was designed to impress. It did its job, and as I steered the car toward the house, the zany early morning high jinks of Lanigan and Webster on the radio provided a sort of bizarre counter-point.

There was an iron statue painted to resemble a black youth in jockey silks, arm extended and holding a ring to which you might want to tie your horse. I shook my head; I thought those things had gone out of favor in the early sixties, a fate richly deserved.

I rang the bell and heard melodic chimes from deep inside the house. I fully expected a butler to answer my summons, but when the door opened a woman stood there, looking some-what surprised and very imperious in a burgundy wool suit that had never hung on a store rack but somehow failed to do much for her besides disguise her thickening middle. Her hair, dyed a discreet golden blond, was pulled back hard behind her ears in an asexual style suggesting maiden ladies of a certain age who organized fund-raisers and bake sales in small towns, and her face seemed to have been drawn back with it. Pale blue eyes peered at me through matronly gold-framed glasses. She looked like the kind of solid, serious woman that rich men marry for security when they are very young.

"Mrs. Morgan?"

She fiddled with her hair, although not a strand was out of place. "I'm Margo Morgan, yes. Did you want to see me?"

"No, actually, I was hoping to see your husband. I thought I'd catch him before he went off to work."

She let a breath jet out of her nostrils in little puffs; appar-ently that was supposed to be a laugh. "You have to get up pretty early in the morning to do that," she said. "When he comes home at all. He's a busy man." The words issued from between her thin lips like mortar shells. "If you're selling some-thing, don't waste your time. He's the best salesman in the world, and as a result he's the toughest to sell." She made a sour face, as though smelling something bad. "Of course, it all depends who's doing the selling."

"I'm a pretty good salesman myself," I lied. "Do you suppose I could find him at the office?"

"He's at the showroom, yes."

"The showroom?"

"Yes. On Mayfield."

I digested the information with barely a gulp. "Thank you, Mrs. Morgan, I'll try him there. Sorry to have bothered you."

I got back into my car and drove down the other half of the crescent driveway and back out onto the parklike street. Now I knew who Henry Morgan was. In the failing light in front of Barrie Tremont's apartment, I hadn't recognized him from his TV commercials.

"Waco" Morgan was a minor celebrity in Northern Ohio. He had opened a used car lot in Cleveland in the late sixties, then a Dodge dealership, than a Ford dealership, and finally he'd gotten a franchise for Asian imports on Mayfield Road that was one of the largest new car operations in the Midwest. Extremely visible in the rich-doing-good-works set, he was in the society columns as often as he was at one of his many automobile showrooms. He had become the symbol of his own business, as many auto dealers have, by appearing between chunks of chopped-up late night and Saturday afternoon movies on television, always wearing his broad-brimmed hat and twentieth-century cowboy drag, a good old boy whose ingenuous sincerity was written all over his smile. No blue-collar car buyer could ever believe that beaming, silver-thatched Waco Morgan, the workingman's pal, might sell them a lemon, and they flocked to him, and to the big-topped minicircuses that provided free cotton candy for their kids and left elephant shit all over his used car lots each weekend. And a lot of them parted with substantial increments of money to drive home in a new or "previously-owned" car, complete with a caricature of Waco on the license plate frame. He claimed he would match or better any other dealer's price, and in a few well-publicized cases his customers had hauled him into court to force him to make good his boast. His specialty was granting loans to bad credit risks, which was possible because he carried his own paper at rates that fell just short of the usury laws. He had a Ford dealership in Toledo and a Jeep-Renault franchise in Akron and was the largest retail car dealer in the state of Ohio.

I thought about driving over to his showroom to talk to him, but then I got a better idea and headed downtown.

* * *

Ohio Mercantile Bank is in the heart of the city's financial district just east of Public Square. Imposing statues of two women flank the entrance. The one on the left brandishes a sword in one hand, and a cashbox in the other. The second stone lady cradles a set of scrolls against her bosom, and her upraised hand is holding what looks to be a severed human arm. I've always supposed the symbolism is that if you want to pry a loan loose from Ohio Merc, it's going to cost you an arm.

Rudy Dolsak is the vice president of something or other at the bank, a lofty position that has earned him an office with walls and a window instead of a desk out in the middle of the huge banking floor under the gaze of small depositors. Rudy is another of my Slovenian friends of thirty years' standing. We didn't know the term *nerd* back then, but in school that's what Rudy was, the class grind and resident math genius. He had idolized Marko Meglich and me with that mute adoration plump, unathletic boys often have for school jocks; he never missed a football game, always cheered louder than anyone else, and could be counted on to run for the Cokes and burgers when we were too busy practicing banging into one another. In return we had allowed him the privilege of helping us with our math homework and invited him to share some of our social pursuits. He was the only one of our crowd whose locker didn't stink of gym socks.

Chronic asthma had kept him out of the Vietnam draft, so while I slogged around in the mud at Cam Ranh Bay getting shot at by little brown people I didn't know and napalming their villages, Rudy was knocking everyone's socks off at Case Western Reserve University, earning several degrees in matters pertaining to the making and keeping of money and marrying the pretty daughter of a stockbroker with offices in a new high rise on East Ninth Street. He alone of the old gang from the parish managed to acquire a house in Beachwood and a Lincoln town car, but what gives him the most pleasure is that his son, Rudy Jr., made the varsity basketball team at Cleveland State. Still a certified sports nut, the statistics Rudy can spew out at a moment's notice have more to do with the Browns' rushing and passing game or the Cavaliers' shooting percentage from the foul line than with the current prime rate.

It was the Browns and their performance against the hapless Steelers on the Sunday past that engaged his interest at the beginning of my visit, and he was duly impressed that I had gone to the stadium and braved the lousy weather. But such a dull game was only good for about five minutes of conversation, and eventually he moved into other areas.

"You're looking fat and sassy," he said to me—this from a man who always keeps his jacket on to hide the rubber tire around his waist. "What's up?"

"I need a few people checked out, Rudy," I said.

He frowned, rubbing the bridge of his nose where his glasses had made two deep red grooves. "I wish you wouldn't ask me. I've done this for you before, but you know damn well that financial records are private."

That was true. According to the law, banking and credit records are as sacrosanct as the confessional. In practice, if you know the buttons to push and the people to talk to, they are about as confidential as the feature page of the *Plain Dealer*.

"I assume you have a case working?" Rudy went on.

"As a matter of fact, I don't. Not in the traditional sense, anyway. A friend of mine has a kid who seems to be mixed up with drugs." I didn't want to tell him it was Matt Baznik's kid.

"That's awful," he said. "And there's no getting away from it, either. That's the damn pity of it. I got lucky; my Rudy never went near the stuff. He's too much of a jock, wouldn't put anything harmful in that perfect body of his." Even while he was shaking his head in dismay at the social problems of America, he was beaming about his son's athletic prowess.

I didn't have the time for Rudy's parental crowing. I pushed a piece of paper across the desk at him. "These are the names," I said.

Rudy tilted his head so that he could read the list through the bottom half of his bifocals. "Morgan I know," he said. "Everybody knows Waco Morgan. He's a pretty important guy in this town. What are you looking for?"

"Whatever you've got on his real estate holdings. And anything else that you might think is of interest."

"What does Waco Morgan have to do with drugs?"

"Probably nothing, Rudy. Let me be the detective, and you be the banker, okay?"

Through his nose Rudy made a pompous noise they must have taught him in banker's school. "Barrie Tremont. Who's he?"

"She. That's why it's spelled with an *i-e* at the end. And I don't know who she is. I was hoping you could tell me."

"Hmmmm," he said, hitting three different notes of the scale along the way. "Cherchez la femme, eh?"

"Rudy . . ."

"Christmas Amboy? Is that a person?"

"Guess when his birthday is."

"What?"

"Just guess."

He put the paper with the three names in his inside jacket pocket. "Get out of here, Milan. I'm busy."

* * *

Waco Morgan 4 Cars was far enough east in Mayfield Heights that the suburbanites from Gates Mills and Hunting Valley were as likely to give him their custom as were the somewhat plainer folks from Lyndhurst and South Euclid. This particular dealership sold Asian imports, which while not exactly exotic anymore were still something of an eyebrow raiser to the good working people of Cleveland. There was a time Asian cars enjoyed their popularity because they were cheaper than their American counterparts, but those days are as dead as the snide titters once evoked by a *Made in Japan* sticker. The top-of-the-line model in the window of Waco Morgan's showroom, a bright red sedan with a roofline like a torpedo, boasted a sticker price of twenty-four thousand dollars and change. *Arigato*, but no *arigato*.

A salesman approached me before I got both feet on the

property line. He was wearing a shiny gray suit and a pink tie with a handkerchief that nearly matched. "Hiya! Ed Johnson!" he said as he pumped my hand and gathered me close to him with his other arm. "Thinking about taking the plunge, eh? Listen, I saw you drive up." He tapped me on the chest with the back of his hand, just over my heart. "I got news for you—this baby here will eat your wheels alive."

As one of those living fossils ancient enough to remember when all cars had grilles that looked like bared metal teeth and headlights resembling the eyes of a giant insect, I had a good time with the mental picture of the sedan devouring my car like something out of a 1950s horror film: *The Big Red Thing That Ate a Sunbird.*

"And smooth?" Ed Johnson went on, giving me another rap with the backs of his fingers. "You'll feel like you're riding around in your living room. Power everything. It takes the work out of driving. Now, don't let the sticker scare you. We can work out the kind of payment plan that'll fit you like your underwear." He gave me another little thump on the chest. It was one too many.

"Don't do that again," I said.

"What?"

I showed him, my backhand smacking his shiny jacket just over his pink handkerchief. I was sorry almost at once; I think I made him feel bad.

"Sorry." He actually blushed. "It's just a habit."

"Work on it," I said. "I'd like to see Waco Morgan."

He recovered, smiling. "Everybody wants to talk to Waco," he said, "on account of him being on TV every two minutes. He's a celebrity. Well, he doesn't do the selling stuff himself. He's the boss, ya know. But as soon as you sign your contract, I guarantee Waco will be out here to shake your hand and present you the key to your new car personally."

"I don't want to buy a car," I said. "I want to talk to Mr. Morgan."

An invisible switch was tripped, and some lambent light deep within Ed Johnson's soul clicked off, along with his smile. I had uttered the ultimate obscenity: *I don't want to buy a car.*

"Office back of the showroom," he said as flat as the plains of Kansas, and walked away, leaving me alone amid the sleek shiny cars. I walked among them carefully, not wanting my rude raiments to rub off any of the gleam.

There was no gleam to the woman who guarded the entry to Waco Morgan's office. It was more of a dull glow, like obsidian. She was somewhere past forty, with dyed black hair worn in a style fifteen years too young for her and sprayed stiff. Her tight black skirt and cream-colored blouse hugged the lines of a sleek figure, but there seemed to be no softness beneath the fabric.

"You have an appointment?" she demanded. The nameplate on her desk, a long thick cube of Lucite, read CLEATTE HOR-NADAY. "Mr. Morgan can't see anyone without an appointment," she said. "I'm sure you appreciate that."

I didn't appreciate it at all.

"There are *no* exceptions," she went on. "I start making exceptions for you, then I'd have to make them for everyone else, and pretty soon we have a state of anarchy here. Anarchy." She tasted the word, relishing its textures and nuances. "You have to have an appointment."

"How do I get an appointment?"

"You call for one, of course."

"If you'd make one for me right now, I'd save myself a quarter."

She went around the hunk of veneered plywood that took up more than half the room and sat down in her chair, swinging tightly-pressed knees under the desk in one fluid, no-nonsense motion. "I'm afraid I'll have to excuse myself now," she said. "This is a place of business."

"You don't even know what I want yet," I said. "Where do you get off giving me the bum's rush? I might want to buy twenty or thirty cars to use in my business."

Her eyes, peering out from under lids burdened by a pound of green eye shadow, examined my clothes and dismissed me in the manner of one perfectly comfortable with making snap judgments about people based on the way they dress, the car they drive, or the ethnicity of their last name. "Not bloody likely," she said.

10

I WENT back to Merle Avenue and hung around, just to see whether anything was up. My muscles were cramping. If I'd wanted to spend this much time sitting in the front seat of a car I would have become a cabdriver. The tough part was that I didn't really learn anything I hadn't known already.

The Seville was in the driveway, and in the two hours I was either parked on the street or slowly driving by the supposedly abandoned house, eleven people dropped by for visits of five minutes or less. I didn't begrudge Deshon his friends—it was just that there were so many of them, and so early in the morning.

At about one o'clock the big Cadillac backed out with Deshon at the wheel and took off with an ostentatious waste of rubber, the bravura move of a guy who'd never dream he was being tailed. This was going to be easy.

I kept a block or so behind him, usually allowing two or three cars to get between us but never losing sight of the Caddy's broad rear deck. The few times I got close enough to see, I observed his head bopping from side to side to the rhythm of the music that was no doubt filling his car's interior, volume cranked to maximum. Deshon was one of those people who drive by with their radios turned up so loudly that everyone for blocks around can share in the enjoyment of the music, whether they want to or not. When I become emperor, those guys will be the first to go.

When he reached Richmond Road he turned south, heading past the glittering Beachwood Mall and the upscale housing tracts of the city of Beachwood, crossing Chagrin Boulevard and passing the Eastern Campus of Cuyahoga Community College to reach the town of Bedford Heights, a blue-collar community geographically close to Pepper Pike and Beachwood, but several million social and economic miles away.

Deshon went east again for a few blocks and then, with a fine disdain for the rules, he hung a left into the parking lot of the Blind Frog Saloon without signaling. By the time I pulled in after him he was on his way through the front door.

I couldn't very well follow him inside; he had seen enough of me to recognize me in a crowd, and at my size I'm not that hard to spot. I would have given a lot to be a fly on the wall in there, because whatever the reason he'd gone into the Blind Frog, I was pretty sure it wasn't just to have lunch. Bedford Heights is a long drive from Merle Avenue just for a greasy burger.

I parked my Pontiac at the back of the lot, nose out, and waited some more. A lot of young sinewy guys were going into the Frog; I figured if they were drinking and shooting pool in the middle of the afternoon, they were either night workers or else unemployed. But they didn't interest me much. I was just afraid I'd have calluses on my butt before this was all over.

After almost half an hour Deshon came out again, accompanied by a slight young man in a denim jacket with a sheepskin collar. He was about five foot six, with the white-blond hair of an albino and pale, vacant blue eyes that he batted a lot. There was a slight space between each of his rabbity teeth; I could see them clearly because he grinned at almost everything. A real space cadet.

The two men talked for a few minutes, and then Rabbit Teeth handed Deshon a paper shopping bag from Higbee's department store. Early Christmas presents? I thought not. I used my camera to record the transaction, thinking of how much fun it would be to invite my friends over to look at the slides.

Deshon hustled the bag over to the Caddy, dumped it in the

trunk, and took off. Rabbit Teeth hitched up his crotch the way ballplayers do whenever the TV camera is on them and got into a black sports car covered with a gray film of dirt and mud. Since I was pretty sure Deshon was on his way either to the school or back to the house on Merle, I decided to direct my attention to his friend.

I followed the sports car to a parking lot just above University Circle. Rabbit Teeth eased it into a small space, got out, and crossed the street to another bar. This one I'd been to before, with Mary; they usually had a pretty good jazz combo on weekends. I parked on the street, fed the meter, and followed him inside.

He was greeted warmly when he walked through the door. Shouts of "Bobby!" "Hey, Bobby!" and "Bobby, my man!" bounced off the walls like handballs. Bobby was obviously a familiar figure here, and he accepted the greetings and accolades with a grin that seemed to get wider and wider and was occasionally augmented by a giggle. He sat at a table and several people came over to shake his hand or slap him on the back. The cocktail waitress kissed him on the cheek and hugged him as she took his order, and that elicited a silly, happy laugh from him. I wasn't sure what had caused it; there wasn't anything intrinsically funny about a Stoli with orange juice.

When she brought him his drink, he stood up, and they walked into the kitchen, arms around each other's waists and chatting like old friends. Sweet kids.

He was back within two minutes, still smiling. I perched on a barstool about ten feet away from him, positioning myself so I could watch him in the mirror, and asked the handsome black bartender for a Stroh's. It cost two fifty and made me remember that there was no client footing my expenses.

Bobby's demeanor was that of visiting royalty, if perhaps a clown prince. Everything seemed to strike him funny, and everything he said seemed to amuse his listeners, but employees and customers alike kept coming up to his table to pay their respects. For whatever reason, he was pretty popular here, and I was acutely aware that I wasn't. That's what happens when you march into unfriendly and unfamiliar territory.

The bartender wiped his hands on a towel and went around

the bar to talk to Bobby for a moment, and whatever the topic of conversation, it seemed to amuse Bobby as much as everything else did. He stood up, and the two of them went toward the back and disappeared into the men's room. Everyone else carefully kept their eyes elsewhere, mostly on the TV set chronicling the vicissitudes of *The Young and the Restless* or one of its many clones. I thought about visiting the facilities myself and concluded it wouldn't be very smart: Bobby and the bartender obviously wanted to be alone together. So I sipped my beer and waited. After a few minutes they returned; Bobby sat back down at his table, and the bartender resumed his station, looking lots happier than he had before.

In the mirror I could see that Bobby's Stoli and orange juice was almost gone, so I finished my beer and went outside, crossing Mayfield to where I'd parked. I got back into my car, which I had begun to think of as a womb I could hide in, and hunkered down to wait. The backs of my legs were aching.

In a few minutes Bobby emerged. He turned the sheepskin collar of his jacket up around his ears before he crossed the street in the middle of the block, deftly dodging cars from both directions and grinning at the drivers who cursed at him and flipped him off.

He trotted to his car, his face wreathed with a grin that told the world he didn't have a care, and I envied him whatever it was that made him such a happy fellow. I even took a photograph of his happy smile. When he pulled out of the parking lot, I noticed what I had been too far away to see before: his rear license plate frame read WACO MORGAN 4 CARS.

I followed him up Cedar Hill, past my own apartment, and on into South Euclid, where he stopped at still another tavern. I waited in my car across the street for about half an hour until he came out again. This time a ruined-looking woman in her early forties followed a couple of steps behind him, and they stood on the sidewalk chatting for a few minutes. Her mouth, painted with vivid red lipstick, was turned down at the corners and twisted as she spoke. She was very animated and seemed to be pleading with him, holding her hands out, palms up in supplication. He kept grinning but shook his head in the negative. The more she gestured, the more adamant he became.

Finally she moved closer and said something into his ear, and his grin widened. He looked around, and then the two of them went to his car, which he'd parked in a small lot beside the bar. They got into the front, but he didn't start the engine. I could see them through the back window, talking a bit more, and then her head and shoulders disappeared below the back of the seat.

I understood why Bobby smiled so much.

After a time the woman's head reappeared above the back of the seat, and she got out of the car and put something small into her purse. She didn't have as much lipstick on as she'd had a few minutes before, and she looked very sad. She patted ineffectually at her hair and went back into the bar without looking at Bobby, her eyes on her feet and a defeated slump to her shoulders.

He sat in his car for a while, wriggling around and adjusting his clothes. He allowed himself the luxury of a big stretch, fists up around his ears and elbows pointed straight out. Then he busied himself with something he took out of his pocket, bent down to it, and threw his head back once, then again. Nothing like a little snort after some cheap sex to enhance the afterglow. Finally he fired up the engine, and headed east.

He stopped in two more taverns, each time for twenty minutes or less, and ended up back at the Blind Frog.

This time I followed him in.

The Frog is a workingman's tavern, the kind you'll find in any industrial city in the middle of the U.S. Country music or rock and roll blasts from the big jukebox, they serve generous messy sandwiches garnished with greasy fries and onions, and they stock about thirty different brands of beer and boast one of the better pool tables on the East Side. At lunchtime there is always a sprinkling of ad executives and secretaries from nearby Chagrin Boulevard, but the guys who hang out in the Blind Frog in midmorning or during the afternoons wear baseball caps, shirts without buttons, and sideburns about three quarters of an inch too long.

I hadn't even been at the bar long enough to order a beer from the sexy lady behind it, who wore a green T-shirt emblazoned with the bar's logo, a smiling bullfrog wearing dark glasses and waving a white cane, when I felt a tap on my shoulder. I swung around on my stool. Bobby was standing there, his smile more questioning than amused. When I'd first seen him I'd thought the grin was a vacant one; up close I saw the cruelty behind those pale eyes with their dark red pupils.

"Do I know you, man?" His voice was thin and reedy, as though he didn't have quite the requisite number of vocal chords. His hands fluttered in front of him; black rainbows of greasy dirt rimmed his fingernails.

"I don't know," I said. "Do you?"

"Didn't I see you someplace before?"

I shrugged. "I get around."

"You following me?"

If I was, it didn't dislodge his ever present grin. He was a real loon, Bobby.

"Why would I do that?" I became aware of someone slipping onto the barstool beside me, but I didn't look over. In the back of the room the pool balls snicked, and I heard the satisfying sound of one dropping into the pocket.

"Why would you?" Bobby said. "If you wanted to talk to me, why wouldn't a man come up and shake hands and introduce himself? You was in University Circle before. I seen you there. Whaddaya think, that I'm stupid or something?"

Bobby obviously never heard that old admonition about never asking a question you didn't want to hear the answer to. "Who are you, anyway?" he said.

"I'm a friend of Deshon's."

"I don't know anyone by that name," he said, but the pink-rimmed eyes narrowed and the grin lost some elasticity.

"Oh, come on, Bobby."

It was hardly a grin at all anymore; one might have characterized it as a sickly smile. "He knows my name, too," he said to no one in particular.

"I know a lot about you, Bobby."

"Sometimes it's better not to know so much."

"Ignorance is bliss, huh?" I was immediately sorry I'd said it. I have little patience with people too dumb to know when I'm insulting them.

"What are you, a cop?"

"No."

" 'Cause if you're a cop, this is harassment."

"I'm not a cop." I didn't add, "anymore."

"This guy hassling you, Bobby?" I heard over my shoulder. I turned around to my neighbor at the bar, a big guy with an enormous beer gut and a ruff of fat around his neck. His scraggly beard didn't make him look like a television hero. Dirty-looking hair the color of wet sand peeked out from under an Indians cap, and a red and blue tattoo of the devil was half covered by the sleeve of his baseball shirt. He'd obviously had some of the Frog's sauteed onions for lunch, and his breath was not nice. Neither was the look on his doughy face. He had the mean, piggy eyes of a bully.

"Mind your business," I said. I could have been more civil, but I was in no mood.

"Fuck you," he said, his huge stomach wobbling.

"Snappy comeback. Tell me, is it tough going through life without being able to see your own dick?"

I thought his eyes were going to explode out of his head, but he stifled whatever clever rejoinder he had planned when the pretty bartender came over and said, "Hey, come on, guys. Take it outside." I ignored her and turned back to Bobby.

"You better back away from me," he was saying. "I don't like people following me around and spying on me."

"If I was trading crack for blow jobs in parking lots I wouldn't like anyone watching, either."

His white face got whiter, and the grin was all gone now. Fear had replaced it. "Jesus," he said, "you're ass deep in shit, man." He started to walk away.

"Bobby!" I said it too loud—it got the attention of everyone in the room; even the pool players paused in their endeavors to look over at us. It stopped Bobby in his tracks. He turned around to look at me, his mouth hanging loosely, showing the spaces between his teeth.

More softly I said, "Come here a minute."

He hesitated, looking at his friend on the stool next to mine.

"Come here," I repeated as if to a naughty child. He came back. Slowly. I leaned forward and got right into his face, close enough to see the clogged wide pores on his nose.

"I don't particularly care if you're feeding dope to every cocktail waitress and barfly on the East Side," I said. "But I want you to tell Deshon something for me. I want him to know that if he so much as goes near St. Clair High School again, I'll make him wish he was still back hustling middle-aged tourist ladies in Montego Bay. And when I finish with him, I'll come looking for you again, and I'll have your head on a pike." He looked blank. That had been a bit too recondite for him. "You know what a pike is, Bobby?"

He knitted his sparse eyebrows. "A fish?"

"Right," I said. It was better than I'd hoped for when I asked the question. I slid off the stool. I hadn't ordered anything, but I think we'd gotten the bartender all upset, so I tossed a dollar on the bar anyway, just to make her feel better. I walked the length of the room and out the door, noting that the sound of the pool game had not yet resumed. Everyone was too busy looking at my back.

I was halfway to my car when the big guy with the belly like a basketball came blasting out the door.

"Hey!" he yelled. I stopped and turned.

"Hey, fuck you, man." The guy must have read the Little Golden Book of Insults every night to prepare his dazzling repartee.

I was tired, and my body was sore and I was pretty disgusted, and I don't like getting braced by rednecks. "If you insist," I said, "but you'll at least have to buy me a drink first."

I figured insulting his machismo would do it. He came at me with the bearlike lumber of a big guy who's out of shape. I sidestepped his rush easily and used his own momentum to slam him against the fender of a nearby Ford Bronco. The breath whumped out of his lungs in an oniony blast, and I twisted his left arm up behind him, bending his wrist in on itself almost double. He made a humming noise between clenched jaws and sank to his knees.

"You aren't half good enough, cowboy," I said. I increased the pressure on his wrist until he got the idea and then let him go. I walked away, leaving him on his knees worshipping at the shrine of the white Bronco.

I was disappointed that it didn't make me feel any better.

101

11

SO Deshon was buying crack from a punk named Bobby and then selling it at the high school, among other places I supposed, and using kids like Paulie Baznik as runners. But Bobby wasn't the one I was after; he was about as small-time as one can get in the drug business, running around to taverns and restaurants dealing drugs to bartenders and waitresses for nickels and dimes, or occasional furtive sex. His vacant look and his nervous little eyes told me he was a conspicuous consumer of his own product, which was another tip-off as to where he fit in the great scheme of things. He was a minnow, almost at the bottom of the food chain, and there he'd undoubtedly stay. The big boys are too smart to put poison into their own systems when they can sell it to other eager suckers for a five-hundred-percent profit. Pinch off the mules and foot soldiers like Bobby and Deshon and there are ten dozen waiting to fill their shoes, waiting for a shot at easy money and hail-fellow-well-met status in the neighborhood.

When I got back home I called the Department of Motor Vehicles and ran a make on Bobby's license plate. I found out his name was Robert DeLayne and that he lived on Rockside, a fairly large street. I guessed it was an apartment building. If I knew my customers, there would be a healthy amount of foot-traffic in and out of that apartment all night. One of the insidious properties of crack is that one can never quite get enough. Buy five bucks' worth and use it up right away, and you want more. Buy twenty bucks' worth, you *still* want some more. It's no wonder everyone on the street is selling the crap—it makes good business sense.

I called Ingeldinger and recounted my afternoon with Bobby DeLayne, clued him in about Deshon, and gave him the address of the crack house on Merle Avenue.

"I thought I told you to tend to your knitting," he said, the words bubbling in such a way I could tell he was sucking a Life Saver.

"I'm just being a good citizen, Ding."

"That doesn't wash. You're starting to get on my nerves. Not that we don't appreciate the tip, but you're messing where you shouldn't be, and sooner or later you're going to step on my toes. Now, I'll tell you once more to butt out, nicely, because you're a friend of Meglich. Then I'm going to hang your ass on my wall."

"I told you, there's this kid—"

"There's lots of kids! Kids not old enough to shave yet knocking over liquor stores for crack money. Twelve-year-old girls peddling head in parked cars to guys that don't even bother to turn off the motor. The department is on top of this and has been since before you knew crack meant anything besides pussy, and we don't need help from well-meaning amateurs."

That stung. "I'm no amateur. I used to carry a badge."

"I used to be able to stay hard all night, too, but that was then and this is now." I heard a crunch as the Life Saver met an untimely end. "It's not a debatable point, and I'm not wasting any more time talking to you." It wasn't exactly a click that broke the connection—more like a clap of thunder against my ear as he slammed down the phone.

I replaced the receiver gently. I owned my own telephone, and I wasn't about to abuse it as though it were city property. I had done what I could. Maybe Bobby and Deshon would take a fall and the crack house on Merle Avenue would be shut down, and perhaps little Paulie would see the error of his ways before some other slime started hanging around the high school passing out crack rocks wrapped in butcher paper. Perhaps, too, Barrie Tremont would receive a slap on the wrist and a fine for unwittingly renting her house out to dope pushers, but that seemed unlikely, especially if she was involved with Waco Morgan and his considerable political clout.

In the meantime I had let down one friend, sent another on a paper chase that was now next to meaningless, pumped my own son shamelessly for information, gotten a gold shield supercop pissed at me, and managed to estrange myself from Mary. My only real satisfaction had been baiting a potbellied redneck and bringing him to his knees with a wristlock in the parking lot of the Blind Frog. And let's not forget the backache from spending so many hours in my car. It didn't seem like much for all the work I had done.

I looked at my watch and found the little hand on the six and the big one just past it. Mary would be home from work by now. I hadn't talked to her for two days, and our last parting, while not acrimonious, was not without strain. I tapped out her number, but all I got was her musical voice on tape telling me to leave my name, number, and the time of day. I did as ordered, but I wasn't happy about it. Talking to the answering machine of a loved one always leaves me with a hollow feeling just under my ribs, especially when you've had a recent disagreement and don't know where they are. A vivid imagination is wonderful for artists and poets and writers; for someone in love it's the curse of the Cat People.

There was nothing in the apartment for dinner, but I wasn't particularly hungry even though I hadn't eaten all day. I didn't even feel like having a beer, which was in itself cause to worry. I went into the den, plopped down in my leather chair, and turned on the news in time to hear the weatherman predict heavy rain for the weekend. I wondered if it might be time to start building an ark.

The news report featured an item about the president's war on drugs that caught my attention, and it would have amused me if it hadn't been so damn sad. All that rhetoric and posturing, and the poor bastard doesn't have any better idea on how to wipe out the drug problem than the rest of us.

Legalization is one solution that is often advanced, and it makes more sense to me than anything else. You take the profit out of drugs and the slimeballs will drop it like a bar of soap in a YMCA shower. Bombing Colombia right off the map is another solution, a hawkish favorite, but it doesn't make any more sense than the liberal proposition that education is the answer. It's pretty hard to convince a kid that he's better off living in a rathole with a family of twelve than driving a new car and wearing sharp threads and having his pals look up to him because he's the candy man. Even Paulie Baznik was a hell of a lot more content with his new stereo and his new friends than he'd be as the class geek.

I switched channels in time to catch a game show hostess applauding for a reason incomprehensible to the rest of us, and then I snapped the TV off and shoved a Beatles tape into the deck. It took me back to an era when we seemed to have more control of our own destinies. Time had proved that control to be illusory, but I had felt better about things back then. I was the Walrus. But not any more.

Before the barber could sell too many photographs in Penny Lane the phone rang, and I reached over and turned down the volume before getting up to answer it.

"It's Rudy, Milan. I got some preliminary information for you; the rest will come sometime in the next few days. I can't work miracles, you know."

"Good enough, Rudy," I said, taking a felt-tipped pen out of a cracked coffee mug on my desk and pulling a yellow legal pad into writing position. "Shoot."

"Well," he said, "I told you Waco Morgan was no candidate for a benefit. He not only owns all his car showrooms, he owns the land they stand on, all of which totals in the neighborhood of eight and a half million dollars."

"That's a nice neighborhood," I said.

"Agreed. His mortgages are worth about half of that, so I guess he's a man who pays his bills."

"Admirable. You bank guys must be thinking canonization."

Rudy ignored me, as he usually does when I get smart about the banking business. "Now, the house on Boyce in Shaker he and his wife own jointly, bought six and a half years ago for three hundred twenty nine thousand and change. They put thirty-five percent down and have been paying monthly ever since, and they were only late once—two days late." He cleared his throat. "Ohio Merc holds the paper on the house, by the way."

"How did I know that?"

"Here's a few things you might not know: He owns a six-flat apartment building on Baldwin and another on Orinoco, both in East Cleveland. At least, they were zoned for six flats. At last count there were eighteen families in one and sixteen in the other."

"Morgan is a slumlord?"

I heard him suck wind through his front teeth. "We don't like that word in the banking biz, Milan."

"Excuse me. I meant, a gifted and aggressive real estate entrepreneur. What else?"

"Four single-family homes, on Orville, Parmelee, Ninety-ninth, and 110th Streets, all purchased within the last three years for the price of a good dinner at Sammy's. All foreclosures except the one on Parmelee, which was a distress sale, so he picked them up for goobers. None of this is unusual, Milan—or illegal. Real estate is always a good investment."

"Sure—especially when you can rent six apartments eighteen times."

"Well, he owns a building near University Circle that only has two apartments in it, and only two tenants, if that makes you feel any better."

I checked my file cards. "It wouldn't be the same building Barrie Tremont lives in, would it?"

"Good guess. You want to hear the rest?" Rudy gets impatient when anyone puts down legitimate ways of making money. "He's overextended. He and his wife have a joint checking account, plus the business accounts he has for his car dealerships. But he seems to have a cash-flow problem, because at the moment he couldn't put his hands on more than sixty K in hard cash."

"Am I supposed to feel bad about that?" I said. "I couldn't put my hands on more than two, and I'd have to hit up every friend I have in the world."

"Yeah, but here's a guy with big successful businesses and lots of real estate, and he's walking around listening to his pocket change jingle." He cleared his throat so I'd know that more was coming. "Now those holdings are not counting any stocks, bonds, or CDs he might own; I haven't been able to get a line on them yet." He lowered his voice, even though I knew he was calling from home. "I know you when you get on one of your crusades, and this drug business sounds like the type of thing that pushes your buttons. The next thing I know this is all going to be in Ed Stahl's column. My ass is in traction if you ever let on where you got it."

"Rudy, be sensible. If I blow the whistle on you, I won't be able to come back to you next time."

He groaned. "Next time?"

I laughed. "Tell me what else you have."

"Let's talk about Christmas Amboy. From what I can glean, he seems to be a respectable businessman. Apparently he came to Cleveland in 1968 from Southfield, Michigan, outside Detroit. He bought an old house on Lamberton in Cleveland Heights for thirty-nine thousand and has lived there ever since. He owns the building his office is in on Eddy Road, and he has several large warehouses near Bratenahl. His cash on hand is somewhere in the vicinity of a hundred forty thou, which sounds a little high, but who knows? Some people don't trust banks." He said it as though it was hard for him to believe.

"When you say ready cash, you mean the accounts you know about?"

"All the accounts in Ohio banks, yeah. Why?"

"I just wondered," I said, "if he still had connections in Detroit."

"Detroit connections? He's an old man, a bachelor, been here more than twenty years, Milan. Don't start seeing the Purple Gang under the bed."

"Okay, I won't. Is that it on Father Christmas?"

"Yessir. And that's just about all I have."

"What did you get on Barrie Tremont?"

"Not much of anything. Her address of record you know, she owns the house on Merle, has a checking account which usually hovers around thirty-two hundred bucks, and that's it. As I mentioned, I don't know anything about any of their stock portfolios yet. The impossible takes a little longer."

I thanked him even more profusely than he deserved. He was too high up in the pecking order to get into any real trouble for divulging confidential information, but what he'd done for me was unethical, and Rudy was another of us guys who see things in terms of black and white. It's a Yugoslavian trait, I guess.

I promised Rudy a lunch at the eatery of his choice and hung up. I was starting to fill in the blank index cards when the doorbell startled me. I didn't have many drop-in visitors. I went to the door and opened it cautiously. It never hurts to play safe.

Rita Marie Baznik stood in my hallway, playing with the strap on her handbag like a rosary.

"What a pleasant surprise," I said. "Come on in."

She took a few hesitant steps in, far enough for me to close the door, and looked around at what was, to her, an alien land. Rita Marie had never been inside my apartment before. After my divorce I had maintained my friendship with Matt, but the close-knit companionship of two married couples who had known each other all their lives and gone on picnics and weekend outings together had evaporated when I broke up with Lila.

"Do you want some coffee, Rita Marie?"

"Don't go to any trouble," she said.

I realized that I wanted coffee very much, or at least wanted the diversion of going into the kitchen and making it, so I said, "No problem. Come on into the den."

I helped her off with her cloth coat and seated her in my leather chair. I'm a fairly diligent housekeeper, but the pile of cigarette butts and ashes in the ashtray next to my chair was a source of some embarrassment. I didn't even know if Rita Marie smoked anymore. She used to, but things have a way of changing when you aren't paying attention. It made me sad that we had grown so far apart.

I went into the kitchen and dumped three scoops of Maxwell House into the basket of my Mr. Coffee, filled the well with water, and checked the larder to see if there was anything else I could offer her. Not even a saltine rewarded my search. I went back inside to my guest, who had a tissue in her hands and was twisting it to its detriment. I'd never seen Rita Marie so ill-at-ease—another casualty of time.

"It'll be just a few minutes," I said.

She seemed to accept that and concentrated on destroying the tissue, leaving me to wonder why she had come to visit.

I tried to be offhand about it. "I haven't seen you for months, and now twice in one week," I said, sitting down across from her on the sofa. "This is a real treat."

"I was in the neighborhood and I was on my way back home for dinner, so I thought I'd just stop by."

I leaned forward and put a hand on hers. "Rita Marie, in the twenty-five years I've known you, you've never just stopped by. What is it?"

She looked pained, as though her shredding of the tissue was an unpleasant but unavoidable consequence of what she'd come here for. "This is so hard, Milan . . ."

"Whatever it is, we're old friends."

"That's what makes it hard."

"Wait and have some coffee. Ease yourself."

"All right," she said. I went in and checked on the coffee. It was almost done, but I didn't want to wait. I removed the pot and placed a mug under the drip. I only burned myself a little. I poured what was in the pot into another mug, took them back in, and gave one to her. She wrapped her hands around it, seeming to take courage and strength from the heat.

"Now, then," I said, seating myself again.

"I made Matt tell me what he asked you to do."

I rubbed my hand over my face in the faint hope that it would buy me a few seconds to think. "Rita Marie, there isn't much anyone can do."

"That's the point. I don't want you to do anything." She put her coffee down on the table without drinking any.

"You don't?"

"Just forget it. We'll figure something out ourselves."

I said, "It's not like I'm some stranger—"

"You don't understand. If Paulie is—doing what you think, and those people find out you're after them because of him . . ." She bowed her head, shaking it, and then the floodgates opened. She sobbed hysterically, trying to wipe her eyes with the shredded tissue. "Paulie's my baby! I don't care what's going on, it's better than him being dead! I'm scared. I'm so damn scared I can't eat or sleep or anything. Those people will hurt him—they'll *kill* him. They don't care! Don't you know what they are?"

"I know exactly what they are. That's why I want to help."

She shook her head, her nose buried in the tissue. "Leave it alone, Milan! Please!"

"Rita Marie, Paulie is in trouble. It's not going to go away if you close your eyes."

"We'll move, then! We'll move to the West Side, or to Toledo or something."

"You think there are no drug pushers in Toledo?"

She glared at me, as angry as I'd ever seen her. "I think my son's welfare is more important than catching every drug pusher in the world!" She rasped. She paused to cough the frog out of her throat. "It'll work itself out in time."

"Have you talked this over with Matt?"

"He's got nothing to say about it."

I said gently, "Paulie's his son too."

"Then he'll understand that you've got to stop."

"Stop what?"

"Whatever it is you're doing. Or I swear to God I'll never speak to you again—or to Matt, either!"

Sobs nearly choked her, and she tilted over sideways in the leather chair, the top half of her hanging over the arm, her face and the now worthless tissue buried in her hands.

I went to her and knelt beside the chair, putting a hand on the back of her neck. Rita Marie Kristic had been my friend almost as long as Matt had, since the days when both of us had pimples, and it pained me to see her hurting. It's pretty hard for a mother to be objective when she perceives something as threatening to her child, and I understood and commiserated with her. If it were Milan Jr. or Stephen in trouble, I might feel the same way she did.

"It's all right, Rita Marie," I said. It killed me, but I said it.

* * *

I sat and stared at the wall for a long time after she'd gone. Long experience has taught me you can't help someone who doesn't want to be helped, and I knew Matt well enough to realize that after all his bellowing and posturing, he'd eventually do exactly what his wife wanted him to. There was a strong case to be made that Paulie was the one in need of assistance, but there was no denying Rita Marie's supposition that if the drug posse found out that Paulie was connected to the guy who had braced Deshon and Bobby, he would be punished for it, perhaps permanently.

I tried to convince myself that I'd done what I could. I had given Bobby DeLayne and Deshon and the address of the rock house on Merle to Ingeldinger. If he could follow those leads to the source, to the big boys, well and good. Perhaps if there was even a brief pause in the distribution it would be time enough for the Bazniks to get Paulie some professional help, and if I had been a small part of that, I guess I could feel good about it. Ding was right: the police were far better equipped than I to handle Cleveland's drug problem. My cape and blue tights didn't fit too well anyway.

His dig about well-meaning amateurs still rankled, though.

I might even deserve it. It had been a long time since I was out on the street chasing after the punks and skels and scum that live in the cracks of any big city. The bulk of my business is industrial security, and usually the worst people I run into are petty embezzlers, industrial spies, and clerks who take home whole boxes of ballpoint pens for their personal use. I couldn't remember the last time I'd met a drug dealer before running into Bobby DeLayne and his pal Deshon, and I couldn't say I handled either one of them very well. Maybe I wasn't in shape to take on whoever was behind them; mental muscles need as much exercise as lats and pecs do. And every so often we all need to use some mental floss to get the decay out from between our ears.

I accepted defeat with as much grace as I could muster and crawled into bed, trying not to think of Paulie Baznik. I tried,

111

too, not to dwell on where Mary might have been when I called earlier. It was apparently not my night.

I don't know how long I was asleep, because I hadn't checked the time before I went to bed. But the pounding on my apartment door got me awake in a hurry, and as I glanced at the clock on the dresser I saw it was just after one in the morning.

I threw on my ratty terry-cloth robe, lurched out through the living room, and opened the door. Ingeldinger was in the hallway, a uniformed cop behind him.

"Get your clothes on, Jacovich," he said. Jacovich. Not Milan anymore. And he'd brought a backup, just in case. A warning bell went off in my head.

"Am I under arrest?"

"Not yet," Ding answered, "but if you don't have your pants on in two minutes flat I'm not making any promises."

12

I PULLED on a pair of jeans and an Irish cable-knit sweater Mary had given me for my birthday the year before and followed the two policemen downstairs. They ushered me into the back of the squad car. The uniform drove, Ding was in the front passenger seat, and nobody would tell me where we were going. When I asked, Ding replied, "Whether you know or not is not going to make any difference in the long run, so why don't you just sit back and enjoy the ride until we get there?" He was none too pleasant about it, so I took his advice and kept my mouth shut.

I wasn't used to the back seat in police cars. It didn't feel right. If I can't be up front where I belong, I'd just as soon forego the pleasure.

It became obvious where we were heading when we turned north on 105th Street. In a few minutes we reached Merle Avenue. The end of the block was cordoned off by wooden barricades, which were quickly moved by the patrolman stationed there when he recognized Carl Ingeldinger. There were at least seven police cars in front of the house, marked and otherwise. There was also a coroner's wagon. It was a jazzy display, one that had brought all the other residents of the street out in their nightclothes to watch the festivities, their dark faces shining in the flashing red, blue, and white lights atop the prowl cars. My throat was closing up; I was beginning to realize why I'd been brought here, and I didn't like it.

We climbed out of the car and made our way up the walk through a crowd of cops, all of whom were very deferential to Ding, either saluting or bobbing their heads in recognition. He was obviously a real department heavyweight, and from the rigid set of his shoulders and his refusal to meet me eye to eye, I knew I was on his bad side. It didn't feel like the best place to be. I've always prided myself on the good relationship I maintained with the force, mostly through Marko but also through the many friends I'd made back when I wore a uniform myself. Ding's hostility was discomfitting.

When we moved through the open front door, the odor hit me with almost physical force, a slaughterhouse stink, heavy and sickening. Marko Meglich was the first one I saw in the practically bare living room, and his presence there as the representative of the homicide division boded ill. He wasn't dressed in his usual sartorial splendor but had on instead a leather jacket, chino pants, and a plaid wool shirt; evidently he'd been called from home. He glowered at me too—everyone was mad at me. I followed his gaze over to a corner of the room. What I saw made me forget about Marko's bad mood—and made me glad I hadn't eaten dinner that evening, because I felt my stomach lurch and tasted bile in the back of my throat.

Deshon's dog, the big wolflike shepherd mongrel, lay on its side on the faded and threadbare carpet, its one visible eye open and glassy, its pink tongue lolling obscenely almost a foot out of its mouth. Both of its forelegs were broken, the sharp white bone protruding through the brownish-gray fur of the left one. The back of the animal's head was nothing but a gray and red pulp. Somebody had beaten it to death with a blunt instrument.

I looked away. I've never been much of an animal person. When I was a kid I was too busy with athletics, and after my marriage Lila hadn't wanted a pet because they were too much trouble to clean up after. But this wasn't right. Deshon might be a dope peddler, but dogs weren't good guys or bad guys, even if their owners were. They were just dogs.

Marko came over to me, his brow still furrowed. He jerked his head at the carcass. "Man's best friend. Make you sick?"

I nodded.

"Wait till you catch the second act." His jaw set at a grim angle, Marko motioned for Ding and me to follow him into the back of the house. We went through a long, narrow hallway floored with sheets of black and white checkerboard linoleum that probably hadn't been new when it went out of style twenty years ago. There were red-brown spatters on the walls and the floor, and the abattoir smell grew stronger.

"Call came in an hour ago," Marko said as we went. "Got me out of bed. Why can't slimeballs do their shit during the day?"

We went into the kitchen at the back of the house. The acrid smell of fresh blood and bodily wastes prickled the membranes in my nose and made my eyes tear. Deshon, or what was left of him, was rolled up into a small, pathetic ball between the stove and the refrigerator. His head, arms and body had been pulverized by a heavy weapon and looked a lot like the dog, only worse. His once splendid dreadlocks were matted with blood and brains. I could feel the sweat popping out on my forehead, and something was pressing against my Adam's apple. I think it was my stomach.

Ingeldinger snarled and gave me one of his patented hard-guy looks. Then he went out into the living room.

"He had his wallet on him; his name was Deshon Garthwaite, a Jamaican national," Marko said. "I know it's kind of tough to tell, the condition he's in, but is this the guy you talked to?"

I was having trouble speaking, so I just bobbed my head.

Marko nodded his understanding. "Somebody was awful mad at him," he said. "We figure a club or a baseball bat or something. The same one that did the dog."

"Lots of baseball fans around here," I said, remembering Deshon's two friends.

Ding came back in with a clear plastic evidence bag and dangled it in front of my face. "You're familiar with evidence, aren't you, Jacovich? An old pro like you."

It was hard to tell with him swinging the bag so close to my nose, but I could see that inside it were two halves of one of my business cards.

"I was here yesterday, I already told you that," I said, and then looked at my watch. "Day before yesterday, if you want to get technical." I've never known a cop who didn't want to get technical. "I talked to Garthwaite—I didn't know his last name then—and I left him a card. I leave cards all over town, lieutenant. That's what they're for."

Ding didn't like that, and I didn't blame him. I hadn't meant to be patronizing, it just came out that way. He said, "Now, if you found a man's business card ripped in half in front of a house where a murder had been committed, what would you think? As a professional, I mean? Wouldn't that just automatically move him into the top ten on your suspect list?"

"Don't be a horse's ass, Ding," Marko said. "Milan didn't off this guy and you know it." He looked at me and grinned. "Football is his game; he never could swing a bat for shit."

"You guys are about as funny as a heart attack. Both of you." Ding waved the evidence bag in front of me again. "I'm keeping this, pressed in the leaves of my memory book." He turned and stomped back out to the front of the house.

Marko dismissed his receding back with a wave. "Don't worry about it. This is homicide's case, not narcotics. I'm not gonna take you downtown." Then he added, "Yet."

I glanced down at the shapeless mess that had once been Deshon Garthwaite and then pulled my eyes away. When they call the brain *gray matter*, they aren't kidding. "Can we go somewhere else and talk?"

"Out back," he said. We both moved gingerly past the broken corpse and through the open kitchen door out into a dusty yard choked with untended weeds. A tumbledown toolshed stood at its far end, tilting to starboard and looking as if the next strong wind would blow it over. A few police lab men were poking around in the dark with flashlights and making casts of footprints with dental stone, so Marko and I just stood on the cement stoop. It was cold and damp outside, but there wasn't too much of a wind, and it was a relief to get into the air and away from the stench that permeated the inside of the house.

"Who called this in?"

"Some woman. The sergeant who took the call said she sounded Jamaican. And hysterical." He took a deep breath. "I would've been, too."

I flashed back to the girl, the "strawberry" with the orange hair and the Carmen Miranda turban whom I'd seen the day before at the house with Deshon. I didn't know whether or not she was Jamaican, because I hadn't heard her speak, but it seemed to be a fairly good guess. I mentioned her to Marko, and he dutifully scrawled something down in his leather-covered notebook. I noticed that he used a gold Cross pen. Marko has style.

"Orange hair and a turban," he said. "Shouldn't be too hard to find." He slapped the notebook closed, pocketed it, and put on his sternest, this-is-difficult-but-friendship-only-goes-so-far look. I'd been on the receiving end of that look many times since we both were kids. The time he and I liked the same girl in high school; the time I quit the force after he'd gone out on a limb to sponsor me; the *North Coast Magazine* case, when every witness I talked to ended up dead.

"Ingeldinger wants to tear you a new asshole," Marko said. "You're in his way. And that business card on the front walk can mean a lot of trouble for you if he wants to push it. He doesn't believe you're a killer, but he'd be just as happy to lock you up to get you out of his hair—what there is of it." He laughed briefly. "Back out of this quick, pal, or I won't be able to help you."

I took a crumpled pack of Winstons out of my jeans pocket and lit one. The cigarette was bent in the middle. Very Bogart. What I said was kind of Bogart too. "I'm staying in. I have to."

He smote his forehead with the heel of his hand, his eyes raised to the heavens, or as much of the heavens as were visible through the relentless cloud cover. I tried to remember the last time I'd actually seen a star in the city. "God damn you—"

"Listen a minute." I let the smoke jet through my nostrils, it being preferable to the smell of death, which lingers for a long while inside your head. "If it weren't for me that kid would still be alive, and the dog too. I've got accounts to square."

"How do you figure?"

I told him about my confrontation with Bobby DeLayne in the Blind Frog saloon. I omitted the part with the redneck, figuring at this juncture they'd just as soon lock me up for assault as not.

"What's your point?" There was an impatient edge to his voice that I didn't like.

"Just this: I let Bobby know that I was onto Deshon, that Deshon had led me to him. He probably told his bosses. They must have decided that Deshon was either getting too mouthy or too careless. Either way, that's no way to run a crack ring. They made an example out of him. Because of me."

Marko stepped down off the cement stoop and paced a few feet away and back in frustration. "Christ, what an ego! You think the whole world turns on what you do? These guys are scum. Lifetakers. There could be a hundred reasons why Deshon bought it, and ninety-nine of them don't have Milan Jacovich's name on them."

"You and I both know that's crap. I did something dumb and now Deshon is dead. I might as well have swung the bat myself."

He ran a hand through his carefully blow-dried hair. "Why are you always so hard on yourself, Milan?"

I sucked in some more smoke. Thinking of Mary, I said, "I'm hard on everybody."

* * *

They had nothing to hold me on, so they let me go. Finally. They assigned a uniform to drive me, and at least this time I got to sit in the front like a big boy. Cold comfort.

It was after four by the time I got home, but I didn't even attempt to go to sleep. The memory of Deshon Garthwaite and his dog was going to act like a jolt of No Doz for some time to come. It's not that I'd never seen a corpse before. What with two years in Vietnam, several seasons in uniform walking a beat in Cleveland's back alleys, and more recently a couple of private cases that had seemed simple when I'd taken them and turned out to be anything but, I've gotten a good look at death more times than I care to think about. But I'd never seen a body so savaged before, and it had left me shaken.

Ingeldinger had told me true—the Jamaican posses that ran crack in Cleveland did indeed play rough.

I didn't particularly want to be alone just then, but it was very late, or very early, depending on your point of view, and there was no one I could call for a friendly shoulder. There was a time I would have called Mary, even at that late hour, but I'd managed to screw up that relationship, too, just the way I'd alienated the police and let down Matt and angered Rita Marie and put Vuk's nose out of joint and used Milan Jr. shamelessly. Just to make sure there was no one left in town still speaking to me, I wondered where I could find a nun to punch around.

A plan was forming in my sleepy head as I drank the coffee I'd brewed to make sure I could keep going until dawn. It wasn't one I much wanted to implement, but given my current relationship with the police, I was all alone and twisting in the wind, and I would accept help anywhere I could get it.

A little after six I heard the thunk of the newspaper hitting the bottom of the door. I went out in the hall to retrieve it and sat back down and read all about the president's trip to Europe without really understanding what I was reading. The president had his problems and I had mine.

I showered, shaved, and dressed in a tweed jacket, a muted plaid shirt, and a tie and headed down Lee Road to Shaker Boulevard at a few minutes after eight. The morning rush traffic was all going the other way, toward downtown, so it only took me ten minutes to reach Waco Morgan's house on Boyce.

Margo Morgan answered the door again, dressed less formally this time in a gray silk dress that didn't flatter her ample figure.

"It's you again, young man," she said. "My, you're persistent."

"Yes, ma'am," I said. I liked the young man part.

"Mr. Morgan isn't going to like being disturbed over his morning coffee. I don't think you're going to make a sale."

I handed her one of my cards. She looked at it and then back at me. "Security? You're selling burglar alarms? We already have a security system here." She pointed to the metal keypad mounted vertically beside the door, on which an intense little green light glowed. I recognized the brand name; it was one of those costly systems supposed to alert a private police force when tampered with. Even a clumsy housebreaker could render it useless in about three minutes.

"If you'll just tell him I'm here, Mrs. Morgan . . ."

She gave the sigh of a martyr and closed the door in my face, but quietly, so I'd know that although I was far from welcome, I hadn't been dismissed. I stood on the doorstep like a mendicant and gazed around at the elegant landscaping, my eyes finally coming to rest on the iron jockey at the edge of the lawn. I knew how he felt; he had to wait outside too.

Finally the door was flung open behind me, and when I turned Waco Morgan was looming in the doorway. He was my height, lean and muscular, wearing a western shirt and a string tie. The cuffs of his suit pants were tucked into butter-colored leather boots, on which the tooling alone had to have cost two hundred dollars. He looked younger than he did on television, in spite of the unruly mop of silver hair. Maybe it was because he wasn't wearing his Stetson. He had my business card in his hand, and he looked mad enough to bite something.

"You better have a pip of a reason for busting into my house at breakfast time, Mr. Jacovich," he said, pronouncing it with the hard *J*, "or else you have stepped in shit."

"I tried to make an appointment at the showroom, but your secretary wasn't having any."

He chuckled. "Cleatte's a dragon lady when she wants. That's why I keep her. Sure as hell ain't for her looks. What do you want?"

"I want to talk to you about your house on Merle Avenue."

He composed his face into a puzzled but serene frown. "I don't own property on Merle Avenue," he said.

"No, but Barrie Tremont does."

His eyes involuntarily flicked over his shoulder toward the inside of the house; then he looked back at me. He didn't look puzzled anymore, he looked mean as hell.

"You're the one went to see Barrie yesterday. Hey, what is this shit?" he hissed. "A shakedown? This is my home, pal. You got the balls of a brass monkey bringing filth into my home."

"Filth? I'm talking about real estate."

"Come off it, Mr. Jacovich, we both know what you're talking about. And I don't like it one damn bit! I've got a good mind to toss your ass the hell out of here."

"I'm not an easy toss," I said. "But let's not get into a pissing contest. Can we sit down and chat, nice and friendly?"

"Not here, stupid. What do you think?" He was still weighing his chances at throwing me off his property bodily, but my sheer bulk must have discouraged him. Defeated, he looked at his Rolex. "Meet me at my showroom on Mayfield in a half hour."

"Thanks, Mr. Morgan," I said.

Suddenly he was smiling again, the late night TV pitchman turning on the charm. For salesmen like him, it was almost instinctive. "Call me Waco," he said.

*　*　*

I stopped at Corky and Lenny's and had some more coffee and ordered a toasted English I couldn't eat. After what I'd seen the night before I wasn't sure I'd ever eat again. When I'd given it enough time I drove over to Morgan's dealership on Mayfield.

Ed Johnson must have been off that morning, because no one pounced on me to sell me a car as I made my way into the gleaming chrome and glass building. Cleatte Hornaday was at her post, today wearing a black blouse and a white skirt that looked like a negative of yesterday's outfit.

"I'm here to see Mr. Morgan," I said, and when she sucked in a breath to tell me off, I added, "And I do have an appointment."

She picked up the phone and bitterly announced me. She was one of those executive assistants who become drunk with power and take any little dent in their authority as a personal affront.

Waco Morgan's inner office, paneled in nut-colored wood with metallic blue drapes covering the floor-to-ceiling window, was a triumph of bad taste. The Naugahyde furniture looked as if it had been purchased from a long-defunct Ramada Inn, and the framed photos were all of Waco Morgan hugging or

121

shaking hands with local dignitaries like college coaches and city councilmen and Browns running backs. Two flags flanked his big blond veneer desk: the Stars and Stripes and the Lone Star of Texas. Against one wall was a huge wrought iron wine rack, stretching from the floor almost to the ceiling, full of bottles on their sides. The wall-to-wall carpet was a shade of red usually only found on the fingernails of loose women.

Waco had his jacket off, and his string tie was looped around an open shirt collar. He didn't rise from his throne like chair behind the desk when I came in; there was no handshake, no how are you, no offer of a chair or a cup of coffee. He simply said, "All right, Jacovich, what do you want?"

This time I corrected his pronunciation. "I have a few questions, Mr. Morgan," I said, sitting down uninvited, "regarding an investigation I'm conducting."

"Maybe you'd better ask them of my lawyer."

"I probably won't get answers from your lawyer."

"You're not getting many from me, either. You're a cheap and very clumsy blackmailer, and a pest. Bothering me at my office—at my *home,* for God's sake. Where I come from, we squish pests with our bootheels."

"I'm kind of big to squish."

His flinty blue eyes became narrow slits. "Don't kid yourself, amigo. I could have you blown away in the parking lot for a buck and a quarter."

"Jumping the gun, aren't you, Waco? You don't even know what questions I want to ask."

"Don't I?" he said. "You force your way into Barrie's place yesterday—"

"Nobody forced their way—"

"You come to my house and start talking about crap I don't want my family to hear. That puts a burr under my saddle."

"I don't care about Barrie Tremont," I said. "What you do and with whom, I couldn't care less."

He was taken aback for a moment, surprised that I wasn't there to shake him down. Then, that out of the way, he relaxed, settled back in his chair, and put his booted feet up on the desk. His soles were new-looking and shiny. "Well, that's good to hear. I thought I was going to have trouble with you. You know, a man works as hard as I do, he's entitled to a little relaxation after work sometimes. A pretty woman, a bottle of wine." He gestured at the wine rack. "You a wine fancier, Mr. Jacovich?"

"Not much," I said.

"I am. Texas wines. Did you know there's a big wine industry in Texas? Acre after acre in the hill country; L.B.J. territory, down by Nacogdoches. I bet you never heard of 'em."

I had to admit I hadn't.

"They laugh at Texas wine—damn New York know-it-alls call it Château de Bubba. But the soil is rich there, and the sun is warm and gentle, and it's damn good wine for the money. And it's going to get better. You got a couple of bucks to invest, you could do worse than putting it into a Texas vineyard."

I glanced at the rack. "Your vineyard?"

"Margo Vineyards," he said. "Named it after Miz Morgan, who I b'lieve you've met."

"I've had the pleasure," I said. "Could we get down to business so I won't have to waste any more of your time?"

"It's your nickel, hoss."

"Do you own the building Barrie Tremont lives in?"

He got mad again. "God damn it, you said you didn't want to talk about her."

"I don't. I'm talking about a building."

He smiled nastily. "Playin' Monopoly with real houses, huh? And other people's money."

"You own the building."

"You sound like you're telling, not asking."

"She lives there rent free?"

He laced his fingers behind his head and leaned back even further. "I always pay my way. My daddy taught me that."

"Did your daddy teach you about real estate too?"

"I'm missing the point here," he said.

"Barrie Tremont owns a house on Merle Avenue."

"That's got nothing to do with me," he said. "What she owns is what she owns."

"But you also own several properties in the same area."

"It's a free country."

"Pretty seedy area."

123

"It is now. You study patterns in a city, patterns and cycles. That area is shit now, but it's going to come back one of these days, and my properties are gonna be worth three times what I paid. That house is a neat little write-off for her, and like most real property it's bound to appreciate. And it's perfectly legal and aboveboard."

"Did you buy the house on Merle for Barrie Tremont?"

"I don't think that's any of your business."

"Seems like a coincidence, that's all."

"Life's full of 'em."

I shook my head. "You're wrong, Waco, there's no such thing as a coincidence."

He ran a thumb across the corner of his mouth. "Let's say that I advised Miss Tremont on the purchase and let it go at that."

"Do you also advise her when it comes to renting it?"

He looked blank for a moment. "It's not rented," he said. "Not that I know of. Who'd want to rent a falling-down piece of crap like that?" He swung his feet onto the floor and leaned forward, resting his elbows on the desk. "Are *you* looking to rent a house, Mr. Jacovich?" he asked, grinning at me.

"You never know," I said.

* * *

When I came out of Waco's office Ms. Hornaday smiled a glittering triumph that he'd only allowed me five minutes of his time. It was a small victory, and I was generous about it. She probably didn't have many in her life. I wondered if she had been one of Waco Morgan's extracurricular activities several years back, before attrition had made her better suited to be the guardian of the gates than the angel of the boudoir. If so, I understood why she was always so angry.

I walked back through the showroom and then across the lot. Ed Johnson had finally arrived, but he was standing talking to another salesman. He saw me out of the corner of his eye and turned with alacrity, ready to tell me he could get me out of the piece of junk I was driving and into one of Waco's cars for the mere price of my first-born child, but after ascertaining who I was, he rather pointedly turned his back on me. Ed, like so many in his profession, pigeon holed people into two classifications: those he can sell something to and make a profit from, and nonpersons.

I didn't like my category.

13

I WAS in over my head and I knew it. The Jamaican posses that controlled and distributed crack were tough and mean and powerful, and what made them so difficult to battle or even to understand was that they operated on a value system that no one I knew could relate to; they were a different culture and employed a different set of standards. They had brutally murdered Deshon Garthwaite, one of their own, because all he'd done was to tell me to get off his front porch when he should have put a permanent stop to me, just as they'd killed Randolph Jones and Garthwaite's dog and God knew how many others who had gotten too close to their operation. Matt Baznik was begging me for some sort of unspecified help, and Rita Marie, his wife, wanted me to look the other way while her son fell deeper and deeper into garbage. The police were about as much assistance as a rowboat in Death Valley; all I could get from them were terse suggestions to get the hell out of their case. But I couldn't do that, not anymore.

When Paulie Baznik was born, my first gift to him was a baby-size football his father put in his crib. He played the Uncle Wiggily game with my own kid in the middle of my living room floor, ate dinner at my house two or three nights a week, and when he got his first bloody nose in a schoolyard fight, it was me he ran to. That made it personal for me. Deshon Garthwaite and his dog made it personal, too, because indirectly it was my fault that they'd died. I needed some help, heavy-duty help, and under the circumstances I only knew one avenue to travel where I might get it. Just my luck, it was someplace where they were likely to shoot me on sight.

I lit a Winston and opened the car window a crack, watching the smoke get sucked out into the gray morning as I headed west down Mayfield Road. Slowly. I was in no hurry to get where I was going; I wasn't even sure I wanted to go there. But I'd spent a sleepless night thinking about it, and if this plan failed me, I was out of choices.

The road jogged at Taylor and again at Lakeview Cemetery. The old graveyard didn't have anything close to a lake view, but I don't suppose any of the residents were bothered by the misnomer. In a few downhill blocks I was in Little Italy, and since it was still early in the morning I was able to find a parking space easily on Murray Hill. I locked the car and walked back to Mayfield, tantalized by the aroma of fresh breads and pastries wafting from the numerous little Italian bakeries that lined the street.

Between a pasta house and the Mayfield Theatre, shuttered up and papered over with out-of-date handbills, was a heavy wooden door to which a small plaque was affixed: FIRENZE SOCIAL CLUB—MEMBERS ONLY, it said. The last time I'd walked through that door there had been a gun at my back. In a way, there still was.

I squared my shoulders and went up the dark uncarpeted stairway. Another door at the top of the steps awaited my knock. There was a fish-eye peephole in its center, and the light behind it changed slightly as somebody inside peered through, checking me out. Then a few lock tumblers clicked and the door opened an inch. A brown eye appeared in the crevasse.

"This is a private club," the eye's owner said. I recognized the voice. The last time I'd heard it I'd been face down in my own blood on my apartment floor, and it had been saying, "Not so tough now, are you, motherfucker?" Something the size and temperature of a hot blintz was pressing against the lining of my stomach.

"Hello, Joey. It's Milan Jacovich."

The eye and the crack in the door both widened about the same amount—a fraction of an inch. I guess in the dim hallway he hadn't seen who it was at first.

"Whaddaya want?"

"I want to see Mr. D'Allessandro."

"He don't wanna see you."

"Ask him."

"Fuck off."

"If he finds out I was here and he *did* want to see me, I'd hate to be you, strunz."

Joey hesitated a bit, and then said, "Wait a minute," and closed the door and relocked it. It was an unnecessary precaution. No sane person walked uninvited into the Firenze Social Club. I waited a second and then the door opened again, all the way, and Joey came out into the hall with another man. Joey pushed me against the wall and his friend patted me down. They didn't find anything; I'd left my gun and holster in the glove compartment of my car. I would have been crazy not to.

"C'mon," Joey said. It was only the second time I'd seen him not wearing sunglasses, and his little eyes were mean as ever.

They led me inside to a large, dark-paneled club room with a bar and several wooden booths and tables. A burnished bronze espresso machine against one wall dominated the room like a golden idol. They must have polished it twice a day to make it shine like that. The two men took me across a wide expanse of uncarpeted floor; the old boards groaned a protest at our weight. We headed for one of the booths against the wall. A swag lamp with a fake Tiffany shade hung so low over the table I had to stoop down a bit to see the occupants of the booth. One was an elderly man with a cheap brown suit and a tieless shirt buttoned to the neck, and he got up and left as soon as I approached, skittering away backward like a sand crab. On the other side of the booth was Giancarlo D'Allessandro.

"Milan Jacovich," he said in a voice like ancient parchment tearing. The first syllable of Jacovich pulled his lips back in a rictus, away from the cigarette-stained teeth that stood in his shrunken gums like a skull's.

"Don Giancarlo," I said, and inclined my head just a bit, not enough to make him think I was being obsequious. But he was the head of the northern Ohio mob, and it didn't hurt to be polite. He looked more cadaverous than when I'd last seen him two years before, if that were possible. His sallow skin was stretched tight over his face, the veins and bones beneath easily visible. Turkey-wattle flesh hung loosely under his chin, and his eyes were the color of water diluted by a drop of walnut woodstain. Deep creases scarred the eyes and mouth of a face wrinkled like an old piece of fake crushed velvet. He couldn't have weighed more than a hundred thirty pounds. But he was still the most powerful bookmaker, whoremaster, and power broker in Ohio, and as a shylock his reputation was more than Shakespearean.

"Sit down," he said. "Have a coffee while I try to figure out why you'd be so stupid to come here."

I slid into the booth across from him, and he looked up at Joey and made some sort of movement with his eyes that sent the younger man over to the espresso machine. As we talked I could hear the steam hissing. "I appreciate your seeing me."

The old man said, "You have things to answer for. Heavy things. Buddy Bustamente."

A wave of memory sickened me momentarily. "You know that wasn't my fault."

"Fault, pah! Buddy was family. A stupid man, but you don't pick your family, eh? Only your friends."

"That's true," I said. Joey came back and put an espresso in front of me. On the small saucer was a twist of lemon peel and a sugar cube. I ran the lemon peel around the edge of the tiny cup, then dropped it in and raised a toast. "Your health," I said. I put the sugar cube between my teeth, and took a sip of the heavy, bitter coffee, letting it filter through the sweetness.

The don coughed to prove me a liar. "My health," he said, "is shit." He took a cigarette from a gold case, and one of the men standing around just out of earshot fell all over himself to light it. The old man took a deep puff and then coughed again, so hard that his frail shoulders shook and the ashes in the little tin ashtray in front of him formed miniature dust devils. When he stopped his eyes were wet. He examined the cigarette and found it guilty. "Goddamn things gonna kill me yet."

"You should quit."

"Sure," he said, "and live longer. That's a good idea. What for? There's nothing left that's fun no more. You eat good food, that cholesterol shit kills you, or you get fat and get a heart attack. Eat rabbit food and the pesticides get you. Good wine, ruins your liver and you turn yellow and die. Smoke, there goes your lungs. A little pussy and you get a disease that eats you away to nothing. Why the hell I want to live longer?"

I smiled. He had a point.

"So, Jacovich." He leaned back, his skinny shoulder blades knocking against the wooden backrest. "I said you pick your friends, yes? Does your visit today mean you're picking me?"

"I'm not your enemy, Don Giancarlo."

"You're a boil on my ass, and that's just as bad." He shook his head as if in great sadness. "I'm getting old. You cross me not once, but twice, and now you sit here at my table and drink a coffee and smile at me. Twenty years ago, you'd of been landfill."

It was a simple statement of fact, not meant to intimidate. I knew D'Allessandro wasn't going to do anything to me. He'd had a long while to think about revenge, almost a year, and I was still alive. But the truth of his simple statement made my flesh crawl.

"Don Giancarlo, I've come to ask you a favor."

He opened his eyes as wide as he could, and then he began to cough again, a real spasm that seemed likely to tear his frail old body apart. One of the men in the room moved toward him, but the old fellow waved him away and kept on hacking. It was terrible to watch at such close range, but there wasn't anything I could do about it. I was afraid he was going to hurt himself.

Finally the don got his spasming throat under control and leaned his head back against the wood, tears running down his face. "Holy shit," he croaked, and wiped his mouth and cheeks with a handkerchief. "Some day I ain't gonna come out of one a those."

While the assembled members of his extended family watched anxiously, it took him more than a minute to get himself together so that his breathing was as close to normal as it ever got. Then he inspected me carefully, my face and my hands and my clothing, the way he would a laboratory specimen of some exotic butterfly, and his eyes crinkled at some private joke nobody else caught. "What are you, tryin' to kill me by making me laugh? You want a favor!" He waved at Joey, who came running to refill his cup and then moved off a respectful distance. The old man was drinking regular coffee, not espresso, and at his elbow on the table was a small pitcher of real cream and a bowl of sugar cubes. He added liberal amounts of both to his cup. "To disrespect me and then come licking around, you must be crazy."

"I don't always agree with you or like the things you do, but I don't disrespect you," I said. "If I did I wouldn't be here asking a favor."

He snorted and snuffled and slurped some coffee, and then smacked his lips and said, "Nobody gets nothing for nothing, Jacovich. What you got to trade? You can't buy a favor here —hell, you couldn't buy that coffee if I didn't want you to."

"You already owe me one."

His bloodshot old eyes glittered, and whatever tolerant humor had been there before was gone now.

I went on, "When you were looking for Richard Amber I helped find him for you. I didn't get paid, not by you. And when someone ripped your hotel off for forty-two thousand dollars, I was the one that got it back for you." I could see the color rising in his cheeks, and I quickly said, "I couldn't help that it turned out badly in the end. You know that, Don Giancarlo. I never asked to become involved with your people; I never wanted to. It was you who came to me, you who insisted." I turned my hands palms up and shrugged—Yugoslavia isn't that far from Italy. "So, I figure you owe me a favor."

His teeth showed when he smiled, brown from sixty years of tobacco abuse. "Bohunk!" he rasped. "Such cogliones you got.

I'm letting you live! Walking around breathing—that's your favor."

I leaned forward and lowered my voice so that he was the only one in the room that could hear me. "Let me put it to you another way, then. How would you like to get back at the Jamaicans?"

The skin on his face stretched even tighter, and he dropped his chin onto his chest and looked at me from under his eyebrows. I could see his eyes, his whole face flickering back to life from the half doze he lived in. The canny intelligence that had kept him at the top of his crime family for thirty years was spreading across his features. He rested his elbows on the edge of the table. At least I'd gotten his attention.

"What Jamaicans?"

I didn't answer him, but I held his gaze, until finally he looked away. Giancarlo D'Allessandro wasn't used to being stared down, and he didn't like it. "What do I care about Jamaicans?"

"I think we both know that, sir."

"Uh-huh." His eyes checked out the room, and everyone suddenly got very busy staring into their coffees or examining their fingernails. "And what do you care about them?"

I told him about Paulie Baznik. He listened carefully, nodding, processing the information better than a computer ever could. Anger tugged at the turned-down corners of his mouth, but I didn't think it was directed at me.

When I was finished, he shook his head back and forth on his skinny neck. "Your friend's kid, huh?" He circled his arms around his coffee cup as if I might try to steal it. "You know, a man—a grown man I'm talking about here—he wants to gamble, to drink whiskey, to run with whores, it's his own business. He's old enough to be in control of what he does. Somebody's going to make a buck or two off it in any case, it might as well be me. That's business. I'm a businessman. I ain't ashamed of that, I ain't ashamed of anything I done. Everybody's a sharper when it comes to doing business. But a kid! A little kid, he ain't even dipped his wick yet, he don't know what he wants. To make a buck off that little kid by putting poison in his body—that's disgusting!"

I took the final swallow of espresso in the little cup, my throat suddenly dry. "Will you help me, Don Ginacarlo?"

His frail shoulders rose up around his ears. "Whattaya want to do, start a fucking war in the streets? My people get killed, their people get killed, and nothing changes except a lot of widows wearing black. You're crazy. I'm starting no war. Not for you, Jacovich. Not even for your friend's kid."

"I don't want a war," I said. "I want to know where the stuff comes from."

He was fast running out of patience with me. "It comes from Colombia, jag-off. Everybody knows where it comes from."

"Somebody in this town is bringing it in. Lots of it, every day. I want to know who it is. It's easy for cops to bust street people, but when one goes down, two more pop up. And most of the mules they use are little kids, ten years old. They spend a night in juvie and then they go home and do it some more. I don't want to hurt them. I want the top guy."

"You want. I'm supposed to jump because you want? You make me laugh, and when I laugh I cough. I hate it when I cough." He swatted a hand at my face. "Go piss up a rope, Jacovich."

"Don Giancarlo," I said, "we disagree on many issues. But I know your feelings about drugs and kids, and I respect them. If it was one of your people I wouldn't ask. All I need is a name."

He rubbed his face with a papery hand and closed his tired eyes for a few seconds, squeezing the bridge of his nose between his thumb and forefinger. "What are you gonna do if you get it?"

"I haven't thought that far yet. But I'm going to stop the son of a bitch, I'll tell you that."

"Somebody else will take his place. Maybe somebody worse."

"Probably," I said. "But I can't walk away."

Even though the room was too hot, he put both hands around his coffee cup as if to warm them. "What if I say no?"

"Then I'll get it somewhere else."

"Where?"

"I don't know," I admitted. "You must realize I wouldn't come here if it wasn't important."

He cleared his throat. "You'll owe me, Jacovich. I don't care how you count, how you keep the score. You'll owe."

I ground my teeth, expelled a breath through them so that it hissed. "I won't kill anyone for you," I said. "I won't do anything illegal, or anything that violates me. I have rules, Don Giancarlo, just like you. That's the only way it can work."

His eyes bored into me, and then he looked down into his cup, his scraggy eyebrows knitted into in a frown. He didn't say anything for a long while, and in the silence I was aware of the old clock on the wall ticking loudly, of the hum of the espresso machine and the knocking of the pipes in the old radiator against one wall, the slap of the cards from a game of hearts going on at a table across the room. And of the don's labored breathing. Nobody was talking, and although no one looked at us, everyone there was aware of our conversation. I brushed at the mustache of sweat on my upper lip.

"Go home, Milan Jacovich," he said finally. "I have to think about this. I'm an old man and it takes me a long time to wake up. It's too early in the morning for favors." He waved me away, and suddenly Joey was there at the edge of the table, waiting for me. I stood up and moved back a step.

"A gentleman pays his debts," D'Allessandro said. "Best you remember that."

I extended my hand, but when he put his out, he held it palm down as though expecting me to kiss it. He'd have to kiss me first, and not my hand either, Paulie Baznik or no Paulie Baznik. I took the brittle old bones gently.

"You know where to reach me?"

"Sure," he said. "Maybe the cemetery."

Joey took my elbow, but I stopped, looked pointedly at his hand and then at him. He looked at his liege lord but got no orders one way or the other. It was a big decision for him, but he finally released his grip, and we walked to the door, our silent audience watching every step. He opened the door and came outside into the hallway with me.

"Still a hard guy," he said. "Still copping attitudes."

"Save it for the guys in the pizzeria, strunz."

"Don't fuck with me, asshole; I don't care what the don says, in my book you're rat shit."

Impressed in spite of myself at his use of three different obscenities in one sentence, I turned to go downstairs.

"You'll crawl before I'm finished with you. I made you crawl once—remember? On your hands and knees."

I turned back to him. He was leaning insolently against the wall, his arms across his chest, one foot cocked jauntily in front of the other. I reached out and pushed his chin back and up as hard as I could, and the sickening clunk of his head against the wall was as satisfying to me as the resonant thunder of timpani. His little pig eyes crossed, his knees buckled, and since one foot was practically off the ground, he lost his balance and slid slowly to a sitting position.

I went downstairs at a leisurely pace. It was lucky for me the members of the Firenze Social Club didn't walk around their meeting room armed, or he'd have shot me in the back for sure.

Coming out into the relatively fresh air of Little Italy, I breathed deeply to get the stale smell of the club room out of my head. Yesterday's cigarettes, last year's garlic, old sweat, past atrocities—even Mayfield Road smelled good in comparison. But as I filled my lungs I remembered a truism: if you lie down in a pigsty, chances are you're going to get dirty.

14

CHRISTMAS Amboy was bent over a file cabinet in the front part of his office when I came in. When he saw me he broke into a smile forty cubits wide. Maybe I had a new best friend and didn't know it.

"Well, Milan!" He came around the desk to pump my hand, his two-handed grip denoting even more warmth and sincerity. "I was fixing to call you, but now you've saved me a dime." He squinched up his eyes to let me know he was only kidding. "I got the poop you wanted on that proppity. Come on inside where we can be comfortable and talk about this."

He led me to his inner office and took his position behind the desk. He was coatless and wearing a light pink shirt, a gray knit tie, and the trendy kind of black and white suspenders you might expect to see on a thirty-year-old account executive in an ad agency downtown. He had on a black plastic belt, though, which was supposed to look like alligator but didn't. It blew the whole image right out of the water.

"You talked to the owner of the house on Merle?"

"I did indeed," Christmas said. "I did indeed. And the news isn't good—depending on your point of view, of course."

I sat down in the visitor's chair and waited.

"The owner doesn't want to sell. She thought about it and changed her mind. She's withdrawing the listing. Wants to wait

136

until the market perks up a little bit. It's a buyer's market out there right now, you know."

"I didn't even make an offer yet," I said.

"I know it. And frankly I'm glad, because I really like you, Milan, and I wouldn't want to see your family in that neighborhood, as I told you. But every cloud has a silver lining." He flipped open one of the metal file boxes on his desk and removed a fresh-looking white card. "This is a brand new listing I just picked up yesterday. It's in South Euclid on Anderson Road, which is right off Green. I know that's a bit further out than you had in mind, but when you see it I think you'll agree it's a better place for your wife and kids. Three-bedroom Georgian, family room, a two-car garage. An older home, but with lots of ambience. It's emotional, you know?" He gave me a conspirator's wink. "That's Realtor talk. But it's true: terrific wood treatment, leaded glass in the downstairs front windows, and they're only asking eighty-nine nine fifty. I'm sure they can be jewed down to around eighty-six." His mouth made a little *O*. "You aren't Jewish, are you?"

"No," I said.

"Listen, I know some fine Jewish people and I'd never say or do anything in any way—What the heck, it's just an expression, you know, because the Jews are so good at gettin' a bargain. They ought to be flattered."

"I'll bet they would be," I murmured.

"Any-old-hoo, this is a dream home, my friend. An enchanted cottage."

I scratched my head so he'd think I was considering it. "I don't know," I said. "I mean, South Euclid . . ."

"Aw, hell, it's only another ten minutes farther out, and that's worst case, with heavy traffic."

I didn't want to buy a house in South Euclid. I didn't even want to look at one. I said, "I'm going to have to speak to Mrs. Jacovich about this, Christmas."

He beamed at my use of his first name. "You do that, Milan, and I'll be waiting for her answer. I'll bet she just jumps at it. But you have to see it first, you really do. Why don't I just make an appointment with the owners for us to amble by and take a gander?" He reached for the phone.

"I'll have to find out when is a good time for her."

"Well, that's fine, that's perfectly fine," he said, and stood up to shake my hand again, effectively ending the interview. "But I want to tell you something now, I don't want you going to anyone else and buying a house. I'll be awful mad if you do that—and you don't want old Father Christmas getting mad at you this time of year. Might end up with coal in your stocking."

"I wouldn't want that."

"Good." He smiled so hard his eyes almost disappeared. "Because you belong to me, now, Milan. You're mine."

I got back into my car and tuned my radio to one of those soft-music stations you don't really have to listen to. Something was bothering me, gnawing away inside my head, but I couldn't seem to get it out in the open to see what it was. For the moment I shrugged it off. It was only two P.M., and already it had been a long day. And I had other things to think about.

It wasn't quite time for school to end, so the grounds and corridors of the high school were fairly quiet when I got there, although with only fifteen minutes to go an air of expectancy crackled in the nearly deserted halls. I glanced though the windows in the doors at some of the classes in progress and remembered sitting in those classrooms, one eye on the clock waiting for the closing bell. Most of the teachers were around my own age and hadn't been there when I was a schoolboy. It made me feel ancient.

Mr. Parker was in his office, looking as harried as a big-city high school principal should. A full pot of coffee sat on the ledge behind his desk. He took off his glasses and laid them down atop a stack of papers and came around to shake my hand.

"I thought I'd be seeing you again," he said.

"Oh?"

"I gleaned from our brief conversation the other day that something was going on here at the school I ought to know about."

"I appreciate your not pressing me then."

He sat down and gestured me into a chair. "I'm a civil servant, when it's all said and done; I learned the art of patience years ago. I figured you'd tell me when you were ready. I gather you are now."

"I'll give you what I can," I said, "if you'll buy me a cup of that coffee."

He smiled and poured a cup for each of us, and then I told him about Deshon. I omitted the more grisly details of his death, and I didn't mention Barrie Tremont or Waco Morgan. When I finished talking, his shoulders were slumping more than usual, and he rubbed his tired eyes with his fingers. I didn't envy him his job. He had a bunch of young minds to mold and shape, but he was so busy staving off attacks from the outside he was lucky to break even.

"I don't suppose you'll tell me who the boy is," he said.

"I can't do that now, Mr. Parker. It would violate a confidence."

He stood up, turning his back on me, and stared out the window, which was covered on the outside with metallic grill-work designed to repel foul balls, rocks, and vandals. He clasped his hands behind him, and the gesture made him seem older than he was. "My wife worries about me," he said. "I go home every night with a knot in my stomach as big as a volleyball. You want to think that what you do makes a difference, but it's like trying to empty out Lake Erie with a teaspoon."

He faced me again and sat down on the ledge next to the coffee machine. "I went into teaching to help kids. Black kids, frankly. The way out of any ghetto is education, and I wanted to do my part, just like my father did his by saving up to send me to college. But this is getting beyond me now. Tell me what to do, Mr. Jacovich."

The coffee was stronger than I usually drink it, and I made a face as I took a sip. "Mr. Parker, the main problem is a gang of young kids from the Caribbean."

He nodded. "Jamaicans. But there are a lot of Jamaican kids in this school."

"I can't give you any names because I don't know any."

"There's a white kid somehow involved with them?"

"I couldn't swear to it—I couldn't swear to any of this—but I think they're all dealing."

He pushed himself off the ledge. "Then I don't need any

139

names from you. The white boy is Paul Baznik, and I know the guys he's been running with." He smiled as my jaw dropped. "You think I'm blind? I can tell you lots of things that go on in this school the kids don't think I know about. I've seen Baznik hanging out with that crowd. The athletes—kids like your boy—are fairly color-blind, and their social groups seem to be pretty evenly mixed racially. When one white kid like Baznik only runs with a group of blacks, it's unusual enough that a principal takes notice." He threw a leg over the corner of his desk. His thigh looked hard-muscled. "Okay, I've got names, and you can feel righteous that you didn't give them to me. Now what do I do?"

I clawed at my necktie, suddenly aware of how warm it was in the steam-heated office. "I think you just watch. Now that Garthwaite is dead, someone else will be coming around. It's up to you to catch that before it starts and call the police."

"I'm not good at watching and waiting," he said. "I had too much of that in the Tet offensive, and I didn't like it any better then."

"I was in Nam too. Cam Ranh Bay."

He nodded. "I could've gotten an educational deferment, but half the people from my neighborhood had to go, so I went. But I was damned if I'd be black cannon fodder for them. So I got into Special Forces."

"I'm impressed. Green Berets was a tough outfit to crack."

An uneasy smile twisted his mouth. "It was simple for a black man—I just had to be ten times as good as anyone else."

I rested my ankle on my other knee. "Not much call for commando stuff around here, I'm afraid. If you could just keep your eyes open . . ."

He thought about it for a moment, then thumped his fist gently on the desk. "The Baznik boy will go down along with the Jamaicans, you know. I won't be able to save him."

I flushed. "I don't remember asking."

"You're right," he said, "and I'm sorry I said it. But we've had drugs at this school for some time now, and I didn't see you coming around until it got personal."

I sighed. "It's not my job to wipe out the crack trade singlehanded. I'm just a private cop trying to help a pal. I can't change the world, Mr. Parker, and neither can you."

"Wouldn't it be nice if we could?" he said. "But we just do what we can."

* * *

I got caught in the corridor when the final bell rang, and was immediately engulfed in a joyous and dizzying rush of humanity all scrambling to escape the halls of academe and get on with their lives. I ran into Milan Jr. just outside the main door.

"Hey, Dad!" he yelled.

"Hey, kiddo."

"I got a game," he said, his face flushed with excitement. "Wanna come watch?"

"I wouldn't miss it," I said. Together we trudged across the athletic field to the mausoleum-type building that served as the boy's gym, and I waited in the wooden bleachers while Milan suited up inside. There were several parents, mostly mothers, already in the stands, and the rest of the seats were quickly filled by the student body.

The football coach, George Hatch, came over to shake hands, and we stood and chatted for a bit. Hatch was a few years older than I and had never seen me play, but he knew of my college football career and was eager to talk about it. I guess when a guy loves football the way Hatch does and he's only five foot eight, the closest he can come to his dream is coaching on the high school level. But Hatch had apparently come to terms with that and was just glad to talk to someone who'd played varsity in college.

"Milan's got ability," he told me as we watched the boys come straggling out of the gym in their scarlet and gold gear. The other team, wearing green and white, was already suited up and getting limber on the opposite sideline.

"Thanks," I said, "but it's too early to tell whether he's got the steam to make it all the way. He'll have to bulk up some."

"Sure," he said, "but he's got it up here." He pointed to his own head. "And most important, he's a team player. A lot of

141

these kids, especially backs and receivers, they come for the glory and don't give a damn for the rest of the team. He likes winning."

"We all like to win, Coach. Even more, we hate losing."

"You got that right." He stepped forward, blew an earsplitting blast on his whistle, and screamed at everyone to take a few laps. "You're lucky," he said. "You have a good boy, a decent boy. A lot of these kids, they got the potential to be decent, but it's tough out there, and there's all sorts of crap they can get mixed up with before they even know it. And we have to stand by and watch with our hands in our pockets, because there's not a damn thing we can do about it."

The assistant coach, a bull-necked young man in his senior year as a physical ed major at Cleveland State, came trotting out onto the field as the pack of kids came around in front of the bleachers after their second lap. Hatch smiled up at me. "Gotta go to work. Come around any time, Mr. Jacovich."

I stayed for the whole game. Milan Jr. didn't score any touchdowns, but he caught four passes, dropped one, and gained about forty-five yards. St. Clair won by nine points. Watching the boys go through the motions that were achingly familiar to me, I ruminated a bit on the brief flicker of time we have to be young. After the game I went down on the field, shook my son's hand and that of the quarterback and a couple of the other boys I knew, and headed home.

When I got back to my apartment I checked my answering machine to find that no one had called me, and then I read my mail, which consisted of a fifty-dollar check from a guy who owed me more than seven hundred, my electric bill, a magazine sweepstakes offer assuring me that I was in the finals for a two-million-dollar drawing, and a catalogue from a cheese-and-wine dealer featuring all sorts of expensive gift baskets for the upcoming holidays. Personal letter writing, it seemed, was a lost art.

I made a call to Ed Stahl to see if he could wangle me four decent seats to the Cavaliers on Saturday, and he said he'd see what he could do. Ed is a good friend, and sometimes I feel as though I impose on that friendship too much. It's one of the hazards of the kind of job I have, but it doesn't make me feel any better about it.

There were lots of things I wasn't feeling too good about on this particular evening. The way this case was unraveling was certainly one of them. I had Reggie Parker on my side, but that was only going to mean grief for Paulie Baznik.

I'd thought a lot about Paulie before going to Parker, and more about him after my brief talk with Coach Hatch. He was right. I was lucky that my own son was too involved with his own body to get into the kind of mess Paulie was in. And I was in a position to do something besides watch. There was no question in my mind that the boy was dealing, and that meant he was going to have to answer to the law. But he was only fourteen, he'd never been in trouble before, and I was betting that a compassionate judge would take that into consideration, and that Lieutenant Mark Meglich would be there to put a word in for the kid. A slap on the wrist beat hell out of winding up like Deshon Garthwaite.

It was a hard decision, but after lots of soul-searching I'd decided it was the right one. Right decisions are often hard. I only prayed that it would work out to be the best thing for the kid, and that Matt and Rita Marie would understand and forgive me.

I almost jumped out of my skin when the phone rang. I'd been deep in my own thoughts and the harsh bell brought me back to the here and now with a jolt. I lifted the receiver. In the background I could hear laughter, talking, glasses clinking, and the droning of a TV set.

"I'm only gonna say this one time," Vuk said, his gruff Jimmy Durante voice like a bulldog's bark in my ear. "They's a guy comes around to some of the other places peddlin' his papers. He gives away free samples, then puts the screws in. He's never been in here, an' he won't be if he values his ass."

"How do you know he doesn't come into your place?"

" 'Cause I woulda remembered," Vuk said. "The way I hear it, he's one of those blond guys—whaddaya call 'em, albeenos. You think I get them in here every day? I never seen one in person."

It would probably please Bobby no end to know he was famous on the East Side. He got around, Bobby. "Who told you this, Vuk?"

"Ass me no questions and I'm not naming no names. You told me to poke around, I poke around. But see, Milan, I told you, not in my place—ever!"

"Who does he work for, Vuk?"

"Do I know? The calypsos, probably. But that's a guess. And Milan—you didn't hear this from anyone you know, right?"

I heard laughter coming from the bar. They were watching the afternoon reruns of *The Cosby Show*. That was the closest black people would ever get to Vuk's Tavern, unless they happened to be playing a professional sport. I thanked him and hung up. I'd pissed him off for a piece of information I already possessed. But he didn't seem angry anymore, and knowing I had at least one friend left gave me a warm feeling inside—or maybe it was just heartburn.

It was twenty minutes to five, and already the winter light was beginning to fade outside and my little den was growing gloomy. I switched on the desk lamp, picked up the phone, and called Mary.

"Oh, hello, Milan." Very businesslike at the office.

"How are you?" I said.

"Pretty good," she said vaguely. "It's been a busy week."

"How does dinner sound? You want to meet me at Sterle's?"

There was a minute pause. "I can't tonight." I waited for her to explain, or to suggest tomorrow night instead, and when she didn't something crawled all over my skin, something evil and green. I'd hoped that a few days would make everything all right, but it obviously hadn't. I'd never heard her sound that way. She'd never turned me down before without offering an explanation.

"Business meeting?" I hated myself for asking. According to the unspoken rules of our relationship, questions like that were out of bounds, and her hesitation before answering only reinforced my regret.

"Actually I'm having dinner with Steve."

"Oh," I said.

144

"Steve Cirini."

"Yeah."

She didn't say anything else for a while. Neither did I. The static on the line was the only sound.

Then she said, "Are you mad at me?"

"I don't know. Should I be?"

She sighed. "I don't know either."

I filled my lungs and let the words coast out on the exhalation. "So this dinner tonight—is this a date, or what?"

"There you go, labeling. Black or white."

"Well, either it is or it isn't. I had lunch with Ed Stahl the other day, but I'd hardly call it a date."

"That's a lousy example."

"You're kind of evading the issue, aren't you?"

"If you're asking if I'm going to sleep with Steve, I'm probably not. But if you want to call it a date, then that's what you have to call it."

I put both elbows on my desk, experiencing the sour feeling in my stomach that I usually only get when I eat brussels sprouts. "Why?"

"Why what?"

"Why are you having dinner with Steve?"

She didn't manage to make it as airy-sounding as she might have liked. "Any reason why I shouldn't?"

"Come on, Mary."

"Damn it, Milan! Sometimes you make me feel this big!"

"I don't mean to, ever."

"I know you don't. But it's the way you are. You can't cut people any slack. It's the Jacovich way or not at all."

"Look, if you're talking about the other night—"

She said, "You know damn well I'm talking about the other night. I'm not a criminal, and I'm damned if I'll be treated like one. By anybody! I'm a person, with good points and bad points and a lot of points that are somewhere in between. I grew up in the seventies, with all that entails, and I did all the things other people did. But you can't accept that."

"I can," I protested. "I have already."

"In your head, sure. But not deep down in your gut where

it counts. It'll always be a black mark, that's the way you are—rigid and judgmental. It's hard having to live under the Code of Hammurabi or something all the time. That's all."

"And so you're going out with Steve Stunning to get even?" It was the wrong thing to say, and the snotty nickname didn't help matters any. She answered me with icicles.

"I'm going because I want to."

I swallowed, trying to get some moisture back in my mouth. "That's pretty succinct."

"I suppose it is."

"The guy's been trying to nail you for months."

"Maybe," she said, "but at least he doesn't pass judgment on me." She sniffled a bit and then sighed. "This isn't a conversation to have over the phone."

"Good. Meet me in an hour at Sterle's."

"You know I can't."

"I know you can do anything you want to do. You told me that once, Mary."

She breathed irregularly into the mouthpiece. "Then I guess I just don't want to."

"I guess you don't," I said.

"We'll talk tomorrow. Tomorrow night. Don't call me, I'll call you at home. Okay, Milan?" And she broke the connection fast because she knew damned well it wasn't okay and she didn't want to hear me say it wasn't.

I sat there holding the handset tightly in my hand as though I were trying to squeeze life back into it. When I heard the harsh dial tone I put it back in its cradle. Gently. Sadly.

Some people say the world will end with a bang, others believe it will be with a whimper. But I never dreamed that for Mary and me it would end with a cliché like "Don't call me, I'll call you."

15

I DIDN'T have anything to drink that night except a pot of bitter black coffee. In my frame of mind I didn't trust myself with anything stronger. I sat like a sofa cushion, staring blindly at the TV all evening, and I couldn't tell you the name or the content of a single program I saw, which I don't count as much of a loss. I do know that by the time I got up and switched off the set, David Letterman was just getting ready to do the top ten reasons Madonna will never win Best Dressed Woman of the Year. I was glad to see him go.

Life is full of endings and beginnings; it's the natural order, and there's no point in moaning about it because that's the way it is. Birth is a beginning, death is an ending, and there are all sorts of smaller ones of both kinds in between. You learn to deal with them if you're going to survive. Endings, however, are a lot easier to take when they're accompanied by the beginning of something else, and there was no new beginning in sight for me. Just the end of a love affair that had bound up and healed some pretty painful emotional wounds, reawakened and revitalized me, sharpened my self-awareness, taught me such things as joy and quiet contentment, reintroduced me to a sensuality I had almost forgotten, and made me happier than I'd been in all my adult life.

As the wind shrieked down Cedar Hill and rattled my bedroom window, I slid between sheets that seemed colder than usual and reflected that all I had to compensate for the empty place inside me was a nonpaying case that might well alienate my son as well as my closest friends—one that I was no closer to cracking than I'd been the day I'd taken it—and a cruel memory of what once was, which now seemed out of reach.

I'd blown it; no point trying to lay blame elsewhere. I'd done it with my little hatchet-shaped head. You can lose weight, dye your hair, get a face-lift, change your eye color with contact lenses, lie about your age, embrace arcane Eastern philosophies, switch your brand of beer, and start rooting for a different football team. But you can't change who you are inside, your values, your sense of what should and should not be. And you can't run away just by falling asleep, because the dreams come and stick out their tongues at you while they buffet you all over your bed in the dark.

I woke up cranky and mean, if "woke up" is the right term for coming out the other end of a long and mostly sleepless night. I'd studied the patterns on the ceiling, including the crack that was the shape of Brazil, the moldings around the top of the walls, the shadows that fell across the floor from the street-lamps out on Cedar Road, and the gradual way the light changed as the world went through its night-into-day transition. Anything you came up with about it, I could have aced a mid-term on that bedroom by morning.

I showered, shaved carelessly, and stepped over the paper on the mat outside my apartment door without even looking at it. For a creature of habit like me that was a radical departure.

You couldn't exactly say that the sun was shining, but the gray cloud layer that blankets northern Ohio all winter seemed thinner than usual, and there was an unnatural brightness outside that was hurtful to my unrested eyes. Downtown, the cop shop seemed to emanate its own burnished glow in the diffused light, despite its dirty walls and the heavy metal grates over all the windows. It was a strange illusion.

At police headquarters the smells of cheap cigars, burnt coffee, and desperation were at war with one another in the upstairs hallway where the squad rooms were. Marko was halfway between his own office and the men's room, talking to a bullet-headed cop whose name I didn't know. He was a huge man with a prognathous jaw like a speed bump in a parking lot, and he wore a heavy-duty shoulder holster. He looked the way cops are supposed to, like the old movie actors; Barton MacLane, Tom Tully, Edmond O'Brien. Cops should look like they could eat you for breakfast and not even belch. Now they're all accountant clones like Ingeldinger or stockbroker clones like Marko, who waved and moved toward me when he saw me. The big cop turned his head to look my way. Getting any sort of mobility out of that twenty-inch neck had to be some sort of accomplishment.

"Who's your little pal?" I said when Marko got close enough to me for the big bull not to hear.

"That's Drago. He's vice."

"What do you feed him? Babies?"

"Yeah, unless he develops a taste for smart-mouthed private stars." He looked at me closely. "You look like the eighth day of a seven-day binge."

"It's my new image," I said. "You got the PM report on Garthwaite?"

"I do. And it's none of your business. You've been told to stay out of this."

"We can't even have coffee together like old pals, Mark?"

He tilted his head to the side like an attentive cocker spaniel, and then he smiled. It was calling him Mark that did it. Just about everyone called him Mark these days, except the guys from the old neighborhood, and I guess he saw my usage of his preferred monicker as some sort of small triumph.

"What the hell, it's a Saturday. Come on," he said, and led me into his office.

He poured some coffee into his ceramic mug and filled a plastic one for me. His concern about cancer-causing elements in plastic cups apparently didn't extend to his visitors. I sank gratefully into the uncomfortable wooden chair while he regarded me with a baleful eye.

"Seriously, are you okay?"

I just waved at him, my mouth full of hot coffee. I was as far from okay as one can get, but I didn't want to discuss it, especially with Marko. I wasn't up to one of his lectures, and

I didn't want to muddle the issue of the coroner's report on Deshon. I swallowed the coffee and asked him about it again.

"Jesus, let it go, can't you?"

"You know I can't. Come on, what'll it hurt to tell me?"

He breathed loudly through his nose and patted at his thirty-dollar haircut. Then he opened his top drawer and rummaged through it until he found the file. "It was a crack house, all right, the Merle Avenue place," he said, scanning the top page. "The perps or somebody else had pretty well cleaned it all out, but the lab guys found a few battered pots and pans with cocaine residue down in the basement, and a dozen empty boxes of baking soda in the trash, along with a couple of glassine bags and a roll of white butcher paper. Fingerprints were inconclusive, it says here."

"Anything else?"

"Upstairs there was a shitty old mattress in the bedroom and some fancy men's clothes in the closet. Also a pair of women's pantyhose in a reddish color with bright red panties attached. A forty-pound bag of dog chow in the kitchen and a box of giant-size Milk-Bones."

"The guy loved his dog, I guess." I lit a cigarette to take my mind off the way I'd last seen the dog.

"Cause of death was massive multiple traumas to the head."

"I would have sworn it was old age that got him."

"According to the angles of some of the contusions," he went on, ignoring me, "there were more than one of them taking batting practice. And traces of the dog's blood were found on him, so they probably used the same weapon on him as they did on Bowser."

I nodded. "All right, tit for tat. There are two guys, both Jamaican, that hung around with him. Apparently they were his muscle. One of them was kind of stocky and had one of those geometric haircuts that made him look like a blue jay. His name, I think, was Javier."

"How do you spell that?"

"How do I know?"

"With an X or a J or an H?"

"Not an H," I said. "The other one, I didn't catch his name, but he wore his hair like Joan Bennett."

"Joan Bennett? The movie star?"

"No, Joan Bennett the clerk at the tie counter at Higbee's in the Beachwood Mall. *Certainly* Joan Bennett the movie star."

Marko patted his haircut again. "I don't think she's made a movie in twenty years. More, maybe."

"I'm not talking about movies. What's the difference when Joan Bennett made her last movie?"

"Because ninety-nine point nine percent of the guys on the force are under thirty-five, and I tell them to go out and look for somebody with hair like Joan Bennett, they're going to stare at me like I've gone around the bend. I can't risk that."

I sighed. "The man's tall, thin, has black hair parted in the middle and falling to his shoulders in waves. Better?"

He scribbled something on a white pad. "Yeah," he said finally. "Better."

"You locate the girl yet?"

"What girl?"

"The kid I told you about, the crack whore. She's probably the one that called it in. And she knows these two guys with the baseball bats."

He thought for a minute, then picked up his phone and tapped out three numbers. "This is Meglich. Send Drago in here, all right?" He hung up and sat back, relaxed. "The Dragon'll know her if she's been around awhile. He knows 'em all."

In about thirty seconds the big cop filled up the doorway. "You want me, Lou?"

"Al Drago, say hello to Milan Jacovich. He's a private."

Drago nodded at me, but if you weren't looking hard you'd have missed it. His neck was so thick that the end of his necktie only came to just below his breastbone. I didn't even think about getting up and shaking hands.

"Milan used to tote a badge like us," Marko said, and Drago's expression warmed up about two degrees, which brought it to a sizzling fifty below. "Sit down, Dragon."

The big man shook his head, about half an inch each way. "I'm fine, Lou." His voice came from a cold subterranean cavern. He leaned on the doorframe, and I worried about the building coming down on us like Samson's temple. His scalp was an unhealthy gray through his buzz cut.

"Dragon, you familiar with a black hooker, light-skinned, long orange hair she wears in a cha-cha ponytail? Probably works Prospect or Euclid."

"She's tall and very skinny," I said. "Freckles."

Drago turned his whole body to look at me, wondering where I fit into the equation, and his scrutiny made me cold all over. He somewhat resembled Frosty the Snowman in that he had a white face, a button nose, and two eyes made out of coal. I shuddered to think what happened when he went thumpety-thump-thump.

"That could be a lot of people," he rumbled.

"This one hung with a calypso candy man name of Deshon Garthwaite. He wore dreadlocks with little silver beads on the ends."

A flash of understanding appeared in Drago's dark eyes. "He wore? Don't he wear 'em no more?"

"Somebody messed them up with baseball bats," Marko said.

"You think the redheaded dingy cunt did it?"

I said, "Material witness."

I waited while he processed the information. "I see her, I'll ask her about it."

He turned to leave, and Marko said, "No rough stuff if you find her, Dragon. She hasn't done anything."

"She's a whore, right?" Drago said. Then he shrugged his shoulders and the earth moved and the mountains rumbled and a tidal wave started way out in the middle of the lake and came rolling in to pound against the shore. And he was gone.

I looked at Marko, who avoided my gaze. "Drago's a good cop," he said, "but he gets overenthusiastic sometimes. God help a hooker who runs afoul of the Dragon. He's messed up more than one."

"Sounds like he's got hangups. Doesn't he have a sex life of his own?"

"I think he sticks it in a hole in a brick wall." He waved a hand in front of his face. "What's the difference?"

"Look, I've already gotten one man and one dog killed. I don't want that girl put in the hospital. She did drop the dime on the Garthwaite killing, after all."

"We don't know that for sure."

"All right then, she's a human being. Does that sit better on your conscience?"

He gave me his hard-guy look again. "I've got no conscience. I'm a cop."

I put down my coffee cup and stood up. "Fine, Marko." I said. "But don't ever ask me again why I turned in my badge. You and Drago are it—in technicolor."

* * *

The glare of the hidden sun was even stronger when I walked down the stone steps of police headquarters, and I wished I had some sunglasses. But you don't wear sunglasses in November in Cleveland unless you're a pretentious jerk or you have something to hide. You even need a pretty good excuse to wear them in the summertime. Cleveland isn't L.A. or Miami or Phoenix, where dark glasses have the designer's name printed on the edge of the left lens. It's a good, honest, working-class city where you squint when the sun hits you in the face, or you shade your eyes with your hand like an Indian looking into the distance for the column of cavalry. I was willing to bet that Jeff Singer, Barrie Tremont's downstairs neighbor, had several pairs of sunglasses.

An uneasy rat gnawed at my stomach when I thought of Al Drago ranging the East side, cracking his oversized knuckles in anticipation and breathing through his mean mouth as he looked for the girl. She might be a prostitute and a crackhead, but she was hardly a menace to society, and I didn't want Drago getting his rocks off by hurting her. I decided to look for her myself.

I went downtown to Ninth Street, past Short Vincent Street, the site of the old Hickory Grill where the gamblers and high rollers and racketeers used to hang out in the fifties, where Shondor Birns and Jake "Greasy Thumb" Guzik would sit in their booth eating ribs and drinking premium bourbon from a bottle they kept under the bar, giving kids five bucks to go out and buy them the afternoon paper or a racing form and letting them keep the change. I wondered what Guzik would think of the Jamaican posses. He probably would have had them off the streets in three days. Just as with cops, they don't make wise guys like they used to, either.

153

I found the western end of Prospect Avenue and cruised slowly eastward, looking carefully at everyone on the sidewalk. At Fifty-fifth I went over to Euclid and headed toward University Circle, past the broken-down rooming houses and the shells of empty buildings that looked like something out of bombed-out Beirut, past the True Holiness Temple where street prostitutes often gather, huddled out of the wind in the recesses in the face of the building. It was still early, and most of the working girls hadn't come out yet. Later in the evening they'd be out in force, shivering in their skimpy miniskirts and vinyl jackets trimmed in fake fur, calling out whatever invitation popped into their minds as the Saturday night johns drove by, checking out the field to make their selections for a quick encounter on some little-traveled side street or alley.

I went around the block just past the Cleveland Play House and retraced my route back down Euclid, then up Prospect once more. There are many beautiful, or at least interesting, scenic spots in the greater Cleveland area—the "emerald necklace" of parks that ring the city, the stately homes of Shaker Heights, the charm of Public Square where the old-world stateliness of Terminal Tower and the Old Stone Church coexist gracefully with the new high-rise office buildings of glass and steel, the bucolic woods of the Chagrin River valley, the miles of unimproved lake front, the romance of the Cuyahoga River, even the high-tech funk of the riverbank, where what once was the best rib joint in the midwest, Hot Sauce Williams', has been replaced by discos and pricey restaurants. It was just my luck to be wandering around some of the places that were as sad and bad as any streets in America. It isn't often a private detective gets to go to the park.

I didn't spot the redheaded strawberry anywhere—I wished I knew her name so I wouldn't have to think of her that way —so I headed up to 105th and drove around up there for a while. The only thing I saw that was in any way unusual was the house on Merle with the yellow crime-scene tape stretched around its periphery and the police seal on the door. I didn't have any reason to go in; I remembered what it was like.

Back home, I collected my mail and messages, changed clothes, and drove over to Lila's to pick up my sons for the basketball game between the Cavaliers and the Knicks that evening. As I started across St. Clair Avenue at Fifty-fifth Street an old man, frail and bent at the waist and wrapped in an ancient woolen coat and a long muffler, stepped off the sidewalk in front of me. I hit the brake hard and he glared at me, then angrily stepped back and waved me to go ahead of him; I had the light. I motioned for him to cross and he waved again even more violently, the wind making his rheumy, malevolent eyes tear. I moved past him slowly, watching in the rearview mirror as he stared a malediction at the back of my head. Maybe he was angry because he was old and knew there wasn't much waiting for him down the road; maybe he had a hardscrabble life fighting traffic and house payments and kids growing up and ignoring him. Whatever the reason, he made me feel bad.

When Stephen opened the door and greeted me with a bear hug and two thousand questions, Lila was in the living room fluffing up the pillows on the sofa. Fluffed pillows are one of Lila's big priorities. I wasn't sure whether Joe was home and hiding in the upstairs bedroom or if he'd taken the day off to do whatever it is nerds do on Saturdays in the wintertime. The boys both had their gym bags in hand, and Stephen was jumping up and down with anticipation. Milan Jr. did not jump for two reasons—first, it wasn't cool, and second, he'd taken a pretty good shot from a defenseman the day before and was sporting a set of bruised ribs. His mother knew nothing of this, and we were all happier for that.

"Don't keep them out too late after the game," she said.

"It's Saturday night. No school tomorrow."

She stopped fluffing and glared at me. "Aren't you taking them to church?"

I folded my arms across my chest. "I get the guys once every two weeks if I'm lucky, Lila. I'm not going to spend a precious hour of that time in church."

"Yay!" Stephen yelled.

I tried forestalling a lecture on piety and obligation by telling her we had to go pick up Paulie, but the strategy backfired.

"Oh, Rita Marie called about half an hour ago. Paulie isn't going with you."

"Why not?"

She sniffed. "You'll have to ask Rita Marie that. I don't know anything about your plans."

I ground my teeth. "I think I will," I said. "Mind if I use your phone?"

"You know where it is," she said airily, and went back to the pillows.

I shot an apologetic look at the boys and went into the kitchen where the yellow wall phone hung next to the door. I dialed the Baznik house, and after a few rings Rita Marie answered.

"How come Paulie isn't going to the game with us?" I said.

After several seconds of silence she said, "The truth is, he's not here."

"Where is he?"

"I don't know. He banged out at about three o'clock and we haven't seen him since."

The phone felt sticky against my ear in the warm kitchen. "Do you want me to go looking for him?" I said.

"I want you to mind your own business!" she said. "I told you that. Paulie's our son, and we'll take care of him."

"If the kid is missing, Rita Marie—"

"He's not missing," she said with some heat. "He's just not here, that's all. Look, I have to finish getting dinner ready. Take your boys to the game and have a good time, all right?"

I leaned against the kitchen wall with the dead phone in my hand and a great weight on my chest. I'd tried to do a friend a favor and wound up the Enemy. How in hell did that happen?

It took about half an hour to get to the Coliseum over in Richfield. Milan Jr. was fairly quiet until I began discussing yesterday's game with him, and Stephen chimed in with "Did you see that guy total Milan out, Dad? Jeez!" About five miles from our exit the freeway became gridlocked; the Cavs were playing well so far that season, and a lot of people wanted to see them cream the hated New Yorkers.

Cream them they did, 103–89, but my mind was only half on the game. I had my own troubles to worry about. Afterward I treated the boys to ice cream, taking childish satisfaction in keeping Stephen up considerably past his bedtime.

16

I AWOKE to the early light pounding against my drapes and the sounds of cartoons in the living room. Stephen was sitting yoga-fashion on the floor in his pajamas, a glass of milk at his side.

"I'm gonna run to the store before Milan wakes up," I said. "Want to come with?"

"Nuh-uh," he said, "I'm watching my cartoons."

I tried not to be miffed. I pulled on a sweatshirt and a pair of jeans with a rent in one knee—not the high-fashion kind of hole that kids make themselves, but a worn spot where my kneecap had finally poked through—and went across the street to the market to buy breakfast for us all. I'm no chef and don't pretend to be, but I always feel obligated to cook the boys breakfast whenever they spend the night. It seems more personal than taking them to a restaurant, which I'm sure they would prefer.

As I raced back across the street in the middle of the block, hugging my groceries against me to keep warm, the wind kicked up a few diehard fallen leaves. The weatherman had predicted badly, and there was no sign of a downpour. In fact, it wasn't a bad day, as winter days go, and I was feeling pretty good about the prospect of spending it with my sons just lying around watching football and hanging out.

I got down my ancient waffle iron, a hand-me-down from someone whose name I can't even remember, whipped up some batter, and set a giant skillet full of bacon to sizzling. I have a microwave, but bacon always seems to taste better when it's fried the old-fashioned way. By the time the food was ready, Milan Jr. was awake and galumphing around the apartment like a sixty-year-old man with a cheap-wine hangover, still tender in the ribs but willing to die before he'd admit it. Breakfast was as quiet as it could possibly be with Stephen on hand, so I opened my Sunday *Plain Dealer*, caught up with the news, sports, and book reviews, and waited for the first televised NFL game of the day to come on.

At about eleven o'clock the doorbell rang. I wasn't expecting anyone, so I looked through the security peephole. Victor Gaimari was standing in my hallway, wearing a charcoal topcoat with Persian lamb at the collar and a natty gray homburg. As always, his hair and mustache were carefully trimmed. Victor Gaimari was Giancarlo D'Allessandro's fair-haired nephew and probable successor, the new breed of mobster with the college degree and the million-dollar vocabulary. He wasn't any less vicious, but the Big Ten polish made him easier to talk to.

"I hope I'm not disturbing anything," he said when I opened the door, peeking around me to see what was going on inside.

"I'm having a quiet Sunday with my kids, Victor."

"Oh, sure. Shall I come back another time, or will you invite me in for a coffee? I won't stay long. I just want to talk for a minute."

Before I had a chance to answer, Stephen had scooted around in front of me and was looking up at my elegantly-dressed visitor.

"Hi," he said, his flower face breaking into a smile.

"And who is this good-looking young fellow?"

"Stephen Louis Jacovich," Stephen said, putting out his little hand. "I'm ten." I swear that some night of the full moon a werewolf is going to come slavering out of the bushes and roar at Stephen and within two minutes they'll be best friends. Stephen has never met a stranger.

"Victor Anthony Gaimari," Victor said gravely, shaking hands. "I'm very happy to meet you."

I sighed and stepped aside to let Victor into my living room. "And this is Milan Jr. Mr. Gaimari." Victor went over and shook hands with my older boy, who was tangled up in the newspaper on the floor and didn't bother standing. I wanted to remind him of his manners, but Victor really wasn't worth it.

"Come on in here where we can talk," I said. "You want that coffee?"

"Not really," Victor said, following me into the den. "I've been up quite a while. I took Mr. D'Allessandro to nine o'clock mass. He's getting to that age where he hates to miss church, especially on a Sunday."

"That's wonderful," I murmured.

He took off his hat and coat, revealing an expensive wool suit beneath, laid them carefully over the arm of the sofa, and sat down next to them. No shiny silk suits and Borsalino hats for Victor Gaimari, the New Breed. "I had no idea you had your kids today or I wouldn't have come. I know what a conscientious father you are. They're fine-looking boys, both of them. The little guy—Stephen? He's a charmer. He favors you."

I perched on the edge of my desk, aware of how splendid he looked and how shitty I looked. "What's on your mind, Victor?"

He allowed himself a small smile. "More to the point, what's on *your* mind?"

I shrugged. "I told everything to your—to Don Giancarlo the other day. It's no big deal."

"I'd say it's a very big deal, for you to come to us for help. It would have to be."

"I thought it was important enough, I guess. And you must think so too, or you wouldn't come to my home like this."

"Your home." He reached into his breast pocket, and I jumped for a moment. Then I realized how silly I was being. Victor Gaimari wouldn't pack a gun to go to church. I'd be surprised as hell if he even owned one. He took a cigarette out of an elegant silver case and fired it up with a matching lighter. "You don't like the idea of my being in your home, do you? With your kids and all."

"It's my day off," I said.

"You feel invaded. Sullied, somehow, as though my being in the business I'm in will somehow rub off on your sons and soil them. You think people like me are contagious."

I didn't like the direction the conversation was taking. Especially since Gaimari was practically reading my thoughts. "Let's not get heavy, Victor."

"You're a heavy guy. A man of deep thoughts and firm convictions."

I shifted my weight uneasily. "I'd like to think so."

That seemed to amuse him. "What you are," he said, "is a hypocrite."

I felt my face flushing, warming, but I didn't answer him.

"I used to like you, Milan, in spite of everything, all our past problems. I used to think you had class. You honored your commitments and took your medicine like a stand-up guy. And when the magazine business blew up you told the police only what you needed to, and you mentioned no names that shouldn't have been mentioned. We appreciated that, and so we didn't make a fuss about Mr. D'Allessandro's nephew. But you disrespect us, look down on us, call us wise guys. You come swaggering around our social club and put your hands on our people like they were animals to be swatted with a rolled-up newspaper and then kicked aside. You take our money, as you have in the past, and then you do everything in your power to rain on the picnic. You even kill, because to you we're somehow a subhuman species. Your head is back in the Capone and Guzik days, and you're so stiff-necked and tight-assed you don't even realize things aren't like that anymore, and they haven't been for years."

"You're a bunch of choirboys, all right."

He waved smoke away from his face. "No, we aren't. We do things that aren't always legal, aren't completely ethical—whatever the hell that means—just like every cop, every lawyer, every businessman in the world. But our names end in vowels and we take care of our own, and by your gospel that makes us scum. And then you have the gall to waltz into Mr. D'Allessandro's club and ask a favor. A pretty big favor, at that."

I started to say something but he held up a hand, his long

160

tapering fingers quivering just a bit. "I know, you thought it was necessary. Because you've found someone who's even worse than we are. We're the lesser of two evils to you. Am I right?"

"Victor, what's the point of all this? You and I aren't friends and we never will be."

"Of course not." He picked up his homburg from the arm of the sofa and waved it at me. "You think this is a black hat, even though your eyes tell you different, because that's how you see life. Good guys and bad guys and nobody in between."

I was putting teeth marks on my tongue trying to keep from telling him what I thought of him and then throwing him out the window.

"Until it's expedient for you to think otherwise, and then you rationalize, you justify in your own mind. You're a narrow, silly man, Milan, and the sad thing is that your morality is selective, and you don't even know it. Your childhood pal, Lieutenant Meglich, for instance. You think he never predated a warrant, aided of course by one of our esteemed judges? Or planted evidence to make a bust he couldn't get any other way? Or dropped his throwaway piece beside an unarmed man he'd just shot? I can give you instances if you'd like; names, dates. And when he was still in uniform, more than one of his collars showed up for arraignment sporting cuts and bruises supposedly incurred while resisting arrest."

"The object of the game is to catch the criminal."

"And the end justifies the means." Gaimari laughed. "It's all right for some and not for others. Your newspaper friend, Ed Stahl, with his Pulitzer Prize gathering dust in his drawer—do you really think he gets all his exclusives like in an old newspaper movie? Or has it occurred to you that much of the time when he isn't buying it, he's extorting it by threatening to expose small indiscretions, which he exchanges for proof of big ones?"

"Reporters are human too," I said.

"Everyone's human—except you. Take that steel rod out of your ass and bend a little. You'll be surprised how good it feels."

"Is that what you came here to tell me?" I said, feeling as though my lips had been numbed by novocaine.

161

"One of the things. Another is that after the *North Coast* business, the overwhelming consensus around our organization was to have you quietly disappear some night and never be seen again. It's something I wanted you to know." He inspected his buffed nails, which seemed to pass muster.

I got up off the desk slowly and walked around to sit in the chair behind it. "Why am I still here then?"

He squashed his cigarette out and laughed. It was a nasty laugh. "Because there were two votes in your favor. Votes that count a lot more than anyone else's."

"You and D'Allessandro?"

His eyes burned. "*Mister* D'Allessandro. You're damn right." He stood up, dropping his shoulders a bit, like a boxer going up against a puncher.

"Am I supposed to say thanks?" It sounded unbelievably lame, hanging there in the stuffy air of the den, dust motes dancing in the light from the bay windows.

"You're not supposed to say anything. I don't want anything from you, I'm sorry I even know you. But you owe Mr. D'Allessandro now, you're in his debt—and we expect you to pay that due bill whenever it's called. We won't ask you to violate your oh-so-lofty principles, but whenever we ask you to do something, you're going to do it. And when you do, you will treat Mr. D'Allessandro with respect; you'll take your hat off to talk to him, and you'll be nice to our other people. You can go play knight of the Round Table someplace else, but you'll be polite and grateful and cooperative with us—or so help me, Milan, votes can be changed."

He smoothed his mustache, shrugged into his coat, and took a sealed white envelope from his pocket and tossed it onto my desk. I picked it up and fingered it without opening it. It didn't feel as if there was much in it, perhaps a single sheet of paper. "What's this?"

"You won't believe this, but I don't know what it is. I don't want to know. It's not my business. I've survived as long as I have by not interfering in things that aren't my concern. It's a good lesson to learn." He put on his hat. "You found this on the street, Milan. It fell out of your morning newspaper. You

162

can't even remember where it came from." He started for the door. "Are you going to see me out?"

I got up and went into the living room with him. The NFL pregame show was on, and Bob Costas was interviewing someone I didn't recognize. It didn't matter, because Costas wouldn't let him get a word in edgewise.

"Thanks for letting me borrow your dad for a few minutes, fellows," Victor said to the boys. "It was nice meeting you both. You have a real good day and enjoy the football games. Are you Browns fans?"

"Yeah!" Stephen said enthusiastically while his brother tried to look as though he was above it all. "Bernie! Bernie!" he chanted, and pantomimed throwing a forward pass.

"That's the way." Victor turned and nodded to me, his movie star charm failing to camouflage the coldness beneath. "Milan," he said.

I locked the door behind him.

"Dad, it's the Raiders and the Bengals!" Stephen said, only he pronounced it "the Radars and the Bingles."

"Yeah, I'll be there in a second," I said.

I went back into the den and shut the door, the envelope still in my hand. I didn't care much about the Bengals game. Any football team that wears tiger stripes like a bunch of imported hookers at a Texas cocktail party could just kick off without me. I dumped the ashtray where Victor had ground out his butt and stared out the window, thinking about what he'd said to me.

Rigid. Stiff-necked and tight-assed. Selective morality. Saint Milan the Hypocrite.

I stared out the window at the light Sunday traffic, listening to the unaccustomed sound of my boys in the other room. I had lived alone for a long time now, almost three years, and the boys were growing up and out faster than I could keep up with them in our once-every-other-week visits. Maybe they thought I was a tight-ass too. It was that which had driven Mary away—and maybe Lila before her. I hoped it wouldn't cost me my sons. It ground at my guts like the gnawing of a timber wolf that, for once in his life, Victor Gaimari might be right.

I shook it off the way an athlete ignores a noncritical but painful injury and sat down at my desk, holding the plain white envelope by its edges. I had a letter opener on the desk, one that Matt Baznik had made for me when I quit the police force and opened my own business. It was sterling silver, with *Milan Security* engraved on it. I slit open the envelope.

A small piece of paper, folded over once, fell out onto the blotter. I opened it and read the two words that were on it. Then I struck a wooden match, held the flame to the paper, and watched it burn up in the ashtray. I sat playing with the letter opener for quite a while, spinning it on the blotter, running it through my fingers, poking its blunt point into my palm. I had what I wanted, but now I didn't know what to do with it.

The door opened and Milan Jr. was there, tall, broad in the shoulders, his black hair as yet uncombed and his cowlick falling into his eyes. "The game's started, Dad."

"Right." I threw the envelope into my wastebasket, put down the letter opener, and went into the living room, where Stephen had opened a large bag of potato chips, most of which were in his lap or on the carpet on either side of him. I'd missed the kickoff. The Raiders had the ball, second and seven on their own thirty-one, but I didn't much care. I was thinking about the paper I'd burned with a wispy, old-man's scrawl on it.

Waco Morgan, it had said.

17

MORNINGS after I have the boys with me for the night, it's always my job to drive them to school. I had gone by the high school first and then taken Stephen to the elementary school about six blocks away. I hugged him hard when we said good-bye, and when he jumped out of the car and raced across the yard, throwing me a backward wave and a grin, the pain was palpable, a sense of loss as if he was leaving me forever.

There were times lately I didn't want to let them go at all but just wanted to keep them willing prisoners in my apartment, helping them with their homework, fixing pancakes, ordering in pizza and Chinese, wrestling with them on the rug, watching them grow at a normal pace and letting reality slide. I knew that if I wanted to see either of them again before two weeks went by, I'd have to come up with a good reason and listen to a lot of negative feedback from their mother first. Without the boys and without Mary, I was back to square one again, the quintessential lonely single, walking around breathing and doing my job but not really alive, my world circumscribed by my apartment and my work. Frozen dinners, reading books till my eyes hurt, watching TV until it put me to sleep, hanging around drinking beer at Vuk's, an occasional sweaty and love-less go-round with some woman whose name I wouldn't remember in the morning—it was like looking ahead toward a bleak lunar landscape.

I sat in the car until I heard the first bell of the morning ring inside the school, and I could picture Stephen, his eyes alive with the sparkle that was uniquely his, sitting at his desk with his hands folded in front of him, hoping the teacher would call on him so he could give her the right answer. After a time the ache in my chest subsided enough for me to drive over and grab a coffee and a bagel with lox at the Bill of Fare, a little Jewish deli that had been on the corner of East Fortieth and Payne ever since I could remember. I read the paper over breakfast, checking out the football scores I already knew. Another exercise in futility. I seemed to be engaged in a lot of them lately. I left the paper next to my plate when I finished breakfast, and the man sitting next to me snatched it up before I'd even gotten to the cash register. I paid my bill and went down to police headquarters to perform what I considered a civic duty.

"You're out of your skull," Ingeldinger said.

"What are you, kidding?" Marko said.

"I'm getting cheesed at you, Jacovich," Ingeldinger said.

"Why?"

"You expect us to go in and bust one of this town's most prominent citizens for murder and drug dealing because a little bird with no name whispered in your ear?"

":I don't expect you to bust him right away," I said. "I do expect you to do something about it."

"What? Bring him in and put him in the basement with three guys like Drago with rubber hoses to sweat a confession out of him? Times have changed. He'd have a battery of high-priced shysters baying like hounds at the front desk before we could get our tape recorders working."

"Besides," Ding said, "the whole thing doesn't compute."

"Why not?"

"Waco Morgan's not Jamaican, or else he's doing a damn good job of passing for white. And it's the Jamaicans run the show on the street. That's why it's so damn hard to do anything about it. They move from place to place, nobody's got a job, nobody's got a social security number. They just vanish."

166

"Could be it's the Jamaicans doing the dancing but somebody else pulling the strings," I said.

"Not according to our information."

"I don't think your information is as good as mine."

Ding smiled, not very sweetly. "Of course we can't make a judgment on that, since you won't tell us where it came from."

"I can't."

"You won't."

"Semantics. I'm not withholding evidence—I'm laying it in your laps like a Christmas fruitcake." I was leaning against the wall next to the window in Marko's office, and I glanced out through the wire mesh at the street, three floors below. It was raining again, one of those fine, cold, late autumn drizzles that wet you to the skin but aren't really heavy enough to make you use your umbrella. The asphalt glistened like in a 1940s musical dream sequence. "When somebody does me a favor, I don't compromise them."

"That's weasel talk," Ding said. "That's how the wise guys think."

I hoped the flush that warmed my cheeks didn't show on my face. Though Ingeldinger was no dummy, he couldn't possibly know of any connection between me and D'Allessandro unless he'd been having me surveilled—a possibility, but a pretty remote one. He was more interested in the drug posses than in Deshon's murder anyway, and he didn't have time to waste on other departments and other crimes. Murder wasn't his table.

"You must have a bunch of pretty worthless snitches if you don't cover their asses for them," I said to him.

Marko said, "Milan's snitches all run banks and write for newspapers, so he don't understand how it works."

How like him to deliberately use bad grammar to make himself one of the boys at the station house.

Ingeldinger mainlined a Life Saver. "Jacovich, if you think we can start bouncing a guy like Waco Morgan off the walls just on your say-so, you're dumber than owl shit. Thirty years ago, maybe. But this is the nineties now, and they've got rules."

"Milan doesn't like rules," Marko said. "That's why he don't wear a badge anymore."

"Stop talking about me like I'm not in the room," I said.

"Then you stop talking like you weren't on the planet."

I ticked off a few points on my fingers. "Barrie Tremont is Waco Morgan's girlfriend. She lives in the apartment house he owns, probably rent free. She also owns the crack house Garthwaite was operating out of. And you'll find Morgan owns several houses in that neighborhood, too. I'd bet the family homestead that Morgan is paying Tremont's mortgage on the Merle Avenue house, and that the rest of his properties are or have been used as crack houses too. It doesn't take a rocket scientist to figure it out."

Ding had been propping up the opposite wall; now he pushed himself off and came over to me. "We stupid and inept cops sure aren't rocket scientists, and we really appreciate your busting in to solve our case for us, but all that's useless without any hard facts to back it up." He worked the candy to the front of his mouth, held it vertically between his upper and lower teeth, and stuck his tongue into the hole. It would have looked obscene if it wasn't so silly. "Why don't you go back to Mr. Anonymous and tell him you need more complete information?" And that was even sillier than trying to put his tongue through the Life Saver.

"Why don't I just call the DEA?" I said. "Maybe they'll be interested, if you aren't."

"Good idea," Marko said. "I've got a big oil painting of those federal pussies elbowing into a local jurisdiction and crawling all over Waco Morgan with nothing more to go on than your suggestion. Grow up, for cry sakes! Federal cops have made covering their own asses an art form."

Ding started talking again from the other side of the room. I felt like a spectator at a tennis match. "Jacovich, I've been on the job eighteen years: walked a beat, vice, burglary. Now it's narcotics, and it's the sleaziest of the lot. I don't like dealers, I don't like users, I don't like people who fuck up little kids. I couldn't give less of a shit about this Garthwaite guy getting pulverized—he's one less slime on the street I have to worry about. I've spent the last eighteen months of my life trying to bust the posses. Full time." He began munching the candy. "You think I wouldn't give my left nut for something I could use? But coming in here and laying down the name of a prominent citizen doesn't cut it, unless you have some proof."

"Isn't it your job to get proof?"

"The only place we'll find it is up Waco Morgan's ass. Hell, we can't bug his phones without a federal warrant, and we can't put a team on him twenty-four hours a day."

"Why not?"

"On an anonymous tip? Come on, you know how it works. We have a captain we answer to," Marko said, "and he answers to the chief, and the chief answers to the commissioner—"

"And the Cabots talk only to God," I finished.

He shook his head sadly and leaned back in his chair so that the springs squeaked. "We can't move on this. It isn't enough." He raised his hands in a show of helplessness. "Sorry, Milan."

I moved away from the window. "You'll have to excuse me, guys. I've got things to do. And I don't have a captain or a commissioner," I said.

Ingeldinger stepped directly into my path in front of the door, and I could smell the butterscotch on his breath. "No, but you've got a license. You want to keep it?"

"You think you're big enough to take it away from me?"

"It'd be fun to try."

Marko stood up. "Damn it, you two, knock it off!"

I moved my shoulders, stretching the muscles, tensing as if for a plunge into cold water. I'd worked it out carefully, all night long, while my kids slept in the next room, and I thought I had it figured. I hoped I did. Because otherwise I was so far out on a limb my only companions would be blue jays. "What if I can bring you the proof you need? You close down the crack concession and grab all the headlines, and I go back into my hidey-hole and track down shipping clerks who steal ballpoint pens?"

Ingeldinger's face was inches from mine, and his eyes burnt holes through his thick glasses. "You bring us good, solid evidence, something we can use to turn off their water, and I'll kiss your ass in Higbee's window at high noon. In front of my mother."

"I don't want kisses, Ding. I want something else."

"I knew it." This from Marko.

"I don't like making deals with the devil, Jacovich. What do you want?"

"Paulie Baznik."

"Who?"

"Our friend's kid," Marko said. "He's selling crack for nickels and dimes at the school. That's what gave Milan this wild hair in the first place."

"What about him?" Ding said. His voice was rough, but he looked interested.

"Free and clear. No matter what other shit spills out of the bag, Paulie walks away clean."

"To you there are good bad guys and bad bad guys, huh?" Marko said, "We know the parents twenty-five years."

"I owe it," I said. "To his mother."

They looked at one another in silent communication, two gold-shield cops deciding the fate of a fourteen-year-old boy. Marko's face was softer than its customary flintiness; he remembered the old days with Matt Baznik as well as I did.

Ding threw up his hands. "I say no, I break a mother's heart."

Reassuring. I had nothing else to say to either of them, and I started to walk around him, but Ingeldinger shifted into my path again, the overhead light bouncing off his sweaty bald scalp. "We never had this conversation, Jacovich. You were never here, and you never spoke anybody's name to us. That's a given."

I nodded.

"One other thing: you fuck up, and you're a bad memory. You, your license, and maybe a lot more too. You'll twist in the wind before we do. You know that, don't you?"

I filled my lungs with the stale air of Marko's office. "We never had *that* conversation, either," I said.

* * *

Trying to find anyone at the Department of Public Works is like trying to locate someone at a late-season Browns-Broncos game when you don't know his seat number. Civil service workers, unlike my friend Renee at the Hall of Records, don't like to be bothered with requests for personnel information, especially when it isn't official business. I had to give my name to no less than four functionaries before I finally stumbled into a huge room where more than a hundred people bent over their desks under the merciless glare of the fluorescent fixtures overhead. Their murmuring into telephones and the various clicks and hums of desktop computers sounded like background noise in a movie crowd scene.

I wandered around through the maze until I found the person I was looking for. I stood at his side for almost a minute, but he was so absorbed in his paperwork that he didn't even notice me until I said, "Hello, Matt."

He started blinking at me. It's always unsettling to see someone out of their usual context, somewhere they aren't supposed to be, and it disoriented him for a moment.

"Milan," he said, drumming his pencil on the edge of the desk. "What are you doing here?"

I ignored the question. "I'm sorry Paulie didn't make it on Saturday. We had a good time. The Cavs kicked butt."

"Yeah," he said.

"You got a second to talk?"

He looked around, his manner scared and furtive. "Uh, I'm working."

"They don't let you take coffee breaks? I thought Lincoln freed the slaves. Come on, Matt, give me a few minutes."

He sighed, put down his pencil, and pushed himself away from his desk, his chair scooting along the sheet of hard plastic underneath. He obviously didn't want to talk to me. I couldn't blame him; in his place I wouldn't want to talk to me either.

He led me down the long row of identical desks, his reluctance as palpable as a weighted sack dragging behind him, and all along the line annoyed heads were raised from papers or telephones, and resentful eyes chastised us for goofing off on city time. We went out into the kind of sterile hallway only found in government buildings, up a wide, uncarpeted stairway, and through a door marked CAFETERIA. Inside, machines offered coffee, soup, soda, and sandwiches, but because it was past the usual break time and too early for lunch, there were no people seated at the Formica tables. I was glad about that.

Matt went to the coffee dispenser and deposited his coins. The machine whirred, dispensing a cardboard cup, and a dirty-brown sludge squirted into it. He brought it back to a table and sat down heavily across from me, a tribal chieftain entering into uneasy truce talks. "Look, I know Rita Marie came to see you—she told me. I guess she was pretty rough on you, and I'm sorry for that. But she's right. This is a family problem. We're gonna take care of it in our own way. I apologize to you. I shouldn't of brought you in."

"But I am in now."

"So get out."

"I can't. I've got to bust this thing. And I can make sure Paulie doesn't go down with the ship."

He ran his tongue around his lips, and after a sip of coffee he did it again, maybe to see if his lips tasted any different. "How can you do that?"

"I've got ways. If you're willing to help me."

His face screwed up, and he smiled in that ineffectual way he has, that he's always had since he was a kid. The kind of look a male elk gives to the dominant bull in the herd to avoid punishment. "I can't even help myself these days."

"All you have to do is come with me for a few nights and wait with me. When it comes down, no rough stuff for you. You just make a phone call and then go home."

Through his glasses I could see white all around the pupils of his eyes. He looked around again, as if his supervisors in the Department of Public Works were listening in and crossing him off next year's promotions list. "Hey, Milan," he said softly, and it was an entreaty. He wanted me to go away.

"Come on, Matt. You always wanted to get in the game. Now's your chance."

"I'm too old for all that now."

"It's for your kid. For your family."

He stood up and wandered around among the empty tables, winding up by the sandwich machine. He leaned his head against the cool metal, his eyes closed, and for a moment I wondered if he might actually have fallen asleep. Then he slammed the side of his fist into the machine, making the shrink-wrapped goodies inside jump. "I'm no cop!" he said with an anger I'd never seen in him before. "I'm just a guy. I come to work, I go home, I watch TV, I go to bed, and every year I take two weeks vacation and go to the Jersey Shore and lay on the beach. I'm no fucking hero, Milan. God damn you for asking me to be."

"Nobody wants you to be a hero," I said. "This is not about guts and glory. It's about Paulie."

He came and leaned on the table, putting his face inches from mine. "Let me tell you about Paulie," he said. "There's a place just outside Chicago I found out about. They know how to take care of kids like Paulie—good kids who just took a wrong step and got off the track. Rita Marie is making arrangements to go there with him. Get him off the streets, away from the scum."

"That sounds expensive."

"Whattaya think, I didn't put something away for a rainy day? This is a rainy day, Milan, it's a goddamm monsoon! And I'm taking care of mine."

"Matt, I can break the back of the drug operation—"

"You're breaking my ass! I told you, I shouldn't of gotten you involved. It's my kid, and that's all I care about. I'm no world-beater; I figured that out way back in high school. I got enough to do just watching out for my family—and now I'm doin' it! You got no right to ask me to risk my neck!"

"You didn't mind asking me to stick mine out."

He looked ready to cry. "That's your thing! Big jock, big cop, big hero. Well not me, okay? I'm just a fat little man with piles and a mortgage and a family to take care of. I don't give a shit for what's right or what's wrong—not the way you do. Maybe that's why I still *got* a family!"

He almost flung himself away from me, turning his back, the muscles in his neck bunched tight. His hands were hard fists dangling at the end of his wrists. He said, "I'm sorry, Milan, that was lousy to say. But it's how I feel." He still wouldn't look at me.

All at once I felt very weary, and not a little useless. Matt was right, of course, and I knew it. I did have a different handle on things, it seemed. But I was getting damn sick of people telling me so.

173

18

I WALKED around downtown for a while, because I was too antsy to sit still in a car. Besides, I didn't have anywhere to go. The rain had more or less stopped, if you don't count the fine mist that always hangs in the air for hours after a drenching, and workers were beginning to stream out of the office buildings around Public Square to do their noontime errands. The Soldiers and Sailors Monument stood tall against the gray sky as a reminder of the difference between real heroes and phony ones.

When my feet started squishing wetly in my shoes, I ducked into Higbee's for a while to get out of the weather, but I didn't buy anything. When I'm low, splurging on some new and unneeded piece of clothing doesn't help my mood any. Maybe it made Lucy feel better to buy a new hat every time she got mad at Ricky, but it just gives me a galloping case of the guilts. I went out again and crossed Huron to the lobby of the Midland Building, where I spent a few minutes admiring the ornate wood carvings and gold leaf on the ceiling in the lobby.

I looked at my watch because my stomach was growling. I went into the restaurant just below street level in the National City Bank Building. It's full of brass rails and mirrored walls and indirect lighting, and its clientele is largely a gathering of stunning, overly made-up young women who laugh too much, talk too loud, and scarf up the free popcorn on the bar, holding the kernels delicately between their long, painted acrylic fingernails. Most were wearing wool skirts or suits and calf-length boots to protect them from the rain. It's a fashion look I'm quite fond of, but my mind wasn't on it. Two of them were having lunch at the next table. A book called *A Complete Wine Course* was open on the table between them, and they were earnestly discussing the best wine to serve with monkfish.

The cornerstone of Cleveland's downtown lunch trade is the corned beef sandwich, but I wasn't in the mood. Mindful of my cholesterol, I ordered grilled John Dory, a fish that always sounds to me as if a ballad should be named after it. Neither the food nor the ambience made me feel like I'd done anything positive or productive by getting out of bed that morning.

I got my car and went east on Euclid Avenue, once more feeling like a john out cruising. When I reached Sixty-ninth Street I spotted the redheaded black girl I'd seen with Deshon Garthwaite at the Merle Avenue house. I hadn't really expected to find her, and I almost drove by her before realizing who she was. She was wearing tight black leggings under a black miniskirt, a fuzzy blue sweater, and her vinyl jacket, and she was holding up the wall of an abandoned industrial building, which was like so many others in the neighborhood a victim of fast-spreading urban blight. She must have left the Carmen Miranda turban at home that day. She looked young and pathetic and a little helpless, which probably stood her in good stead in her profession—the sex-for-sale trade flourishes because there are an awful lot of very insecure men out there. I slowed to a stop and rolled down the window on the passenger side, and she pushed herself off the wall and crossed the sidewalk to the curb.

"You wanna date?" she said in a Caribbean lilt. It was the first time I'd heard her speak. Her voice was hollow, as if she'd been dead for several weeks. Living the way she did, I guess she might as well have been.

I opened the door in silent invitation and she slid in beside me. On closer scrutiny I saw that her left eye was swollen nearly shut and there was purple discoloration under the carelessly applied make up. Her lower lip was bruised and puffy, too, and her nose was running.

"What's you name, mon?"

"Milan. What's yours?"

"Denise. How much you got to spend, Myron?"

I let it go. "I just want to talk to you."

She turned her head fully toward me so she could see out of her good eye. Then recognition kicked in, or seemed to, and she shrank away from me, her hand groping for the door handle.

I grabbed her arm. "Don't be afraid of me, Denise. I want to help you."

She tried to pull away from me. "Shit. I got to make money, mon."

"Fifty dollars," I said quickly. "I'll give you fifty dollars for fifteen minutes.

"I don't got nothin' to say," she muttered, but she stopped struggling. I imagine she didn't get many fifty-dollar tricks, and none that just wanted to talk. She huddled down in the seat, a still life of misery. "You a cop?"

"No," I said. "I'm private." I thought about showing her my license but I wasn't sure she'd know what it was. "Do you remember me, Denise? We've seen each other before."

She stuck her chin out. "I remember you okay, Myron."

I turned off Euclid and onto Chester, where there was less chance of being observed, and headed back toward downtown. It seemed as good a place as any to go. "You were the one who called the police about Deshon, weren't you?"

She sniffled. "You said fifty dollars, mon."

I dug into my pocket and gave her two twenties and two fives, a pretty big bite for a guy who didn't have a client to foot the expenses. She wadded the money up, hiked up her skirt and put it into the waistband of her tights. "Why you be comin' roun' axin' questions?"

"Because I still want to find out who killed Deshon."

"How come?"

I said, "Lots of reasons. And you've got fifty reasons to talk to me now." She touched her waist as if to make sure the money hadn't been snatched away somehow. "Did you call the police about Deshon that night? Were you the one that found him?"

She nodded, her eyes downcast. People like Denise weren't supposed to call the police under any circumstances, and to admit she had done so was to spit in the eye of the strange underworld code by which she lived.

I tried to help a little. "That was the right thing to do. Tell me what happened."

"I don' know. I come to de house jus' after midnight. I almos' always come by den. Dat be when I fin' him." She squeezed her eyes shut as if to banish the sight. Deshon had treated her worse than he did his dog, I had seen that myself, but there was an emotional connection there nevertheless, and his demise must have hurt her, maybe more than she cared to admit even to herself.

"Did you see anyone? Hanging around?"

She shook her head.

"Who did it, Denise? Who killed him?"

She looked out the window intently, as if Chester Avenue was one of the world's scenic marvels. After a time she said, "I din' see who." A tear ran out of her swollen eye and over her freckled cheek. "I din' see no one."

"He'd been beaten with baseball bats. Was it Javier and that other guy? The ones with the funny haircuts?" I shook my head; the haircuts probably weren't that strange to her. More softly, I said, "Was it them?"

She shrugged in such a way as to let me know I was probably right but allowed her to feel better for not having told me.

"Why? Why'd they kill him?"

She glared at me, hatred and despair commingling in her dull brown eyes, and my stomach lurched a bit because I knew I'd guessed right—Deshon had been killed because of what I'd said to Bobby DeLayne.

"I'm sorry, Denise. I never meant for him to get hurt." I reached over and touched her hand, and she jumped at the contact, shrinking away from me again. I said, "What happened to your face?"

She turned away as though I hadn't already seen the bruises.

"Was it a cop?" Her body jerked, her head going wildly from

side to side looking for an escape. But there are no exit signs in nightmares.

"It was the Dragon, wasn't it? Did he do that to you?"

The muscles at the base of her jaw jumped, and a sob shook her skinny shoulders.

"What did you tell him, Denise?"

"Nothin'. I don't tell dat fucker nothin'. Even he beat me aroun', make me give up pussy, I don' tell him."

Her face looked like she'd gone three rounds with a welter-weight. Beating up and raping a skinny young girl must have made Drago feel like a pretty tough guy.

"Don't worry," I said. "He won't bother you anymore."

She lifted one hand off her lap and then let it flop back down again as if it didn't matter much one way or the other.

"Do you know Bobby?" I said.

Even her swollen eye opened wide, and the look on her face was sheer terror. "Wit' de white hair an' funny eyes?"

I nodded. "Did you see him around the day Deshon—"

"I got to go, mon!" She opened the door very suddenly. I called out her name and made a grab for her, but she was too quick for me and was out and away before I could stop her. The traffic on Chester was fairly heavy, keeping me from going more than twenty miles an hour in the far right lane, but she jumped from the car while it was still moving, and her momentum sent her staggering, up over the curb like a burlesque drunk. Luckily she had lurched across the sidewalk and onto the grass of a vacant lot before she fell flat on her face.

I braked hard, but by the time I got the car in park and started to get out, she had scrambled to her feet again and was running across the lot, deftly avoiding the broken bottles, old auto parts, and other urban detritus hidden in the high weeds. The wet ground sucked at her shoes, finally pulling one off, and she slowed for half a step, looking back at it, and then continued running away from me until she disappeared between two buildings, a street-smart Cinderella on a broken-field run in the inner city.

I watched her go without much regret. I wasn't going to get anything else out of her, because she was too angry, too fright-ened. And she probably didn't know much more than she had already told me. My fifty bucks hadn't bought me much, but it was more than the Dragon's fists had managed to pry from her. I made a note to speak sharply to Sergeant Drago. Very sharply.

The guy in the green Volvo behind me, a well-dressed marketing-analyst type with a tweed overcoat, a pompadour, and a brush mustache, was leaning on his horn, impatience turning his face a bright red. I got back in, but by the time I'd shifted into drive the light had turned red and we had nowhere to go. I glanced in the mirror and watched the guy mouth *Asshole* at me. It burned me up, but I didn't do anything about it.

He shook his head angrily, frustration fairly bristling from him, and put the receiver of his car phone to his ear. He was calling his office to tell them he would be two minutes late. I'll bet he was wearing designer suspenders under his coat and jacket.

When I finally got the car started—and I made the little shit wait through still another red light—I turned right on Fifty-fifth and went back over to St. Clair, then headed east again. It took me about ten minutes to get to the high school.

I had spent so much time sitting in my car in front of that place I was beginning to wish I had some dirty pictures to sell. What with the dampness, the insides of my windows were fogged up, and I could hardly see through them. I heard the final bell ring and watched while the liberated kids came flying out. I didn't see Milan Jr. and figured he had used one of the other exits, but I was more interested in the Paulie Baznik group. They finally straggled out, more slowly than usual, and gathered on their accustomed corner. Today they seemed distracted, unfocused and without purpose. Some of them paced up and down on the pavement, searching the street in both directions. They were waiting for Godot, but Godot wasn't coming today.

Paulie looked particularly miserable, pale and scared in a world that was alien to him. My heart hurt for the kid. I knew what it was like to feel like a nonbelonger. Not when I was young myself and had my pals and my football team and later my buddies on the police force, but now, on the threshold of the Wonder Years—those years when you wonder what it all means, wonder where it's all going, wonder whether it'll be worth the trip—I seemed to be losing lovers and friends and strangers at an alarming rate. Forty is a hell of an age to find yourself cast adrift.

When the group had smoked enough cigarettes and gotten damp enough from the hanging mist, they dispersed uncertainly, most going off in one direction. Paulie was heading toward his home, and I suppose I was grateful for that.

After a few minutes the faculty began its daily exodus, as happy for the reprieve as the kids were. It was depressing all over again: you know you're really over the hill when teachers are younger than you are.

Reggie Parker was last to leave. I watched as he double-locked the main doors and then slipped a heavy padlock chain through the two door handles. He was a careful man. He had to be. I waited until he turned from his task, then got out of my car and hailed him. He crossed the street, a deep vertical crease between his eyebrows.

"You keep hanging around out here, Mr. Jacovich, I'm going to start assigning you yard duty."

"Actually I wanted to talk to you, Mr. Parker."

"Call me Reggie," he said. "I took a lot of heat about that for a while because of Reggie Jackson. We're the same age, and I look a little like him, especially with the glasses. But it's my name, what can I do." He put his hands in the pockets of his car coat. "You could have come inside," he said.

"I wanted to talk to you privately."

He started to say something and then thought better of it. He turned up his collar. "I've got to make a tour of the place, see that everything's buttoned up. You want to walk? I don't mind the rain if you don't."

"No, that's fine," I said.

We began a slow parade around the perimeter of the school, the principal checking the locks on the various gates and entryways. "I kind of like it when it's cold and damp," he said. "Makes going inside seem that much warmer. Isn't that how you'd characterize this town? Houses, restaurants, taverns—they make you feel nothing can reach you, as long as you're in out of the cold. The wind howls, the rain comes down, or the snow, and you're all cozy and safe inside. That's what I like about Cleveland. One of the things. And the Browns, of course. Hard not to like the Browns. Think they'll go all the way this year? Your expert opinion, of course."

"No chance," I said.

"That's what I think, too." He jiggled the gate that led to the athletic field and nodded in satisfaction when it didn't open. "I also think you've got something on your mind."

I ducked my head in agreement.

"Let's hear it, then."

"You said you wanted to help."

"I've been watching what goes on, but I haven't seen anything yet."

"I mean help of a more personal kind, more specific."

He frowned, and his glasses slipped down his nose. He pushed them up again. "I said I'd help."

I took a deep breath. The air was icy and seared my lungs. It felt good. "Enough to put your ass on the line? Look, I have no right asking you this, and if you say no I'll understand completely. All I ask is that if you decide you don't want to get involved, you forget I ever said anything to you. Is that a deal?"

He stopped and leaned against the cyclone fence, hands in his pockets. "What are you getting me into?" he said.

I told him.

19

SURROUNDED as it was by the night the automobile dealership glistened like a highly-polished jewel. The office building next door and its adjacent parking area were dark, and the arc lights shining down on the cars on the lot lit up the night. There was one light on inside the showroom, a spotlight aimed at the top-of-the-line sedan, which had the interior floor all to itself like an emperor's coach. On the roof of the showroom, blue neon spelling out WACO MORGAN 4 CARS nicely set off the red neon that had been fashioned in the image of Waco Morgan's face, complete with cowboy hat and wide grin. Out on the lot a night watchman, obviously a retired pensioner, dozed in his five-by-five booth behind the security fence as his little black-and-white TV flickered with the late news.

I looked up and down Mayfield Road. Cleveland isn't a night-time town, and with the exception of the traffic signals, a few streetlights up near Lander, and the advertising signs that stay on twenty-four hours a day, Morgan's dealership was the only illumination around. There were no cars on the streets, and the cold mist had disappeared on the edge of an arctic wind that had swooped south from Canada, picking up the icy air that hovers just above the surface of Lake Erie. A cold night for surveillance. Winter in the Midwest at night.

I consulted my watch, which was not digital but one of the

old-fashioned kind with a minute hand and an hour hand. You have to be able to tell time to read it. It was ten minutes past eleven; the place had been closed for more than two hours, and we had been on the job since just before they locked up. During that time only the watchman's single foray away from his space heater at about ten-thirty for a pee break and a quick tour around the building had broken the monotony of the stakeout. I looked over to where Reggie Parker slumped behind the steering wheel of the car, his car, a Ford Taurus wagon. He endured the waiting with admirable and surprising stoicism. The red and blue neon reflected in the lenses of his glasses to give him a spacey look.

"I hope you know what you're doing, Milan," he said. "My wife thinks I'm having an affair." He chuckled softly.

"Reggie, I don't have to tell you how I appreciate—"

"That's right, you don't," he said.

His eyes were half closed, but I knew he was wide awake and alert. Reggie Parker impressed me. I had watched him the past two nights as we sat across the street from the dealership, waiting for who knew what. He seemed relaxed, his glasses low on his broad nose and his collar up around his ears against the cold, but I could tell that inside he was wired, finely tuned, and aware of every passing car, every shift in the breeze, every subtle changing of the light in the sky. His senses were keen as a wild animal's. I already knew he was a skilled combat veteran, a Green Beret, but after two nights of surveillance with him, no one would have had to tell me. And no one had to tell either of us that this was war. We'd both experienced war before, the same war; we knew what it could mean and how it could end, and that even the rear guard had to be vigilant and watchful. The difference was, this time we *knew* we were the good guys.

"Here comes something," he said, and slithered lower in the seat. I did the same, not easy for a man my size, as he reached up and adjusted the rearview mirror to get a better angle. The beams from the headlights coming up behind us bounced off the silvered glass onto his taut brown face. He was silent, watchful, a bird of prey.

The pavement beneath the car vibrated as a huge truck rumbled by. My eyes were just at window level, and I watched as it passed us, slowed, and turned into the driveway of Waco Morgan 4 Cars and stopped. The night watchman stirred from his dreams of a winning pick-four ticket and hastened to unlock the sliding gate so the truck could go through.

It was one of those automobile transports that resemble a mastodon in the dark, huge and hulking and ominous. This one carried ten cars on its two levels, all two-door midsizes imported from the Far East. Three were red, three blue, one silver, two black, and one was white. They all had price stickers on their rear right windows, and I imagine all were loaded with options that upped the price by several thousand dollars. I could see two men in the cab of the truck.

"What do you think?" Reggie said.

"Let's watch."

"Funny damn time to be getting a delivery."

"Maybe," I said.

The truck pulled to an open space at one end of the lot, and the two men got out. One of them I didn't recognize; the other was Bobby DeLayne. He was wearing a pair of blue mechanic's coveralls under the jacket he'd worn the day I'd tailed him. The arc lights made his white hair whiter, his pink scalp showing through. He lit a cigarette and chatted with the watchman for a moment, then waved him off to his little hut. Perchance to dream. Bobby and the other man began backing the new cars off the transport, the top row first, and parking them in front of the locked bay of the service department.

"That's Bobby," I said, and Reggie nodded. Watching.

It was a painstaking operation, stretching over forty-five minutes. Bobby and his friend didn't seem to be in any hurry, taking turns driving and directing. The process was agonizing to us, since we couldn't move or sit up straight for fear of being seen. A million little needle-toed centipedes began dancing on my left foot, and I wiggled it to get the circulation back.

"This is as much fun as watching haircuts," Parker said.

"I never promised you dancing girls."

"Dancing girls would be nice."

Finally the cars were unloaded. Bobby and his companion stood deep in discussion for a few minutes; then Bobby signed a bunch of papers on a clipboard, took two sheets for himself, and shook hands with the driver, who climbed into the empty transport. It backed slowly out of the car lot, its skeleton silhouetted against the lights.

Reggie Parker squirmed in the seat. "Follow him?"

I shook my head. "Bobby's our main man."

"Waiting makes me nervous."

"Me, too. What do you suggest?"

"I'm not suggesting, I'm merely observing."

"Don't get testy."

"I haven't slept in two nights."

"Don't feel like the Lone Ranger. Neither have I."

"But you get to go home and sleep. I have to go to school and watch those little bastards' faces break out."

We kept on waiting. Even though it gets lonely, I prefer one-man stakeouts. When you're accompanied, you begin getting on each other's nerves. I guess it's the same principle as that if two formerly peaceful rats are put into a cage only big enough for one, they become warlike and aggressive. We two rats weren't used to sitting in a closed car together for eight hours at a time, and it was starting to tell on us.

Bobby lollygagged for another twenty minutes, going in and out of the service department several times. Then he strolled over to the guard shack and had a cup of coffee with the old guy, who clearly would have preferred being left to his napping but still wasn't as impatient as we were for Bobby to make his next move. I envied both of them the hot coffee.

Finally Bobby waved a good-night at the watchman and climbed into the white car that had just been delivered. He futzed around inside the car for about five minutes, feeling all around the doors and the headliner, then fired up the engine and drove it slowly out of the lot and onto Mayfield Road, heading west, as the watchman closed and locked the gate after him. I waited until the white car was nothing more than two red taillights bobbing in the distance. Then I said, "Hit it. No lights until you have to."

The Ford's engine rumbled and caught, and we made a quick U-turn and cruised off in Bobby's wake.

"Don't get too close," I said. "And no Indy Five Hundred stuff."

185

"Yeah, yeah," Parker answered.

Bobby didn't know he was being followed, so he made no effort to lose us. He was such an airhead he probably wouldn't have noticed if we'd tailgated him the whole way. He turned north on Superior and wound through Forest Hills Park. There aren't many streetlights there, and Parker was leaning all the way forward in his seat, cursing his lack of headlights. We eventually wound up on 135th Street, heading toward the lake.

"What if he's just driving the sucker home?" Parker said.

"He's not. He's going somewhere else."

Nobody lives in the area Bobby led us to. No one would want to. It's all industrial: small plants, warehouses, vacant lots where manufacturing and storage buildings have long since bowed to the wrecker's ball, suddenly obsolete in the midst of a technocratic revolution, and an occasional junkyard, plumbing supply house, or corner grocery store that survived selling six-packs and wrapped sandwiches to the workers on their breaks. There were no cars anywhere on the street, and we were careful to stay at least three blocks behind our quarry.

Bobby stopped the white car in front of a large, squat warehouse that bore no identification, sign, or legend to let the curious know what went on inside. That wasn't unusual in this neighborhood. It was an anonymous building, made of red brick, with a big steel door that raised to admit tall trucks. He got out and unlocked the chain link gate and rolled it open on its track and then drove the car through into the yard. He stopped again to relock the gate behind him, and Parker and I watched from down the street as the big bay door creaked upward like a theater curtain, obviously controlled by someone inside. The opening stabbed a shaft of yellow light into the darkness. We were at the wrong angle to be able to see anything inside. When the car cruised through into the warehouse, the door rolled down again and swallowed it.

"Okay," I said, "you get to a telephone right away; there's a convenience store on 135th Street that has one. Call the number I gave you and ask to talk to Lieutenant Ingeldinger. If he's not there call his house. You have change?" Parker just looked at me with disgust. "Okay. Give Ingeldinger this address and tell him to hurry up. Then go home."

186

"The hell I'm going home," Parker said.

"The hell you're not."

"This is the fun part."

"Reggie, we've been through this. You're a private citizen, and you've got your whole career on the line. Nobody wants a principal who's a commando. Just make the phone call and then beat it. I'll contact you as soon as I know anything." He started to talk and I cut him off. "That was our deal. I don't go back on my word and I don't expect you to go back on yours."

He drummed on the steering wheel with his index fingers, a riff that sounded like Krupa's in "Let Me Off Uptown." He wasn't bad. Then he said, "Watch your ass, Milan," and turned and shook my hand with both of his. I got out of the car and watched as he backed up around the corner, turned on his lights, and headed off the other way, toward 135th Street and the all-night market on the corner, where I hoped the phone was working.

I was alone in the dark.

I walked the block to the warehouse I'd seen Bobby DeLayne enter, feeling the .357 digging into my side. I took it out of its nylon holster and checked to see it was fully loaded, even though I knew it was. I'd cleaned the weapon and loaded it before I left the house that night. Checking was simply a habit, a good one to get into. I also had a mini–tool kit hanging from my belt, including a few tools not purchased at the local hardware store. Burglar's helpers, in the trade.

The chain link fence around the warehouse was about nine feet high. The steel curtain Bobby had driven under was the only entrance at the front of the building. I began walking the fence line. On one side was a people-sized door painted with rust-resistant paint. It was marked NO ADMITTANCE and secured with a large padlock hanging on a hasp that looked as if no one had used it in years. Obviously whoever visited the warehouse gained entry through the steel loading door most of the time. The windows, which were about twelve feet off the ground, were painted black, but a few little slivers of light shone through the holidays in the paint. Around on the other side of the warehouse I found another steel door, but it was flush with the side of the building and had no handles or visible locks.

The place was buttoned up tighter than a rusted lug nut.

I had no idea how I was going to get in, or what I was going to do when I got there, but I knew I was on the wrong side of the fence to do anything. I went around to the back of the building, a blind wall without windows or doors, and boosted myself up onto the fence, finding tenuous footholds between the links with the blunt toes of my work shoes. It took more of an effort than I expected. Too many bagels and sausage sandwiches.

At the top I swung my legs over and then hung for a moment before letting go. The landing wasn't as gentle as I'd hoped, and it jarred my ankle, but it wasn't anything I couldn't live with. What did make me uneasy was that a minute ago I'd been outside the fence with no way to get in; now I was inside with no quick way to get out.

I went around to the front and checked the loading door more closely. There was a steel box on the wall beside it at about eye level, and I was sure there was some sort of electronic mechanism in it that opened the door from the outside. However, the box was locked, and I didn't want to go in that way anyway; it would be too noisy.

I made my way around the building to the entrance with the padlock, and pressed my ear against it. I could hear very faint sounds coming from inside. Voices. Either Bobby DeLayne was not alone, or he was carrying on an animated conversation with himself. From the sound of the voices they were on the other side of the building, near the loading bay.

The padlock on the door was extra-heavy-duty. Nothing less than a hacksaw was going to get through it, and I didn't have one with me. I did have a small screwdriver, however, and I took it from my pocket and began working on the hasp. It was tough going, as the screws were rusted tight in their grooves. It took about two minutes to get the first one out; after that it was easier.

I looked at my watch. Parker had been gone for seven minutes, enough time to have gotten to a telephone by now. Whether or not he had managed to track down Ingeldinger I didn't know.

I pulled the hasp out of the wall, but the door was locked besides. I carry a set of lock picks in my tool kit to make things like this go a bit easier. The lock picks are illegal. So is selling crack. It's all a matter of degree.

It was an old lock on an even older door, and like most things in our society, they don't make them the way they used to. I can open a new lock in thirty seconds or less, but the old ones are more complicated, made back when people meant business, and I spent a precious three minutes or so fooling around with it until the tumblers finally clicked.

I had to shove hard with my shoulder to get the door open, and I moved quickly inside and closed it behind me, leaving myself in inky blackness. I stretched out one arm, then the other, and encountered beaverboard walls on either side of me. I was evidently in some sort of hallway. I moved down the narrow corridor slowly, putting one foot in front of the other with great care, since visibility was zero. Sandy dirt crunched under my shoes. Not far away a mouse or two had died recently.

Somewhere at the other end of the building there was light, and the voices grew a bit louder now, although still too far away for me to make out specific words. I headed for the sound, for the vague light. On my right I felt two doors, possibly bathrooms. I kept going, relying mostly on instinct in the darkness. My adrenaline was pumping, but I figured I wouldn't have to do anything. There was no need to do anything but wait until Ingeldinger and his troops arrived.

Unless Bobby and his friends attempted to leave, taking the evidence with them. Then I'd have to step in and be a hero, to somehow stop them. I reached inside my jacket and caressed the butt of the Magnum. That would do it, all right. Anybody who knew anything about guns realized the kind of a hole a .357 can make.

At the end of the long corridor I turned left. There was nowhere else to go; to the right was a blank wall, a blind corner. I got the idea that some of the walls in the place had been put up as an afterthought. I went through a doorway without any door and found myself inside an enormous storeroom with high ceilings, completely dark except for a thin shaft of light coming from a partly opened bay on the far side. I was aware of strange

189

shapes around me in the blackness, skeletal steel like the pieces of a giant Erector Set. I'd always liked playing with those things when I was a kid. But I wasn't playing now.

I headed for the door. I could hear the voices more plainly, Bobby's saying, "Easy, Javier, don't tear the headliner. We wanna be able to sell this car. Don't be in such a damn hurry."

My old friend Javier. The gang's all here.

I peeked through the opened bay door. Bobby was standing by the car; Javier was crouched inside it. The headliner was hanging down loose, and Javier was removing some small packages that had been hidden inside it.

I took the pistol out and held it loosely in my hand. I didn't want to use it, didn't even want to reveal my presence, but there was no sense in not being prepared.

There's no way to prepare for something crashing across the back of your neck with sickening force. A hot red pain spread across my shoulders and down my spine, like someone had just electrified my nervous system, and a vivid light engulfed me behind the eyes, turning the whole world bright red. Suddenly I was ten years old and on the Thriller again, high above Euclid Beach Park. The car was hurtling downward, the wind roaring in my ears, the rest of the world a blur on the periphery of my vision so that there was nothing but the downward plunge, dizzying and terrifying, as the earth sped up to meet me with a rush that closed my throat and took away my breath.

I don't even remember hitting the floor.

20

THERE is a limbo land between waking and unconsciousness, like the sea a few feet before you surface, where the tangled kelp parts and light is visible but not yet attainable, where the brain becomes aware before the rest of the entity responds. It's almost an out-of-body experience, as the consciousness kicks back in to see what's going on, as if it wanted to check things out and decide whether it was worthwhile showing up. So it was grudgingly that I came out of a blackness as deep as any I had known, with my eyes still closed, knowing that as soon as I opened them or tried to move, the pain, which was at the moment a dull memory in my head and neck, would blossom into a morning glory of agony. I thought about never opening my eyes again, but that didn't seem practical.

A musty smell enveloped me, one of long-ago cooking odors and dust and neglect, of rotting wood and the leavings of small creatures. I was lying on my left side on some sort of mattress. It must have been pretty old, which accounted for part of the smell. It was soft, at any rate, and I shifted in a tentative, pathetic effort to roll over. The pain came, shooting through my head in a million starbursts of intense white light, liquid fire from my crown to the base of my spine, and a groan forced itself through my teeth. I tried to rub the back of my neck with my hands, and that's when I discovered that they were fastened

191

together behind me in some way, and that my feet were bound as well.

I opened my eyes. It wasn't as simple as it sounds. My own juices had glued them shut, and opening each of them took a specific effort. I should have kept them closed. The light slashed through my pupils like a scalpel, all the way through to the center of my head, and somewhere in there was a muffled buzz like that of a neighbor's snow blower coming from down the street.

When everything came into focus—a Herculean struggle on my part—the first thing I saw was Bobby DeLayne's gap-toothed grin, close to my face and distorted as if through a fish-eye lens.

"Wake up, sleepy head," he said in that high-pitched whine of his. And then he slapped my face hard with his open palm and then again backhanded. The second slap brought the taste of blood in my mouth. The sting of the blows was nothing compared to the pain they set off in my head and neck, the kind of pain so excruciating and deep-seated that it snatches at your sanity, the kind you remember for a long time.

I thought for a moment I was going to black out again. I fought against it, struggled to keep my head above the waves of unconsciousness that lapped at me. The exertion left me soaked with perspiration, and nausea pushed at the back of my throat.

Bobby simpered at me. He'd enjoyed the slapping. Standing there with my .357 Magnum tucked into the pocket of his me-chanic's overalls, he was a perfect specimen of Loony Tune, sadistic, amoral, spaced out. He drew his hand back as if to hit me again, but the thought went away in the middle, leaving his face completely blank except for the vacant grin, and he walked out of my field of vision.

I looked around as much as I could. I was lying on a daybed covered with a cotton spread printed with faded but still bilious cabbage roses, in what seemed to be the living room of a house. It was an old house, with peeling wallpaper and flaking paint on the ceiling, and the cold in my bones went deep, the kind of chill you get when the furnace has stopped working long ago. The floor was hardwood, and its planks were splintered and rotten. The light fixture in the middle of the ceiling had been removed, leaving bare wires hanging out of a hole in the plaster, and the only illumination came from the kind of standing floor lamp you can purchase in a discount store for $9.95.

There were a couple of unmatched wooden kitchen chairs around the room, and a butterfly sling chair with a wrought iron frame and a faded orange cover. Javier was sitting in that one giving me a mean look, and his buddy with the Joan Bennett hairdo was leaning against the wall, a baseball bat held loosely in his hand as though it were an extension of his anatomy. A second bat was lying on the floor near the wall as though tossed there by a careless Little Leaguer. I had no doubt that one of them had been used to bring me down from behind. I was lucky to be alive.

But perhaps not for long. My stomach was leaden as I realized that they'd probably gotten me out of the warehouse immediately, which meant that when Ingeldinger and his troops arrived they wouldn't find much. They certainly wouldn't find me.

I tried to move my hands behind my back, but they were fastened with what felt like duct tape. Much more secure than ordinary rope. I could only assume they'd used the same stuff on my feet. I was helpless, trussed up like a Christmas turkey.

My mouth was dry and my tongue was swollen, but I managed to croak out, "Bobby."

He came to stand in front of me, turning his body in profile and looking over his left shoulder. His lower lip hung away from his teeth, which made him look even more stupid than usual. "You talkin' to me?" he said. He was playing Robert De Niro in *Taxi Driver*. He must have practiced the line in the mirror for hours, the way the character had in the film. How To Be Macho, or Self-Esteem Through Intimidation. "Are you talkin' to *me*?"

"I want to sit up."

"Is that so?" he said. He looked at Joan Bennett. "Help the man sit up."

The young black man's soft hair swung around his ears as he moved away from the wall and crossed the room to the daybed. He looked down at me, his eyes like brown marbles and twice as cold, and then he bared his teeth and raised the baseball bat over his head, and I prepared for the impact, for death. I didn't wince, didn't try to roll away from the blow; I just prepared. Called up the memory of the faces of my sons, maybe a prayer or two, vaguely remembered from childhood and run through my brain at quick time.

The bat wavered. He looked over at Bobby and they exchanged dumb grins. Just having a little fun.

"The man don't scare easy," Bobby said. "Let's see what happens when Ricardo gets here. He's gonna be plenty scared, man. He's gonna be piss-your-pants scared. Help him sit up."

Joan Bennett looked disappointed at not being allowed to hit, but he was a good soldier who followed orders. He grabbed me by the shirtfront and yanked me upright. Exquisite pain swam around through my neck and lower back, resettling itself into different nerve endings, but I regained my equilibrium in a few moments and was better able to observe my surroundings.

It was indeed the front parlor of an old house, similar to the one on Merle where Deshon had died. Three tall windows formed a bay at one end of the room, but they were boarded up, with the dark of night showing through some eight-inch chinks in the cheap lumber. A large archway with crumbling gingerbread molding gave onto a small vestibule where the front door was. Just off the vestibule a stairway went up to a second story. Sliding double doors separated the room from the rear of the house. The neglected timbers creaked and sighed, sounding pretty much the way my bones felt.

Joan Bennett made sure I wasn't going to fall over again, then regripped his bat and moved back to his primary job function, holding up the wall. Bobby came and beamed in my face. He was having a wonderful time.

"You're making a mistake," I said through my thickening tongue and the blood that was collecting in my mouth. My words slurred the way they did after too much red wine; I knew I had a concussion.

"You made the mistake, man."

He seemed about to say more, and I was looking forward to his erudition, when from the back of the house came the sound of a door closing. Bobby was instantly alert, his hand stroking the butt of my gun protruding from his pocket. Joan Bennett came away from the wall, tightening his grip on the bat, and Javier scrambled up out of the butterfly sling chair as quickly as was possible, and reached for his own Louisville Slugger.

The double doors opened and a handsome black man in a calf-length leather trench coat hanging open stood between them, posing as if for a paparazzo's camera. A thin Little Richard mustache shadowed his upper lip. He was dressed for effect, to look dashing, European, unique. I thought he looked like a pimp.

"Messy," he said, looking at me but talking to Bobby. "You been messy to let dis mon track you down." He smiled easily, the kind of smile that lets you know the smiler isn't happy with you. He had a definite flair for the dramatic. "Not once, but twice. Messy." There was the upward Jamaican lilt in his speech, but it wasn't nearly as pronounced as it had been in Deshon's. This one had been in the States for a while and had picked up some of the flat vowels and cadences of the Middle West.

"He didn't see nothing," Bobby protested. He seemed nervous, licking his slack lips and blinking a lot.

"He saw enough, dumb shit." He held out his hand in an imperial gesture, and Bobby handed him something. It turned out to be my wallet, which they must have taken from me when I was out. The man in the leather trench coat flipped it open and looked at my driver's license, my PI license, and for all I know the pictures of my kids. Then he came over, leather skirts swishing, to stand in front of me. His fists were on his hips, his legs apart, his head cocked jauntily as though about to sing "Is a Puzzlement."

"How you say your name? Jacoveech?" With the hard *J*.

I corrected him, as if it mattered a damn, and he nodded. I said, "How do you say yours? Ricardo?"

He looked startled. Then his eyes narrowed and he glanced over at Bobby again. Apparently his feelings were hurt, because he shook his head with a sorrow deeper than the Atlantic trench. "Dumb shit," he said.

Bobby seemed to shrink like Alice when she ingested the

potion marked DRINK ME. He moved back into the corner, as far from Ricardo as he could get. The two designated hitters stirred around uneasily. Ricardo had a little clout around here.

He turned his attention back to me. "So," he said, "dis de mon been pokin' his nose where it don' belong, eh? When dey call an' tell me you been at de warehouse, I t'ink, Why he does dis? What we do to you ever?"

"I'm a conservationist," I said. "I hate guys who wear leather coats."

He leaned over and punched me in the stomach. It wasn't a particularly hard punch because his angle was bad, but with my hands behind me and my ankles trussed together I could neither protect myself nor even tense for the blow. It knocked the breath out of me and jarred my already aching body, and the bile rose in my throat, mixing with the blood in my mouth. My already concussed brain dispatched a million little dots to dance on my eyeballs.

"Don't fuck wit' me, smart guy," he said.

I was gasping for air, in no condition to fuck with anybody. He waited until my breathing became more or less normal and I straightened up and lifted my head. Then he resumed his spraddle-legged King of Siam pose, looming over me.

"Next time," Ricardo said, "I let Javier smash your knee-caps. See what a smart guy you be wit' no kneecaps."

I leaned back and pressed my shoulders against the wall and levered my bound feet upward as hard as I could between his legs, toes pointed. He let out a scream that had to be an E above high C, grabbed himself, doubled over, and vomited all over his pretty leather coat. See what a smart guy *he* be with no balls.

The other three men in the room, Bobby and the two bats-men, simply froze. They couldn't believe what they had just seen and as a result were unable to act. Finally Bobby jumped like someone had jabbed him, came over to Ricardo, and helped him stand up straight. That seemed to be Javier's cue to jump into the fray, pummeling me in the head and face with his fists, awkward and hurried blows that weren't too bad in and of themselves, but the jarring to my head and neck produced a festival of red pain and strobe lights in the brain.

196

It would have been so easy just to lose consciousness, to slump down into the murk again and not worry about any of it. But I knew I had a concussion and if I went under I'd be in big trouble later—assuming there was going to *be* a later. So I squinched my eyes shut and waited until Javier wearied of hitting me and backed off.

Ricardo staggered over to the sling chair and fell into it, his hands cupping his crotch, grunting at regular intervals like the little engine that could. The kick had been pretty stupid, I suppose, but it was instinctive on my part. I figured I was a dead man anyway, and I didn't want to die with the score so lopsided. Up until then I hadn't even made a dent in the drug operation that was choking my city and tearing my friend's family apart. A kick in the stones didn't seem like much in the way of payback, but at least it was something. It made me feel better.

Ricardo waited a long time for the pain to fade. He took out a flowing white handkerchief and wiped his mouth and the tails of his trenchcoat where he'd thrown up on himself. Then he balled up the soiled handkerchief and threw it on the floor and turned his eyes on me. His mouth curled in a snarling grimace, and his chest rose and fell with his heavy breathing. I met his gaze and stared him down—I had nothing to lose at that point.

He looked away and motioned to Bobby, who bent down so Ricardo could mumble into his ear. Bobby straightened up, grinned at me, and disappeared through the sliding double doors, leaving them open slightly. I could hear him banging around in the back. Probably in the kitchen fixing us some sandwiches.

"I could have dese boys break every bone in your body," Ricardo said to me through gritted teeth. "Slow. One by one. While I watch. I'd like to watch."

He waited for me to answer, but I had nothing to say to him. There didn't seem to be much point answering anyway. In the meantime, the two muscle boys stood up a little straighter, ready to do or die.

"Or we could take a chain saw to you. Carve you like a barbecue pig and leave your pieces all over town." I thought of Randolph Jones and tried not to shudder. I didn't want to give him the satisfaction.

"Den you be a message to ever'one," Ricardo said, struggling to sit up straighter in the chair. "To mind dey own business. Den we don' get no more fuckers like you gettin' into our face, 'cause dey be afraid. Nothin' make people afraid like a nice atrocity." He pronounced the word carefully as if it was one he'd only read but never said aloud before. "But, my shitty luck, mon, dat be a bad idea. Den de po-lice, dey get all upset 'cause a white man get kill like dat, dey come lookin' for de posses, bust some head, fuck us up. We can' have dat. Don' need no more po-lice. So I come up wit' somethin' better."

The sliding doors rumbled, seated inexactly as they were in their metal runners, and Bobby DeLayne came back in. He was holding a hypodermic syringe in his hand, point up, like a sadistic pediatrician terrorizing a four-year-old. It was one of the disposable kind so favored by junkies.

"You know what a speedball be?" Ricardo said. I didn't answer him, but he wasn't to be denied. "Do you?" He heaved himself up out of the chair and came over to the daybed; it was a source of satisfaction to me that he was walking funny. He kicked me so hard in the shin that tears sprang to my eyes. "Answer me, fucker."

I shrugged. Shrugging hurt. "As opposed to a curveball or a slider?" The blows to my head had done some damage, and I was tripping over words like the town rum pot.

Ricardo laughed. He went "Hee, hee, hee," so it was at least a reasonable assumption that he was laughing. "Dat be pretty good. No, Jacoveech, a speedball mixes up coke an' horse, you know? Dat be a high an' a low all wrapped up in one. Get a mon flyin' like he never flied before. Good stuff." He smiled. "If you take too much, naturally, not such good stuff. Make your heart go bippity-bippity-bippity, real fast like dat, an' den it blow right up in your chest, an' you're gone, you know?" He snapped his fingers. "It be a damn shame, a mon to take too much. Be ugly."

Despite the dank coldness of the room, sweat ran down my back and dripped off my chin. The death he described was preferable to being carved up by a chain saw, but I'd always envisioned myself going quietly in a big brass bed, surrounded by weeping grandchildren.

He took the syringe from Bobby and waved it under my nose. "Sooo," he said, enjoying the drama, "we gonna shoot you a nice speedball an' watch while your heart go boom! Den we take you home an' leave you by your house, an' when dey fin' you, you be jus' one more damn dead OD junkie. De po-lice dey shake dere heads an' say too bad, and nobody come lookin' for us."

"If you think the police don't know I've been chasing you guys, you're dumber than I thought," I said, and then I clenched my teeth together to keep them from chattering. I've never been quite so frightened.

A frown knit his handsome brow. "Okay," he said, "maybe dey do. But speedballs ain't our way. How you say, it ain't our *MO*. De po-lice maybe stir up some shit for a little while but dey need some proof. Otherwise you jus' a OD junkie corpse." He leaned close, his dark eyes sparking hatred, his mouth a rictus of hate. His breath smelled of exotic spices and dirty rice. "Myself, I much rather do de chain saw," he said. "But dat be too messy. Count yourself lucky, Jacoveech. An' kiss your ass goo-bye."

I wasn't quite ready to do that, but at the moment I was spared the stress of any decision making. Ricardo turned to Bobby. "Roll his sleeve up," he ordered.

Bobby jumped again, and came over to the daybed. His obedience was instantaneous and unquestioning, and now I could see him for what he was, a functionary, a minor cog in this machine, which seemed bigger than I'd ever imagined. "Which sleeve?" he said. A real rocket scientist, Bobby.

Ricardo rolled his eyes. "De lef' one, stupid. De guy, if he right-handed, he gonna put a spike in his lef' arm, ain't he? You be one dumb white mon, Bobby."

Bobby's chalk-white skin flushed as much as it ever could. He thrust me to one side like a sack of dog chow so he could get to my sleeve. He was being needlessly rough, humiliated at the way Ricardo had spoken to him in front of the rest of us and taking it out on me. I felt him fumbling at my hands behind me. I was wearing a shirt, a sports jacket, and a heavy corduroy car coat, and with my wrists tightly taped together, rolling up my sleeve was proving to be a labor beyond Bobby's limited capabilities. In his clumsiness, his fingernails scratched the tender flesh on the inside of my arm just above the tape. I had noted the dirt under his nails when I'd first met him, and the scratching seemed oddly worse than anything else that was going on. I shuddered in disgust. It was not the best time to be concerned about tetanus, but that's how I am.

"I can't get his sleeve up," Bobby said, and added with a prideful note, "we trussed him up too tight."

Ricardo took a nickel-plated police special from the pocket of his leather coat and pointed it at my head. I could tell from there it was official PD issue, and I wondered idly where he'd gotten it. "Den untruss him, mon. He's not goin' noplace." As Bobby started to do so, Ricardo barked, "Watch your heat, mon!"

Bobby leapt away from me as if burned. Shamefaced, he took my Magnum from his pocket and handed it to Ricardo, who shook his head, a mother grown weary of the antics of her toddler, and jammed it into the pocket of his trench coat. Then Bobby came back to me and pushed me over on my side on the daybed like a sack of grain. I felt him behind me, unwinding the duct tape from my wrists like a little boy opening a well-wrapped Christmas present. His face was near my ear, and I could hear his breath whistling through his nose. He was bending my arms a lot farther up than necessary, straining my shoulder muscles; one more pain to go with the rest.

As Bobby tore the tape off my wrists it pulled the hair out by the roots. Compared to everything else on me that hurt, it was a mere trifle, but for some reason it made me furious—and all at once I felt the fear drain out of me, leaving only rage. Through the shooting pain in my head and neck and spine, the bad bruise on my shin, and the blood in my mouth, I resented the hell out of having my body tossed about so casually, treated like a thing, an inanimate object. I was prepared for death as well as anyone can be, I suppose; I was expecting it. But I wasn't prepared to accept degradation. I'm not a thing, I'm a person. I'm Milan Jacovich. And if I was going to die I'd damn well not go gentle.

I felt the circulation returning to my hands, a painful tingling sensation that was a relief. My wrists were finally free, and I tried to flex my fingers to get the blood moving, but Bobby kept a tight hold on my left hand while he tossed the wadded-up tape across the room. He pulled me upright, none too gently, and started to take my jacket off. As his face came close to mine, I looped my free arm around his neck, hooked my fist under his chin and butted him in the nose with my forehead. It set temple bells clanging in my ears, but I ignored them and turned him around so his back was to me and pulled, hard. My knees pressed into the backs of his until they buckled, and I brought him back and down so he was sitting on my lap. His legs thrashed out, and he threw his head back, gagging and sputtering, trying to bang my hands loose. I turned my face to the side to protect my nose. In the meantime I concentrated on crushing his windpipe.

Javier and Joan Bennett had been mere spectators until then, and my move caught them unawares, flat-footed, and they looked at one another for a clue as to what their next move should be. Ricardo, his gun now trained on Bobby, whose body was shielding mine, only hesitated for a second. Then he took a breath, straightened his arm, and squeezed the trigger of his police special.

In the high-ceilinged room the shot sounded like a nuclear bomb blast. The .38-caliber bullet passed through Bobby's body and slammed into my right pectoral muscle like a mailed fist. It rocked me back against the daybed cushions against the wall. Bobby's body convulsed in my arms and he screamed, but it was a wet, bubbly scream that boded no good. The bullet had pierced his lung. I grunted and loosed my hold from around his neck. He slumped against me and slowly slid forward off my lap and onto the floor, rolling over onto his back, his eyes wide open and fixed on some point on the ceiling. His grin had changed to gaping astonishment, maybe at the blood running out of his mouth, and his body jerked like a spastic puppet. As he slid off me I instinctively clamped my left hand against my own bullet wound to keep from bleeding too badly.

The rotten-egg stink of cordite in the closed room made my eyes tear. I looked up at Ricardo. His own eyes were glittering insanely, bloodshot, the edges of the brown irises somewhat blurred into the whites. A sheen of sweat made his features glisten as if he'd suddenly sprung a high fever. His eyes flicked to the pile on the floor that had been Bobby and then back to me. "God damn you, Jacoveech," he said, and I could see as if in slow motion his finger tightening on the trigger of the gun again, the muzzle pointed at my chest and looking a mile wide. At that range he couldn't miss.

And then there was another roar, even more deafening than the first, accompanied by shattering glass. The gun disappeared, as did most of Ricardo's hand, bits of blood and bone flying through the air and spattering against the wall. He dropped the syringe from his other hand, whirled away from the middle of the room, and started to shriek. He banged off the wall a few times in an agonized frenzy, and finally sank down onto the floor in a corner. His face, contorted with pain and pouring sweat, had turned a dirty shade of gray.

The other two men started for the sliding doors and the back of the house until a voice commanded, "Freeze!" They stopped in their tracks and put their hands on top of their heads, fingers interlaced. They knew the drill. I turned in the direction of the sound and saw a 9-millimeter military automatic extended through one of the chinks in the boards covering the bay windows.

The same voice said, "You two clowns—get your pants down. Now!" It was a voice accustomed to command.

Javier looked at Joan Bennett in a kind of outraged wonderment, but when the voice barked, "Do it!" they hastened to do as they were told, unbuckling their jeans and letting them puddle around their ankles. I think they were more humiliated than anything else. Joan Bennett was wearing silky gold boxer shorts with a rearing black horse stitched on one hip, and Javier wore bright red bikinis. I would have been embarrassed too.

"On your bellies on the floor, hands behind heads. Now!"

They did it. They looked at the hunk of blood and gristle that had been Ricardo's hand and they seemed eager to.

"Milan, pick up the piece," the voice commanded. My ankles were still taped together, so I awkwardly crawled over the crumpled body of Bobby DeLayne to where Ricardo had dropped his gun on the floor. I got up on my knees and covered Javier and Joan Bennett, who lay on their faces with their pants at quarter mast, effectively hobbling any escape attempts. I tried to keep my right elbow against my body to minimize the flow of blood from the gunshot wound. Apparently the bullet had passed clear through Bobby and clear through me, because I felt the sting of the exit wound on the right side of my back. At that, I was better off than Ricardo, who was still screaming in the corner. There wasn't very much left of his hand, and through the blood I could see the white splinters of bones that once had been fingers.

"Never mind them, I got 'em. Unlock the damn door."

I stumped over to the vestibule on my knees; I felt like Toulouse-Lautrec. I fumbled with the lock until I reasoned how it worked and then swung the front door open. When I stuck my head out, the cold air turned the sweat all over me to ice, numbing the holes Ricardo had put in me. The night smelled like winter.

A wide, swaybacked wooden front porch ran the entire width of the house, and off to my right I saw Reggie Parker kneeling in front of the bay windows, his hand stuck through the boards and one eye pressed to the small opening.

"*Now* get back in there and cover 'em," he snarled.

With my good hand I clawed at the tape around my ankles, finally managing to pull it down over my feet. I lost one shoe, but I was finally able to stand up and walk. Every move brought waves of pain and another dollop of dizziness. I went back into the living room and pointed my pistol left-handed at the two designated hitters, both belly-down on the floor with their pants around their ankles, and noticed that my hands were shaking almost uncontrollably. The whole thing was hitting me now, and I realized I'd probably never get any closer. I swayed— or else the room did.

Ricardo's howls had de-escalated into a rhythmic whimper, almost a chant, and he quivered in shock. I went over to him and removed my gun from his coat. With the blood and the vomit, that lovely leather garment wasn't very elegant anymore.

Parker came in through the front door and looked at our captives. "Is that all of them?"

"I think so." The room was still rocking, and the big bass drum in my ears was the pounding of my own heart, each beat sending a little trickle of blood down my side. I said, "I thought I told you to go home."

"I was a Green Beret captain," he said. "I don't take orders, I give 'em." He allowed himself a half smile. "If you've got any complaints, have the chaplain punch your TS card."

I heard distant sirens screaming through the cold night, coming closer, but I was hearing them and Parker in an echo chamber.

Parker went over to Ricardo and looked at his hand. Ricardo whimpered like a small puppy, partly from pain and partly from the knowledge that henceforth and forever more he'd be picking his nose with his left hand.

"This man needs medical attention," Parker said.

"Him? What about me?"

"You," I heard him say as the room rocked again and everything faded to a fuzzy blue, "only need your head examined."

21

THE old saying about hospital food being lousy is not just a generalization; it shimmers like pure crystalline truth. I'm not crazy about Salisbury steak, I loathe mashed potatoes in any form but especially when they're made from powder, and I think lime gelatin with little pieces of canned pear trapped in it should be declared unconstitutional. I also don't like orange juice. I was thankful that my treatable injuries consisted only of a simple flesh wound, which was cleaned out and stitched up in the emergency room, and a concussion, made slight by Joan Bennett's lousy aim with his bat. Maybe his hair got in his eyes. Were he to swing at a ball that way, he'd undoubtedly undercut it and pop up to the first baseman. He had aimed for my head but connected with the back of my neck, which means that I only had a headache I could complain about intelligibly, instead of being dead or in a lounge chair in the solarium with a beatific smile on my face, staring at the TV and drooling oatmeal onto my pajamas.

As it was, I had a bandage wrapped around my chest, the serious part of it under my right arm and in the back where the exit wound luckily was pretty clean. I was uncomfortable and sore, and I was delighted to settle for that instead of a punctured lung. Getting shot, like baseball, is a game of inches.

The ache in my head and neck had diminished to a low

rumble, the contusions on my face from Javier's pummeling were not serious, and as for my bruised shin, it was such small change I don't think anyone at the hospital had even taken a look at it. They'd given me a semiprivate room, but I guess business was lousy, because the other bed was empty. It was just as well. I didn't need a roommate telling me about his gallbladder all day long. Instead I watched TV or looked out the window, bitter because for the first time in weeks the sun was shining and I was stuck in bed.

Through my various aches something was sticking in my head, but I was doped up with pain pills just enough that I couldn't get it out. The constant drone of the TV set didn't help me, but if I turned it off the silence would be worse.

My nurse was a chubby little lady in her fifties whose underpants showed through her white nylon nurse's slacks. She brought me white pills, yellow pills, and pills of the most delicate turquoise hue in little paper cups the size of a shot glass, and she came in to raise and lower my bed so often I began thinking she had entered her noble profession just so she could play with the controls. She scolded when I didn't take my medication and was chirpily efficient, optimistic, and motherly. I hated her an awful lot.

I also discovered that being visited by loved ones while hospitalized is a rare and subtle form of mind destruction on the level of playing a radio loud enough for someone to hear but too softly to understand what it's saying. When I finally came to life just before noon the next day, I had a parade of visitors to rival that of a medieval prince dispensing favors with a wave of his scepter, and Nursey announced each one like a footman at a royal ball.

"Mr. Baznik," she intoned.

Matt carried a bouquet of flowers, white carnations, but he slunk in rather than walked, and as much as I hurt I couldn't help pitying him.

"I feel like a shit," he said.

I managed a weak, brave smile. He *was* a shit, but that would have to be old news if I wanted to maintain a friendship that had lasted since childhood. "Thanks for coming, Matt."

"Jeez, I mean, you coulda been killed."

206

"I wasn't, so let's not talk about it."

He held the flowers out and I took them, realizing too late I had no place to put them. So I sat there holding them on my chest, white on white, the flowers and the sheets and my face and my hospital gown, like a bride awaiting the wedding night visit of the seigneur.

"When are they letting you out of here?"

"Tomorrow, if I'm lucky," I said.

"Does it hurt?"

That was too dumb to rate a reply.

He didn't know what to do with his hands. "Okay if I sit on the bed? I don't want the nurse to yell at me."

"She won't yell at you."

He lowered himself gingerly onto the bed, perching on the end of it so as not to jostle me. I said, "Matt, I'm not a burn case. Relax, will you?"

He did, his back going from a ninety-degree angle to his lap to eighty-five degrees. "I didn't go to work today." He chewed on his lip, his eyes tormented behind his glasses. "Marko called at seven o'clock this morning to tell us what happened, and me and Paulie and Rita Marie had a long talk." He attempted a smile and failed miserably. "A good talk. Quiet. No yelling. I told Paulie what happened to you."

I nodded. Nodding hurt, but it beat talking hands down.

"I told him it was all his fault you got hurt."

Nothing like a little old-fashioned Catholic guilt passed down from father to son to get the day started. I began a protest, but he stopped me. He'd rehearsed this and he would be heard.

"He feels pretty lousy about it, Paulie. He cried. It's okay, it was good he cried. Sometimes you hafta cry. I never thought so, I raised him not to cry, but it was good that he did. He told me everything, about the guys at the school and how he's been picking up some extra money." He had dropped his chin onto his chest while he spoke, but now he raised his head and looked straight at me. "He's not gonna do it no more. He said he'd even see somebody about it. You know, get some . . . help."

It wasn't that Matt didn't know the word *psychologist*, but he somehow couldn't bring himself to say it. Good Slovenian kids don't go to shrinks, and Matt wore it like a hair shirt. "Jeez, and I wouldn't even help when you asked me."

I thought of what might have happened had it been Matt with me the night before instead of Reggie Parker. Then I decided not to. "It worked out better this way."

"You're a good friend, Milan," Matt said. "A better friend than I deserve." He sniffled, and a tear rolled out from under his glasses. He wiped it away quickly. "Jeez, look at me," he said, turning his face away so I couldn't.

"It's okay, Matt," I said. "Sometimes you have to cry."

After he left, the nurse put his flowers in a vase and cranked my bed down despite my beefing that I preferred to stay upright for a while. I'd gotten involved in *The Young and the Restless* and wanted to watch the rest of it. That Cassandra was really something. All the actors and actresses on that show were. Firm silhouettes, with less than one percent body fat, flawless skin that had never borne a pimple, thick hair coruscating with the glow of health. Where do they find such beautiful people?

My Auntie Branka called. Apparently Lila had heard about my problems from Marko and phoned her. Branka had never learned to operate a car and was too old to be running around on buses, so she was effectively imprisoned in her Euclid neighborhood unless one of her children or the lady next door drove her somewhere, but she still apologized for not being able to visit. She was full of old Slovenian folk remedies that she instructed me to pass on to my doctor and promised as soon as I got out of the hospital that she'd cook me a good old-fashioned Yugoslavian supper of *girice*, *raznjici* with *sarma*, and *palacinke* for dessert, which she inferred would clear up my concussion, heal my gunshot wound, and put me back into the mainstream of vibrant well-being. Her broken English was difficult to understand even in person, more so over the telephone, but I wouldn't have traded her phone call for a million dollars. Apart from my sons, she was the only family I had, and at those times when it seemed the whole world had either forgotten about me or just plain didn't give a damn, Tetka Branka was always there.

I watched the TV at an awkward angle until I decided it

208

looked better that way. Then the bustling little nurse came back in and announced solemnly, "Mr. Parker is here."

Reggie came in, dressed as conservatively as a high school principal should be. But I wasn't seeing him that way any more. He looked tall and wide to me this morning, a black John Wayne in dirty camouflage, and though there was no beret on his head, I could still see it shining there.

"You look a hell of a lot better than the last time I saw you," he said. "You aren't green, for one thing."

"I feel green," I said. "And part of it's envy. I guess you're the hero of the day, Reg."

"A hero's just a guy who was too scared to run."

"Maybe. But I wouldn't be here if it wasn't for you."

He put his hands up to stop me. His palms were pink and scrubbed-looking. "I'm not up for any long speeches of gratitude, okay? I didn't get much sleep last night."

There's nothing more aggravating than wanting to thank someone for a real biggie and not being allowed to. I think Reggie Parker knew that and was enjoying it, and I decided to let him have his fun. God knows I owed him that much. I said, "I'm a little foggy on the details. All they'll tell me in here is what's on my chart. And they're pretty secretive about that too."

"They probably don't want you upset in your delicate condition," he said. He sat down in the visitor's chair, looking awkward, hands clasped between splayed knees. "Well, I did my big job; I went to the convenience store and called Ingeldinger. He wasn't happy to hear from me, and he didn't quite believe what I told him. Anyway, after I hung up, I decided I didn't want to miss the fun, so I went back to the warehouse. Next thing I know, that white car is driving out again, with three guys in it 'stead of one, and no sign of Jacovich anywhere. So I follow them to this house on 119th Street and I see them dragging something big and limp and heavy out of the car. I recognized your jacket. I hauled ass to the nearest phone booth and called the police again, and then I went back to 119th to see what was up." He chuckled. "I'd've been a lot better off with a car phone, but I never saw anyone with one of those

209

that wasn't an asshole. Every time they stop at a red light they have to make a call."

"Where'd you get the gun?" I said.

"From the glove compartment of my car. I didn't know what you were getting me into, and I wanted to be ready."

"You could've caught a bullet."

He raised his eyebrows, which caused his glasses to move down on his nose. "I could've gotten hit by a truck too."

"What happened after I passed out?"

He said, "Ingeldinger and company arrived with sirens rampant. They came blasting in there with weapons right out of *Star Wars*, and naturally since I'm black they figured I was the boss of the outfit." He squeezed out a mirthless smile. "I'm not sure Ingeldinger still doesn't think so."

"What happened to those guys at the house?"

The smile went away. "The one I nailed will make it all right, but he doesn't have much of a hand left. The others are in the slam." He looked away, out the window, anyplace but at me. "The white guy—Bobby? He died on the way to the hospital."

I knew what he was feeling. I'd been there. "It's not easy being the Great Puppeteer, is it?"

"It never has been. Not when the puppets were guys in black pajamas whose names you didn't know and couldn't pronounce anyway, and not now." He shook his head to shake loose some memories. "They never get it right in the movies, do they? The killing." He stood up. "I've got a school to run, but I just dropped by to say hello. And to bring you a visitor."

"Just what I need," I said.

"As a matter of fact, I think it is," he said. "That's why I used my not inconsiderable authority to get him here." He waved and walked into the corridor. I heard murmuring out there, and after a second or two my next caller appeared in the doorway.

"Hey, Dad," Milan Jr. said. I held out my good arm, and he moved into the crook of it so I could give him a hug.

We talked a little, cried a little, and he told me his mother and brother were worried about me too, which made me feel pretty good, and then we talked football and basketball and the other crap kids like to talk about, and I wasn't sure but I think he might have been proud of his old man, if not downright impressed, and that made the pain and everything all worthwhile.

* * *

At about three o'clock the nurse interrupted my nap to get the latest update on my temperature and blood pressure. After she had ascertained that I was still alive, she said with reverence, "Lieutenant Meglich is here." The title must have impressed her as much as it did Marko. It didn't have the same effect on me, but I pushed the button and cranked up to a sitting position anyway.

He came in with a tall man in his late thirties who wore a sprayed-on blue suit and a haircut that looked ten minutes old.

"Milan," Marko said, "you have to start being more careful. Say hello to Dave Urbancek."

I did as I was told. Dave Urbancek nodded as if the secret of eternal life had just been vouchsafed unto him, and flipped a leather wallet open under my nose to reveal some sort of badge and ID. I couldn't tell what it was, but it had an American eagle on it, which meant he was federal. He didn't need to show me the badge. Guys who dressed that way were either government cops or field representatives for IBM.

"DEA," Urbancek said. "How're you feeling?"

"Much better, thanks. The concussion isn't serious, and the gunshot didn't hit anything vital, although it'll probably stiffen up on me in cold weather. And please thank the president for sending someone here personally to inquire."

Something died behind Urbancek's eyes, a diminishing of whatever passed for warmth in the federal bureaucracy. He glanced at Marko, who jumped in to cover my gaffe.

"You were right about Waco Morgan," he said. "We found nearly seventeen pounds of crack cocaine in the headliner of that car. By the time it got stepped on, it would have been worth a couple of million bucks. Nice work, Milan. Ding asked me to tell you specially how much he appreciates your help."

I looked Marko dead in the face and saw a smile working

the corners of his mouth. We have our differences, but we've been friends too long to bullshit each other. If he was speaking for the record in front of the fed, it was okay with me.

"Just being a good citizen," I said.

"We were hoping you'd feel that way, Mr. Jacovich," Urbancek said, coming over to the bed. The sun was still shining, coming through the window and hitting the back of his head. How can you take a guy seriously when the sun is behind him shining red through his ears? "We'd like your help some more, if you would."

I waited for the pitch. I knew what was coming.

"Lieutenants Ingeldinger and Meglich tell me that you found out about Waco Morgan through a tip. Is that correct?"

I nodded. It still hurt to nod.

"Where did you get that information?"

"I can't tell you that."

The slit between his nose and his chin flattened out in what was supposed to be a friendly smile. "Sure you can."

I shifted around in my bed, feeling a twinge under my arm where they'd stitched me up. "Mr. Urbancek, the closest I've ever been to being a government cop was when I was an MP sergeant in Vietnam. But I was a policeman here long enough to learn a few things, and one of them is that you protect the identity and integrity of your snitches, or pretty soon you don't have them anymore."

"Whoever it is," Urbancek said, "the government will take into consideration their cooperation in this, I can assure you."

"The party wasn't involved in any way with the crack operation. So they don't need your assurances."

"Let's let us be the judge of that, okay?"

"I'm afraid it isn't okay."

He put his right hand in his jacket pocket, fingers pointed straight down and thumb hooked over the edge, but the resemblance to John F. Kennedy ended there. "This isn't some piddly-ass street bust. This is a major drug operation, and as such falls under the purview of the Drug Enforcement Agency of the United States government. And frankly, whatever little private code of conduct you might have picked up in the Cleveland Police Department isn't worth a pitcher of warm piss."

I didn't like the edge in Urbancek's tone when he said Cleveland, as if he was talking about West Jibipp. I looked at Marko. "Huh. Who's he, anyway?" I said. In the local patois, that means that a guy has a hell of a lot of nerve saying what he said, doing what he did, being where he is. The appropriate response on the East Side of Cleveland is, "Yeah."

But Marko didn't say that. He didn't say anything, which wasn't a hell of a lot of help.

I said to Urbancek, "It may not be worth much to you, but it's worth plenty to me, because this is where I live. And when you live someplace you play by the local rules. You should wear your jacket a little looser, Mr. Urbancek. I think it's impairing your judgment."

Urbancek's expression was a blank piece of paper. He looked over at Marko. "Tell him," he said. "I'll meet you downstairs." He walked out of the room without another glance at me.

Marko glared after him. "G-men always wear their suits too tight. Why is that, you suppose? You think they're all gay? Or is it regulations they all visit the same tailor?"

"What are you supposed to tell me?" I said. "I want to take a nap."

Marko came over and perched on the edge of my mattress. "Morgan's claiming ignorance. About the drugs."

"The stuff's being brought into his car showroom and then being cut and distributed through houses that he or his girlfriend own, and he says he's innocent?"

"Stranger things have happened."

The pain behind my eyes became a little sharper, and I closed them for a moment to shut out the light. "I suppose. But you can't tell me that Bobby DeLayne was running the show. Or Ricardo whatever-his-name-is, either."

"Morgan's hollering frame. His lawyer's mad. He's ready to sue someone."

That made my eyes open. "You mean me."

"You and the city and the United States government. Unless you give Dipshit there what he wants and take some of the heat off yourself."

I thought of Giancarlo D'Allessandro and Victor Gaimari explaining things to Urbancek or one of his brass-buttoned pals

213

after I dropped a dime on them. But that's as far as it got. You just don't do things like that. Even to guys like them.

"I can't and you know it."

"I told him that. But these guys figure their federal tin gives them a special dispensation from the pope. They don't give a shit about local jurisdictions, they just move in and take over. It won't look good on Urbancek's personnel folder if Morgan sues Uncle Sam. Like it or not, he's the Man, and he wants a name. He doesn't get it, he'll settle for the next best thing, which is your ass."

"What can he get me on? Using the account of a Major League game without the written consent of the commissioner?"

Marko got up and went to the door. "He'll figure something out, Milan."

I took the electronic control in my hand and pushed the button with my thumb, and the top part of the bed slowly lowered, my head with it. Sunset. "So will I," I said.

* * *

They woke me up to eat. The hospital dinner was the usual yummy—two pieces of dust-dry roast chicken devoid of any seasoning, a dollop of potato buds in yellow gravy, and some peas the bright green of Bambi's meadow, accompanied by the ubiquitous lime jello and a glass of grapefruit juice. After she removed my dinner tray it was time for my favorite nurse to go off shift for the day, but she had one more visitor to present.

"Miss Soderberg to see you," she said, and stepped aside so Mary could come into the room.

"Hello, Milan." She had a bouquet of spring flowers for me. Where she found spring flowers in November I'll never know, but that's Mary.

The nurse stepped between us, took the flowers from Mary, and stuffed them into another ugly milk glass vase she found in the closet. "Aren't these pretty?" she said, putting them on the table next to the carnations Matt had brought me earlier. "I'm going home, now, Mr. Jacovich. Don't let me hear from the night girl that you've been difficult."

"I won't let you hear it," I said. After she was gone, Mary took off her coat, came over and leaned down to kiss me. It was the perfect kiss for a friend in a hospital bed wearing one of those silly gowns, quick and warm and fleeting.

"You gave us all a scare," she said.

"Who's us?"

"The people who care about you."

"Are you one of them?"

"Don't be silly. Of course I am."

The hospital dinner was a wad of warm cotton in my stomach. "That's good to hear."

"How are you?"

"I'm okay, Mary. I'm going home in the morning, if I'm not difficult with the night girl."

"Well, that's good," she said. It seemed pretty pale for someone who's bed you've been sharing. We had never been this formal, this awkward, not from the moment we'd met.

"Why don't you sit down?"

"That's okay," she said. "I really can't stay long."

"Oh."

"I just wanted to see how you were."

"I'm here. I'm alive. I hurt, in several places. But I'll get over it."

"Sure you will," she said, and squeezed my hand. Her dry touch reminded me of Auntie Branka.

I squeezed back. "So what's the deal?"

Her eyelids flickered, "The deal?"

I smiled at her without having a thing in the world to smile about. That kind of smile. "Come on, Mary . . ."

She shook her head, hoping the conversation would go away. "I don't think this is the time—"

"It's the perfect time. They're releasing me tomorrow, presumably to get on with the rest of my life. I'd kind of like to know what that's going to consist of."

She walked around the room, touching things as she went, taking inventory with her fingers. Bed, hospital-type; two each. Chair, straight. Table, metal. "I'm a little confused," she said.

"About what?"

With a deep breath she sucked up half the oxygen in the room. "What I want right now. For my life. I just need a little time to think."

215

I waited for her to elaborate. It was a long wait, garnished with Mary not meeting my gaze. That wasn't like her. Mary was the lady who always said what was on her mind, who didn't like to play games. She'd always been forthright and direct, and her failure to be that way now started my head pounding again.

"It's a lot of things, Milan," she finally said. "It isn't that I don't care for you—"

"Care for me? How polite."

"We're very different kinds of people. I guess we always have been, but I didn't realize it for a long time. You see things in a certain way—"

"Black or white. I know."

"And because of it you wind up in situations like this." She indicated the hospital room. "Broken bones, broken heads, guns and killing. I'm just a nice Swedish girl from Boston. I'm not equipped to handle it."

My throat was closing around a lump the size of a volleyball. "Does Steve Stunning have anything to do with this?"

Two spots of color rose on her cheeks; she was all at once a little girl who'd gotten into her mother's rouge pot. "I don't want you to think that."

"That's evading the question."

"It's not a question that can be answered yes or no."

"Black and white again. Are you sleeping with him?"

The red spots got brighter, and she walked over to the window and looked out. The setting sun haloed her blond hair. "That's a lousy thing to say."

"It'd be an even lousier thing to do."

She whirled around to face me. "Is that your considered judgment, Milan? Black and white? Some things are good and some are lousy?"

I hated having to do this lying down, but the hospital gown with its air conditioning made it impossible for me to get out of bed and retain any dignity. "Some things are," I said. I reached for the water pitcher on the table and poured some into a waxy cup. My mouth was dry. "Look, you don't owe me any explanations. And I don't owe you any. You say you need some time to think, go ahead and take it."

216

Her eyes widened. "You mean that?"

"Sure," I said. "You've got thirty seconds."

A vertical line appeared between her beautiful eyebrows. She knew me so well, but she still didn't get it.

"Mary, when two people want to be together, they want to be together. There's nothing to think about, nothing to decide. I know what I want, but I want it right. I'm not going to worry every day that I'll say the wrong thing or do the wrong thing and you'll be gone. I think what we've had together is terrific, and I don't want to sit around and watch it shrivel up without being able to do anything about it. That's worse than dying. I'm committed, and if you aren't it's no good. I love you. I think I loved you from the first second I looked at you. But if you don't want to be with me, then I don't want to be with you. It's that simple."

She stared at me, tears welling up in her eyes. She picked up her coat before they could get out and went to the door. "I hope you feel better, Milan. I really do. Call me, okay?"

"Thanks for coming," I called after her. I waited until she was gone and then I lowered the bed to sleeping position. I couldn't think of a single reason to stay awake.

Some things are good, and some are lousy.

22

IT was Ed Stahl who came to collect me from the hospital in the morning like a package from Will Call. In ways known only to newspaper men, he had managed to get into my apartment and put together a set of clothes, and after delivering them he waited downstairs for me because the rules kept him from smoking his pipe above the first floor. My Favorite Nurse was back at her post, apparently freshened by a night's sleep and armed with a whole new set of platitudes. It fell to her to take me down to the main entrance in a wheelchair, and she chattered all the way. In most hospitals the wheelchair ride is mandatory, as though after the poking and prodding and temperature taking and blood-pressure cuffs and enforced pill swallowing that strip your dignity away in chunks, they want to retain their absolute control over your poor body right up until the last second.

Except for a soreness under my arm and a mild though persistent headache, I felt fine, but that wheelchair ride took a lot out of me. The helpless dependency that comes with being pushed around like a toddler in a stroller did little for my mental well-being, only reminding me how close I had come to taking my ride that morning in a hearse. When you have a concussion and a hole in your side that close to your lung, it's pretty hard to think straight anyway. But as we sailed down the hospital corridor and I shut out the chatter to concentrate on my own thoughts, something was still nagging at me, something that had to do with getting hit on the head. I figured it would eventually come to me.

Ed drives a four-door Audi sedan, and I settled into the seat for the journey home. I live just up the hill from the hospital, but this morning it seemed a long haul, especially the way Ed drove. He handled a car the way an eighty-year-old man might, hunched forward, both hands gripping the wheel with a desperation that belied the snail's pace he maintained. The wind blew cold off the lake, and once more the skies threatened rain; a good morning to stay inside.

"You're topic A around town," Ed told me as he helped me up the stairs to my apartment. "Big hero. Broke up a drug ring, caught a killer, got a lot of dope off the street." He chuckled. "The feds are mad as hell at you for stealing their thunder."

I didn't ask Ed who told him. He wouldn't have admitted it anyway. He had an ear to every wall in town, like the great reporter he was. I said, "There's nothing to it. You just let them brain you with a Louisville Slugger and then shoot you and presto! you're a hero."

"Too bad you can't pay the rent with gold stars. It's all going to turn to shit when Waco Morgan takes you to court."

I put my key in the lock, noting that my hand was shaking a little. "What'd you hear about that?"

"Only that he's going to sue you for everything from slander to letting your dog crap on his lawn."

"I don't have a dog." I opened the door. I'd only been gone about thirty-six hours but the apartment already had an uninhabited odor. Or maybe it always smelled that way and I was just noticing for the first time. It made for a lonely homecoming.

Ed came in behind me and guided me into my den and over to my favorite chair. The climb upstairs had winded me, and it felt good to sit down. "What can I get you, Milan?"

"A good lawyer."

"I can do that," he said, sitting on the sofa. "You'll need one, for all the good it'll do you."

"What's that supposed to mean?"

He began filling his pipe from a leather pouch that might have been older than he was. "As soon as I heard what went on the other night I did some checking. In person, even—first time I've been out from behind my desk in years. I went to Mayfield Heights and talked to Waco Morgan."

"And that fire-breathing secretary let you in?"

He looked over his glasses at me. "Power of the press."

"Did he offer you a glass of 1989 Château de Bubba?"

"You better start taking this seriously, young fella."

"Why? Who the hell ever heard of a criminal suing someone for saying he was one?"

"He's not a criminal yet, not till they convict him. He claims he's innocent."

"Prisons are full of guys claiming that."

Ed struck a match and held the flame to the bowl of his pipe, and a blue haze rose around his head. "He was more than happy to talk to me. He's scared, sure. Who the hell wouldn't be, with a federal indictment staring him in the face?"

"He's been indicted?"

"The U.S. attorney is going to try. But Morgan swears he's been set up."

"What else would he say?"

"Milan, I've been around a long time. I've talked to con men, kiddie-porn peddlers, welfare cheats, booze smugglers, ax murderers—you name it. And Waco Morgan, for all his Texas bullshit, doesn't fit the pattern. He makes a pretty convincing case that he doesn't know anything about any drug ring, and I'll lay you odds that when the dust settles that indictment never comes down. And if it doesn't, you're looking at a lawsuit that won't even leave you the fillings in your teeth."

I put my head back in the chair, and he leaned forward, concerned. "Are you feeling okay? If you aren't up to this . . ."

"I'll never be up to it, Ed. What do you suggest?"

"You've got two options. First, you can give the feds your source, which will take the heat off you and put it on him—"

"That's no option at all."

Ed sucked noisily on his pipe, wet dottle gurgling inside the stem, and then smacked his lips. "Okay," he said. "Then the only way you'll calm Morgan down is to get him off the hook by hanging someone else on it."

I rubbed the back of my neck. It still hurt. "Ed, I'm tired and beat up and several chunks of my life have cracked and dropped off. I don't want to hang anybody on any hook. I want to rest and spend some time with my kids."

"Then that's easy," he said. "Name a name."

"How long would you last in the newspaper business if you turned your sources?"

"Not long," he admitted. "But then I'm not tired and beat up and whatever else you said. Look, you need someone to stay here with you and make you chicken soup. Is Mary coming over?"

I felt a muscle in my eye twitch. "Mary and I . . . aren't seeing each other right now."

"I'm truly sorry to hear that. She was good for you."

I didn't say anything.

"Sometimes when you get divorced and you start seeing someone new, even though you think it's the best thing since sliced bread, what it really is is a transitional relationship. You just accept it for that and be thankful for it." He tried a brave smile, and though it didn't work I appreciated the effort. Mary had been no transitional relationship.

"Thanks for coming to get me this morning, Ed. I wasn't quite up to a taxi ride."

He waved at me as though it had been nothing. "Listen to me, friend. I know this Urbancek character. He's been around town for about eight months. He's a mean, snotty son of a bitch, and a good cop. But he's your dyed-in-the-wool government man, which means he has no use for local police. You can just imagine how he feels about PIs, especially ones that play it close to the vest. And the book on him is he takes no prisoners." He stood up. "Watch yourself. You're on the downside of the hill and your brakes are just about shot."

He leaned down and squeezed my shoulder—the good one, thank God—and let himself out. His pipe smoke hung in the air of my room, and I knew it would be days before the slightly sweet tobacco smell went away. I sat and stared at the wall, my mind churning almost as badly as my stomach. I was thinking about Mary and feeling the big empty place in my chest that had nothing to do with a bullet wound. I was thinking about Paulie Baznik and about my own kids and a lot of other people's kids that I'd never even met. I was thinking about that bastard Urbancek, about what Ed had said, and what I was going to do with the rest of my life. And I was considering my options, which were really down to one. In my weakened condition it was too much for me to handle. I slumped down in the chair, put my head back, and closed my eyes. Within seconds I was asleep.

I dreamed about roller coasters.

23

FRIDAY morning, six days before Thanksgiving. All over Cleveland the holiday decorations were appearing in the stores and on the streets in premature anticipation of the shopping frenzy that invariably pollutes the end of each year. The Browns were back in town that Sunday, riding the crest of a win over Houston, the Cavs were playing solid basketball, the current show at the Play House was a hit, the grocery stores were hawking turkey and ham for the holidays in newspaper ads that featured pilgrims in wide-brimmed buckled hats. Everyone seemed geared up for the season and in a festive mood.

Not me. I awoke early, feeling enervated and stiff after snoozing the entire night away and most of the previous day. I staggered into the kitchen and made a pot of coffee, of which I wound up drinking only half a cup. That's a red flag that all is not well with a coffeeholic like me. I was at loose ends, nothing to do and nowhere to go.

At about nine o'clock Lila called. "I wanted to see how you were doing," she said. "The boys were worried about you. So was I. And so was Joe, by the way. He was really good with the boys, asking me what he could do to help. The world is full of people who care about you, if you'd only realize it, Milan. You have to stop feeling so sorry for yourself. It's unattractive."

"I've never been known for my logic, Lila. I always go with my feelings. And right now I'm feeling not real terrific."

"Well, there are two little boys over here who feel pretty terrific about you, buddy, so shape up."

I had to smile at her characterization of Milan Jr. as a little boy. But Stephen still fit the description, and my smile widened as I thought of his bright, inquiring face, his quick blue eyes, his ready smile. "Can I have them on Sunday? I don't know if we can do anything real strenuous, but I'd just like to be with them for the day if I can."

"Sure," she said. "Maybe take them to a movie."

"Sounds great."

"Now, make it a nice movie, Milan, they're just kids. None of those violent cop films."

After she hung up I sat around in my robe for a while. My headache was gone, but there was a band of tightness around my head that I assumed came from excessive deep thinking. Lila usually triggered that in me, but something else gnawed at me today. As everyone has told me, I tend to divide the world into good guys and bad guys. But one of the things that separates me from the badge toters, that had driven me off the force along with my dislike for regimentation, is my sincere belief that a bad collar isn't better than no collar at all. If Waco Morgan was being set up, I wanted to know about it. Whether or not I liked him, whether he was an admirable human being, whether he was going to haul me into court on a variety of complaints really had nothing to do with it. Innocent is innocent; guilty is guilty.

I couldn't take showers yet, according to my doctor, so I ran a hot bath, sat in the old claw-footed tub, and washed my upper half as best I could with a loofah sponge, taking care not to get my bandage wet. For nearly forty years I made do with a plain old washcloth, but Mary had turned me on to loofahs, the way she'd introduced me to herbal shampoo and whole-grain mustard and extra virgin olive oil and so many other things that had changed my life in small but significant ways.

I shaved my battered face and put on a turtleneck and a pair of khakis. Then I slipped on a gray tweed sports jacket and a trench coat, because my car coat had a bullet hole in it and was in the trash. I usually only wore the trench coat when I was going out somewhere fancy, but at the moment it was the only thing I owned that would keep me warm besides a ski parka that I reserved for January and February when the temperature dipped below zero and the wind blew the snow off Lake Erie sideways.

I can be pretty stubborn sometimes, a Slovenian trait, and there are things I can't simply take someone else's word for. I got into the car and headed east toward Deep Shaker.

* * *

"I don't think Mr. Morgan wants to see you, Mr. Jacovich. He's been too upset even to go into his office." Margo Morgan was an awkward and uncertain sentry at the entrance to her mansion with her arms folded across her chest, possibly to ward off the cold wind blowing up the driveway. But her hair was pulled back severely, her glasses rested on her nose, and her entire stance recalled an angry dean of women. "I'm frankly surprised you'd even come here. Mr. Morgan's attorney has advised him—"

"I know all about his attorney. I'm not your husband's enemy. I'd like to convince him of that. Just ask him. Please?"

She pursed her lips in disapproval and raised one eyebrow. "Wait here," she said, and went back into the house. Though she didn't invite me to step inside out of the wind, at least this time she didn't close the door in my face. I looked into the interior of the house, where a maid in a gray uniform bustled around doing whatever maids do. Since I've never had a maid, I wasn't sure, but whatever it was, she was awfully busy at it.

Waco Morgan came stomping out of a room off to the side of the entryway and barreled toward me. He was wearing boots, jeans, and an open sports shirt of velvety silk. I thought for a moment he was going to hit me. Normally that wouldn't have caused me a flurry of consternation, but I was in no shape for any Marquis of Queensberry stuff on this particular morning. At the last moment he changed his mind, standing framed in the doorway with his balled fists on his hips. Finally he said, "Well, if you don't take the blue ribbon!"

"Waco, I have to talk to you. Maybe I can help—"

"We'll talk in court, amigo. You've helped enough. I wish I could show my true appreciation—with a couple barrels of bird shot. Since I can't, I'm going to litigate your socks off."

"Suing me isn't going to get you a damn thing because I don't *have* anything. It's just going to wind up costing you money."

He smiled nastily. "I can afford it. I'm a big drug kingpin, haven't you heard?"

"Ten minutes. Then you can sue to your heart's content."

He was breathing heavily, thinking it over. Finally he stepped aside so I could come in.

"We'll talk in the den," he said, walking past me into the room from which he'd just emerged. I followed him inside. His den smelled masculine and leathery, and was as tasteful and low-key as his office was tasteless and garish. Built-in bookshelves stretched the length of one wall, holding volumes on many subjects that looked as if they'd been read, and a window opened onto a sweeping side lawn so well-tended it was hard to remember it was the beginning of winter.

Morgan sprawled onto a burgundy-colored leather sofa that appeared to have spent fifty years in an exclusive British men's club. "Sit down and speak your piece."

I sat across from him in a matching club chair. The leather felt soft and weathered under my fingers. "I know you're pissed off," I said.

"You got a real talent for understatement, boy."

"And if you're telling the truth, I don't blame you."

"Somebody set me up," he said.

"Not me."

"Hell, I know that. But you pulled the trigger, by going to the cops and telling them I was running a crack ring. There are laws to protect innocent people from false accusations, thank God, and I'm going to invoke them and ream your butt." His shoulders relaxed a bit. "You want some coffee?"

"Under the circumstances, that's very nice of you."

He shrugged. "I'll add the price to what I'm suing you for. One cup of coffee." He pointed at a tray of coffee and fixings on his desk. Apparently his graciousness didn't extend to pouring it for me, so I leaned forward and did it myself.

"Who set you up?"

"If I knew that I'd be a happy man." He reached a long arm out to the end table and took a thin dark cigar out of a humidor. He lit it with a gold table lighter, and though I'm not a cigar smoker, I know fine tobacco when I smell it. "Look, I've done pretty well in the last few years with the dealerships," he said. "I've got an instinct for making money and I make it. I'm not ashamed of it—hell, I'm proud of it."

"It's the American way."

"When you make a lot of money you don't sit on it. You make it work for you. That's why I bought the winery in Texas—that and a little Texas pride. But I figure Ohio made me rich and I should give some back, and I looked around for something nearby to spend money on. They say real estate is a good investment, so I invest; couple of inexpensive houses, an apartment building or two. The rents come in, they aren't exactly making me millions, but they cover the mortgages, and in the meantime the property appreciates. It ties up some cash, but so what?" He waved a languid hand around the room, dissipating some of the cigar smoke. "Do I look like I'm hurting for spending money?"

I took a sip of the coffee. It was strong, exotic in flavor, and obviously more expensive than the Maxwell House I use. "Didn't you know who you were renting to?"

"Hell, no, and I didn't care. Jacovich, you probably never had two nickels to rub together—I didn't either, until a few years ago—but when you're rich you just hire people to do things you're too busy or too lazy to do yourself. And I am rich, amigo. Too damn rich to mess with anything as ugly or dangerous as drugs."

"There's no such thing as too rich," I said.

"I've heard that. But once you make a pile, there's more important things."

"Such as?"

"The Three Ps," he said. "Position; prestige; power." He took a deep puff on the cigar and then admired the ash. "That's what you never get enough of. I've been working at it. And that's why the idea of me running a drug ring is out-and-out silly."

"I'm not sure I'm getting your point," I said.

"I'm not sure I give a bull's patoot if you do or not."

"Maybe if I did I could help you."

He squinted at me, whether because of the smoke or for effect I wasn't sure. "Did you come here to hustle yourself some business?"

"I came because I don't want to get sued, and because if you're being set up I want to find out by whom."

"By whom?" he said, and laughed nastily. "You're an educated man, are you?"

"I even read without moving my lips." I wasn't about to trot out my master's degree for his approval.

"I'm not. Educated. I barely made it through high school. I got my learning where it counts—in the streets and in the business world."

"That explains the money," I said. "Not the Three Ps."

"Money helps you get the Ps," he said. "And I aim to get mine in a way that should convince you I'm clean."

He checked me out through the cigar smoke the way he'd scrutinize a used car or a racehorse or a new woman, weighing risks and calculating possibilities. Making a decision, he jammed the cigar between his teeth like Gary Cooper in *Bright Leaf*, reached into his pocket, and produced a roll of cash the size of a tangerine. He carefully extracted five hundred-dollar bills from the middle of the roll and tossed them onto my lap.

"Isn't it a little early for Christmas presents?" I said.

"I'm hiring you. You want to find out who's trying to frame me, you may as well get paid for it. Unless you already got a client?"

I thought about that and smiled ruefully. All I'd been through, and I really wasn't working at all. I didn't touch the hundreds; they lay there on my thighs like crumpled paper napkins at a ball game. "This is what I get per day," I said.

He waved the roll at me. The loss of five hundred dollars hadn't diminished its size much. "I got more."

"Businessmen don't usually spend money where they don't have to," I said. "As you mentioned, I'm going to work on this whether you pay me or not."

"I know the rules—and I know that once you accept my case, whatever I tell you is confidential."

228

"I'm not a lawyer," I said. "Lawyers can invoke confidentiality, private detectives can't, unless they've been hired by a lawyer."

I started to hand the money back, but he said, "Then just consider you're working for my attorney. Don't be such a hard-ass, okay? It's a waste of time, and I don't have a lot of time."

"A minute ago you were suing me for my first-born child."

"I still might," he said, "so don't get too comfortable."

I neatened up the bills, folded them, and put them on the end table next to me. "I still don't understand why—?"

"Hush up," he said, "and you might learn something." He uncoiled himself from the sofa and ambled over to a closet, unlocked it, and went inside. I heard the tumblers of a combination lock clicking and a metal door clanking open, sounding a lot like when Jack Benny used to go down into his vault to visit his money on the old radio show. It wasn't the most original place for a safe, but I figured Waco Morgan didn't keep vast sums of money in his home. He finally emerged, cigar still in his teeth, and tossed an oversize leather loose-leaf binder at me. I caught it awkwardly, because the toss took me by surprise, then turned it around so it was right-side up in my lap. Stamped into the rich pebble-grained cover in gold was the name and corporate logo of a well-known political consulting firm in Columbus. Beneath it, in a different and bolder type style, it read *Henry Morgan*.

"What's this?"

"Read it," he said. "Remembering that it's in the strictest of confidence."

I opened the binder to the title page:

Proposed Campaign:
Henry Morgan
for the
Governorship of Ohio

When I looked up he was beaming like a benevolent uncle. I began turning the pages slowly. Each page was encased in a clear plastic sleeve and backed with thick black three-hole construction paper. It was all there, a step-by-step account of how

229

to get nominated as the Democratic candidate for governor. Fund-raising techniques, endorsements, position papers, speeches, strategies, names of possible supporters and investors, power brokers, political strong-arm boys, committee chairpersons. Areas of the state in which to concentrate certain efforts, and those areas to ignore. There were more than two hundred double-spaced typewritten pages. It was a thorough professional job.

Waco had sat back down on the sofa, one leg slung over the side. When I'd finished scanning the report he said, "Now you know why I'd have to be crazy to be peddling drugs."

I closed the binder. "The world is full of surprises, all right. Tell me something, though."

"What's that?"

"When you're talking about honest government and the common people and cleaning up the state, how will you explain Barrie Tremont?"

He laughed out loud, throwing his head back. When he was done he looked at me with dancing eyes. "First of all, we're talking an election campaign two years down the road. By that time Barrie is going to be out of the picture, out of the state."

"Does she know that?"

"Why sure she does, amigo. There's never been any commitment there, she knew it from the start. That's why I put that house on Merle Avenue in her name, why I had Christmas put it up for sale. Kind of as a good-bye present."

"It may come out," I said. "If I found out about it, others could too."

"Well, what if they did? My God, Jacovich, no one much cares any more if a feller gets his weiner wet once in a while."

"What about Gary Hart?"

"Hart only fucked up when he challenged the press to catch him with his pants down and then lied about it. I'm sure not gonna bring Barrie up, and if someone else does, I'll just admit it, say I made a mistake but it's over now, and let it go at that. These days if you're a letch, they think you're a hell of a fella. But if people find out you're a crook, why that's a different story." He reached out for the binder, and I leaned forward and handed it to him. He took it into his lap, caressing it as though it were a kitten, a serene and peaceful look smoothing out the planes of his face.

"You'll pardon my saying so, but we already have a Democratic governor in Ohio. I've met him. And George Kinnick doesn't look like a man who's ready to quit. What makes you think you can win?"

He looked at me and smiled, probing an ear with his finger. "I don't," he said. Seeing my puzzlement, he widened his smile. "You're forgetting the three Ps," he said, ticking them off. "Position: a pillar of the community, a concerned citizen, a leader. Prestige: a man so highly regarded that those in control of such things think enough of him to nominate him to the highest office in the state."

"And the third P? Power?"

"If I make enough noise," he said, "the governor will give me anything I want to withdraw gracefully from the race and throw my support to him. Behind-the-scenes power beats a title hands down, and I don't have to stop making money to get it."

"That's neat, Waco," I said, shaking my head.

"Isn't it? Slicker than a snake's ass."

"I think they call guys like you troublemakers."

"Not quite," he said. "They call us kingmakers. That's how it's done, amigo." He gave a luxurious stretch, and got up to put the loose-leaf binder back in the safe. When he came back out of the closet he said, "Now you understand why I could never be involved in anything as pissy-assed as selling crack."

"A million-dollar business isn't pissy-assed."

He sat down again. "With all my dealerships I can gross that much on a Labor Day weekend sale. I'm sorry to wreck your little theory, but you can see by that report that I'm aiming a lot higher than a few lousy dollars." He examined the tip of his cigar and found that it had gone out. Frowning with annoyance, he lit it again. It didn't smell as good the second time. He gestured at the neatly folded bills beside me. "Now you pick up that money, Jacovich, and you do what private detectives are supposed to do. Detect. Go find out who's trying to make old Waco take a fall he doesn't deserve. You been poking around in this business for more than a week now, you must have some idea where to look. So go look there, and come back

231

and tell me. Or I'm gonna take you to court and wipe my ass with your license."

I didn't move. He got up, picked the money up off the end table, folded it again, and stuck it into the pocket of my coat. "There's a good fella," he said.

24

VUK stood with his arms crossed over his chest and his butt resting against the edge of the backbar. It was two o'clock, and there weren't many customers left after the lunch rush, but Vuk had been busy, and there was a light sheen of perspiration on his forehead. He chewed on his mustache, deep in thought, and watched me drink my beer.

"I don't think you oughta be drinking, Milan," he said. "I know about concussions, and drinking won't help it much. You gotta start taking better care of yourself. You're pushing the big four oh, you're no kid anymore."

"One beer won't kill me," I said. "As a matter of fact it's the first thing I've been able to keep down since I got hit."

He nodded. "Maybe so. But after one, you're cut off."

"Vuk, you're not my father."

"Your father never knew when to quit, either." He moved around a bit against the backbar, switching cheeks. "Matt stopped in on the way home last night and we talked some. I guess him and Paulie are getting things squared away. Says he's got you to thank for it."

"I didn't do it for thanks."

"Didn't do it for money, either. Why did you?"

"Guilt. I beat him up once when we were eight. He was a lot smaller than me, and I've felt lousy about it ever since."

"That's not guilt. That's friendship."

"Whatever," I said.

He fixed his eyes on a point somewhere above my head, which, come to think about it, was probably more fascinating than watching me drink Stroh's. "Look, I didn't mean to chew your face off the other day. You know how I am."

"Yeah, I know how you are. But you've got the coldest beer in town, so I come in here anyway." I shoved the empty at him. "One more," I said, "and I promise I'll go quietly."

He thought it over, then shrugged and snatched it off the bar, tossing it into a galvanized can. "It's your ass." He got another one out of the cooler, opened it, and slammed it down in front of me hard enough to make it foam over. "I'd think you had better things to do than sit here and brood, though."

"I'm going through midlife crisis," I said, and instantly regretted the sarcasm. Vuk didn't read much, and the only TV he watched had to do with oversize grown men doing things to balls of various sizes and shapes; he'd probably never heard the term before. "I've just got a lot on my mind. I'm getting sued, I can hardly move my right arm, and my girl and I have split up. And I can't think of a single thing to do that has nearly the appeal of brooding." I wiped the neck of the bottle and swallowed. It was so cold I got a white-hot pain behind my eye.

He looked at me and grinned, perversely enjoying my discomfort after I ignored his advice. Then he took the half full bottle out of my hand and tossed it after the empty one. "No charge," he said, "Go home, Milan. Heal up. Get your act together and come back in a few days and I'll buy you the first beer."

"Are you eighty-sixing me?"

He shrugged, not wanting to put a name to it. "If you're gonna act like a jackass, you can do it in somebody else's bar."

* * *

The chill wind nipped at my pants legs as I stood by my car in the vacant lot that served as Vuk's parking area. He was right, of course, but only partly. In the course of my brooding, the thing that had been eating at me ever since I'd been socked on the head in the warehouse was beginning to crystallize. And yet it didn't seem possible, it was like a strange dream that you can only remember in bits and pieces. I decided to check it out. I slipped off my glove and reached into my trench coat pocket for my keys, and my fingers met the folded bills Waco Morgan had put there. I wasn't going to use them just yet, not until I was sure about where they'd come from. I'm not a germ freak, but I have a strong aversion to spending dirty money.

I drove up St. Clair Avenue as I'd done ten thousand times before. The familiar sights and sounds and smells of my childhood and youth all around me, the storefronts and the various Serbian and Croatian and Slovenian clubhouses and restaurants of Slavic Town wrapped around me like a reassuring cocoon, and the warmth of the car's heater and the merry sounds of WMJI made a cold day cozy. At 135th Street I turned north, past the 7-Eleven where Reggie Parker had made his phone call before riding in to save my life like a one-man cavalry in an old Western. Half a block later I stopped, parked behind a Lincoln Continental, and walked the rest of the way to the corner.

The red brick warehouse was even uglier in the dull gray light, squatting in unlovely dominance on a street where the buildings maintained a depressing anonymity. Stray newspapers, street trash, and paper bags from fast-food joints swirled around the edges of the building like brats at the skirts of a reluctant nanny. Deserted, the neighborhood was an industrialized wasteland, cold and forbidding.

On the main gate there was a yellow police department crime scene seal, but this wouldn't be the first time I'd ignored one of those. I walked around back to the blind side of the building, this time familiar with the problems of gaining entry, and once again scaled the cyclone fence, being careful to avoid the sharp ends of exposed wire along the top. It was a more difficult climb with a stiff and bandaged side. The shock of impact when I finally hit the asphalt inside the fence sent shooting pains up through my left armpit into my shoulder and neck, and I had to blink away big black spots that appeared on my field of vision like ink blots. I stood there in the chain link cage, shaking my head like an ungainly bear. Vuk was right—I should have gone home to heal.

I went around to the door where I'd broken in before. The rusted hasp had been screwed back into the wall and the old padlock had been replaced with a dull black one from the police department. I removed the hasp with my screwdriver as easily as I had two nights previous. The lock on the door only took me about a minute this time, old hand that I was.

I left the door open so I could see where I was going. On my left was an office with a window looking out into the corridor, but it didn't appear to have been occupied for years. The only furniture was a battered desk, and there were several empty cartons piled up on the floor. Everything was covered by half an inch of grit. The place smelled as moldy as it had the first time, but somehow I didn't notice it as much, perhaps because this time I had something to look at. It wasn't much, granted, but I was grateful for the visibility. I rubbed my nose to try to keep from sneezing.

I made my left turn through the doorless doorway and into the storage room and lost a good bit of what light I'd had, but the skeletal shapes I thought I'd noticed in the nighttime were more visible to me now. Fumbling against the wall by the door, I found a light switch and flipped it upward, gasping as the enormous room sprang into yellowish life in the illumination from the single ceiling fixture. Surely I'd fallen down Alice's rabbit hole.

The room was stacked high with swooping metallic tracks, as if a narrow-gauge railroad designed by an engineer on acid had been dismantled and stored there. Against the left wall they were simply piled one on top of the other in a bewildering maze of steel; on the right, though, was a section of track that seemed to have been assembled in some fashion, arching up on unsteady wooden supports almost to the ceiling. And up there, some twenty feet above the concrete floor of the warehouse, was what made the whole thing recognizable. I remembered the sensation, just before I'd passed out from the blow across the back of my neck, of being on a roller coaster, the ground rushing up to meet me, the dizzying plunge, and I vaguely recalled my roller coaster dream. Now I knew why. Even in the dim light of a seventy-five-watt bulb, there was no mistaking the shiny red car from the ride that had once delighted and scared me at the same time, along with thousands of other kids and adults at the old Euclid Beach Amusement Park, back in the days before high-tech and video arcades and theme parks had ever been thought of, when such magical places flourished all over the country and eased the process of growing up.

The Thriller.

I had probably sat in that very car twenty-five years ago or more, holding on to the bar that came down over my lap and locked into place, perhaps with my arm around Lila or one of the other girls I'd dated in high school, both of us yelling at the top of our lungs as the car racketed downward, the noise of the wheels and the rush of the air and our own screaming combining in an incredible din, the wind making our eyes Chinese. It was what had flashed into my mind just before unconsciousness, what had been nibbling at me ever since. It had finally come together for me while listening to Vuk's lecture, and so I had the answer I sought.

I wandered around for a bit, checking things out. There were two other cars hidden in the corner behind the stacked-up tracks. The one section of track that had been assembled was pure showpiece, the car at the top frozen in that moment just before it begins its dizzy downward rush. A large wooden block was jammed under its front wheel to keep it forever at its apex. As when the Thriller roared over Euclid Beach, the anticipation was more keen than the experience itself.

What I wasn't anticipating was the sound of the steel bay at the other end of the warehouse groaning open, and a car driving in. A door slammed with the quiet snick that characterizes new, expensive American cars, then the bay closed again. It clanged shut against the concrete floor with a disturbing finality. Footsteps came closer, the sound of soft soles on the crunchy dirt of the floor. I turned to face them, leaning back against the structure of the track.

"I'm in here, Mr. Amboy," I called.

He appeared in the big archway separating the two main areas of the warehouse. "Hell, I know where you are, Milan," he said. "I been follyin' you since early this morning." He smiled, and the light danced on his lenses. "An' I thought I told you to call me Christmas." He was carrying a baseball bat in his right hand. It wasn't a kid's bat, either, but one of the big thirty-two-ouncers that the Major League power hitters use. I couldn't see very well in the dim light, but it looked like there were several large spikes or nails protruding from all around it, and the nail heads had been filed down to vicious points. He wasn't brandishing it at me; it dangled at his side like an afterthought. I could see that it had a dull black finish and it was big. He came toward me, close enough to hit me with one swing.

"You carryin' a piece, Milan?"

I wasn't. The stiffness in my right side and the heavy bandage under my arm would have played hell with my shooting accuracy anyway. I said, "You expect me to tell you?"

He smiled his warm, reassuring salesman's smile, and he brought his own weapon up partway. "It don't matter. I'm pretty good with this. When they find you, they'll figure it was the boogies. A white man don't use a ball bat on another white man."

"You've got it all figured, don't you, Christmas?"

"I try," he said. "What gave it away? That picture of the Thriller in my office?"

"That was one of the things."

"Rolly coasters always fascinated me. So I figured when they shut down Euclid Beach Park, I'd just make a bid an' put the ol' Thriller in storage here until they got sense enough to open another amusement park just like it. They never did, but that really don't bother me none. Sometimes I jus' come over here and look at it." He glanced up at the car on the track. "Sometimes I even sit in it. Good place to think."

"So you're running the whole northern Ohio crack operation out of a roller coaster?"

"You might just say that. Seems fitting, don't it? It's all got to do with cheap thrills. If anyone's gonna be dumb enough to pay good money to go up in the sky and get dropped down faster than hell, they'd pay good money for a drug that does the same thing." He looked at me shrewdly. "But you didn't put all this together just from a picture on my wall."

"When I first came to you about the Merle Avenue house, you told me the owner couldn't be reached during the day because he worked. Then I found out Barrie Tremont owned the house, and she doesn't work during the day. I didn't really think about it until I was in the hospital. I had a lot of time on my hands."

Christmas sighed. "Damn, I wish you'd of minded your own bidness."

"You've been playing Waco Morgan like a violin, haven't you? A busy, wealthy guy walks in and hands you a lot of money to play with, and you've been buying properties and using them for crack houses ever since. What did you do, pay the rents yourself?"

He nodded. "It costs money to do bidness. But it was worth it."

"And Waco Morgan never knew?"

"Waco got political ambitions. He's too damn busy to see what's been goin' on right under his nose."

"And Barrie Tremont?"

He laughed. "She's just an airhead. Only good for one thing. That's what else's been keepin' Waco busy. Let that be a lesson, Milan, never let pussy get in the way of profit."

"And in the meantime you have the Jamaicans out there getting their hands dirty, and even they don't know it's you behind it. They all think it was Ricardo."

"Nobody asked 'em to come here," Christmas Amboy said. "They got to take their chances if they want a piece of the American pie."

"Deshon took his chances."

"Deshon was an uppity little shit!" Christmas said with some heat. "I never liked him to begin with. Thought he was better'n everybody, and took too damn *many* chances. Lettin' you get a lead on him was jus' goddamn dumb."

"So you made an example of him?"

"*I* didn't do nothin'," he said. "I was at a Board of Realtors dinner that night, an' I got a hundred witnesses to say I was."

"So you had Javier and his pal do it for you?"

He laughed, comfortable in his own skin. "I don't even know them," he said. "Never had the pleasure. They answered to Ricardo. If they got caught, hell, them boogies're nothin' to me."

239

"Bobby either?"

"Bobby was a gooney bird, Milan. Anybody puts that shit in their bodies is a gooney bird."

"How'd you do it, Christmas? Bring the stuff in from Southeast Asia hidden in the import cars?"

"Idden' that a good idea?" he said. "The police just naturally figured that with all the Jamaicans on the street, the stuff was coming in from Central America or the Caribbean. Never occurred to them it was coming from Cambodia right into Waco Morgan's showroom."

"How did Bobby figure in all this?"

"He was a two-bit pusher when I met him, but he had this kind of animal good sense and had never got caught. No record. I put him to work for me, doing various things, paying him just enough to give him a little sharp edge. Two years ago, when he got hungry enough, I set him up in the auto transport bidness and had Waco use him as kind of a favor. After all, I was making Waco a lot of money on his real proppities; the least he could do was give my nephew some bidness."

"Bobby was your nephew?"

"That's what I told Waco."

"And you've been banking all your profits in Michigan?"

He raised his eyebrows. "You know about Michigan? Yeah, I was connected back there when I was younger. Nothing really this big, though. They was real impressed when I came to them with the idea."

"So the Detroit boys bankrolled this whole operation?"

"At first," he said. "Now I use my own money. Of course, I still give them a little taste. That's how I stay in bidness." He shook his head sadly, disappointed in me. "Damn, Milan, you're a bright guy. I'd druther have sold you a house than have to kill you."

"Me, too."

"Don't know what else to do. Can't have you tellin' what you know to everyone."

"You think I haven't told the police all this?"

He smiled some more. It was a disarming smile. "If you'd told 'em, you'd've told 'em yesterday, and they woulda been all over me by now. And you didn't tell 'em today because I've

240

been on your tail since you left home this morning. I'm clean with everybody. I got paperwork for the house rents and everything. They gonna try to nail Waco and not gonna get anywhere, and pretty soon it's gonna blow over and we'll be right back where we was. I'll back off for a while, and they'll have their Jamaican Task Force lookin' for boogies again, an' in about six months I'll just gear up with a new set of players. You wasted a lot of time, Milan, an' all you did was put me behind schedule."

"Sorry about that," I said.

"You're gonna be sorrier."

Quicker than I thought he could move, he swung the baseball bat at me one-handed. It smashed against my left bicep, numbing that whole side of my body, and I felt one of the nails slash through my clothes and gouge a little hunk out of my arm. The blow sent me staggering a few steps to the right. Luckily he had to reset himself before he could swing again.

"Hold still, Milan, and I'll make this as quick as I can," he said. The next one was two-handed and came down toward my head. I ducked out of the way, and the bat clanged against the steel tracks of the Thriller behind me.

I'd been lucky that time, but I was boxed in, my spine against the tracks, and Amboy standing between me and the nearest escape route. I moved toward the corner, not where I wanted to be but at the moment my only option. My arm throbbed. All the injuries I'd suffered two days before started to hurt more, and a wave of dizziness made the room swim. I knew that if I put my arms up to shield myself from his next swing, the impact would shatter them and I'd be helpless. I had to get away from him.

I turned away from the next blow, and it glanced across the middle of my back, the spikes again ripping through my clothes and tearing at my flesh. I could hear his heavy breathing behind me. I was moving along the slope of the tracks, and when I felt them across the back of my thighs I jumped upon them. At least now if he hit me again it wouldn't be in the head—he couldn't reach that high. I kicked out at him, but he moved out of the way.

"You got nowhere to go," he said, and swung at my legs. I

241

was able to turn around to protect my kneecap, but the bat crashed into the side of my calf with sickening force, my leg buckled under me, and I fell forward onto the tracks. I held onto the rails and tried to pull myself upward. The end of the bat jabbed into my ribs, luckily not on the side where I'd been shot, but still the pain jetted all the way through me, snatching at my breath. The blood drawn by the first swing was trickling down my arm and onto my hand, making the rail I clutched slippery.

I crawled forward, upward, toward the red roller coaster car, twisting away from another blow, which landed just beside my face and made the steel vibrate under my hand.

"Shit," Christmas said, and I heard him groan with the effort of a heavy set man exerting himself.

I looked over my shoulder. Christmas had heaved his bulk up onto the track and was starting up after me, one arm out to keep his balance, the other clutching the murderous bat. He was moving faster than I was on my hands and knees, and when he got within range he crashed the bat down on the back of my legs. I felt a nail go all the way into the fleshy part of my calf, and I couldn't believe the pain, but I mule-kicked back at him with one foot and felt it connect, and he grunted and slipped about seven feet backward down the track. I had to hang on to keep from backsliding too, pulling myself up with aching, traumatized arms.

I clambered higher, moving away from him. The various injuries to my body had merged into one big pulsing pain, and I could feel blood on me, warm and running. It seemed that if only I was able to reach the top of the tracks where the Thriller car waited, I would be safe. It was my ally-ally-oxen-free, that silly car where once I'd sat, hanging on, howling with excitement and delight at a world gone crazy with speed below me, and I dragged myself up laboriously toward the shimmering scarlet haven.

He was coming after me again, panting from the exertion. I was now about twelve feet off the ground, and the red car was nearly within reach. Calling into play the second effort I had learned so well in my football days, I propelled my body forward and upward and grabbed onto the front of the roller coaster car with one hand, pulling myself up, hanging on to the sissy bar. I swung my body around, the torn muscles in my side protesting at every move, and with my feet I kicked loose the wooden block from under the front wheels. As I felt the car begin to move I hauled myself up and into it head first, my legs up in the air.

After a few feet it picked up momentum, and I raised my head over the front just in time to see his shocked and terrified eyes behind his glasses as the juggernaut mowed into him. The heavy car, augmented by my not inconsiderable weight, smashed both his legs in the opposite direction from which they normally bent, and he fell backwards as it wedged them against the metal track. The baseball bat flew crazily into the air, clattering noisily against the wall before it fell, and the only other sound was of Christmas Amboy's screaming.

25

I GOT a different room at the hospital this time, but on the same floor and with the same nurse. A stroke of misadventure, if you want to look at it one way. The way I saw it, I was the most fortunate guy in the world. Massive contusions, multiple stitches in my arm and legs and back, and a giant tetanus shot to make sure it didn't get any worse than that. But I remembered Deshon. And Deshon's dog. And I counted myself Mr. Lucky.

They kept me two days for observation this time. Still not long enough to make me like lime Jello. And I had a lot of visitors again, some of the same ones and some others. They were all announced with grave formality by my nurse. Milan Jr. came back and brought his mother with him, and the way she clucked and fussed over me I almost forgot I hadn't been married to her for a long while.

Marko returned as well on the second day of my lying-in to tell me that Christmas Amboy had his right leg amputated above the knee and was in federal custody, and that the prospect of spending many Yuletides yet to come doing his Christmas shtick for the appreciative audiences in his cell block was making him sing like a bird, songs that had nothing to do with wassail and decking the halls. Apparently Urbancek the Junior G-Man was going to forget how pissed off he was at me, because he was now taking credit for the big drug bust, and that made him a hero in the hallowed halls where he normally stood around posing in his tight suit, and Ingeldinger had simply run his hands through his nonexistent hair and said "Son of a *bitch!*" and hadn't mentioned my name again. Marko also said he'd talked to Matt Baznik, and Paulie had agreed to go to a drug rehab center on the West Side, ten days living in and twice weekly visits after that, and that Matt's city employee's health plan would pay for it.

Rudy Dolsak dropped by, as did Milan Jr.'s orthodontist, my old school chum Alex Cerne.

And Ed Stahl stayed for a long while, sitting on the edge of the bed with his tape recorder running, and that time I did all the talking.

The biggest surprise walked in wearing a cowboy hat and hand-tooled elkskin boots and looking just like he does on his television commercials, to thank me for the great job I'd done. Before he departed, he told me anytime I wanted to buy a new car he'd sell me one at cost. And then he pulled out a roll of bills and left it on the blanket for services rendered. He probably would have tucked them into my pocket, but the hospital johnny I was wearing at the time didn't have any pockets. I felt like a high-priced hooker. Later I counted it, just out of curiosity. There were thirty one-hundred-dollar bills. That wouldn't begin to pay the medical costs; it was a good thing I carried insurance.

After they released me from the hospital and sent me home, I didn't go out much for a while. It hurt to move around, for one thing. For another, I didn't have anyplace to go. I caught up on a lot of reading. I watched TV shows I hadn't even known were on the air before and discovered I hadn't been missing much. Thanksgiving dinner came frozen in a package, and I ate it alone. I explored brand new dimensions of napping.

I rarely answered the phone but kept my machine on so I could monitor the calls. If it was Milan Jr. or Stephen, I'd pick up the receiver and talk. If not, I wouldn't. Mary called once and told the tape she just wanted to know if I was all right. I didn't answer or call back, and after she hung up I erased the tape and reset the machine. I couldn't think of anything I wanted to say to her.

Waco Morgan's money, including the first five hundred he'd given me, was in my dresser drawer wadded up inside a rolled pair of socks I hardly ever wore. I don't know why I didn't deposit it. It somehow didn't feel right to me. It's not that I hadn't earned it, I just hadn't earned it from Waco Morgan.

The Monday after Thanksgiving I was sitting in my den watching an old movie starring Audie Murphy, which tells you how far I'd dropped out of things, and I got to thinking about Waco and his plans for brokering power before the next election, and the money seemed a tangible and unwelcome presence in the apartment. I made a decision.

I switched off Audie Murphy just before his final face-down with Lyle Bettger, went into the bedroom, and took the money from the rolled-up green socks. I removed five of the C notes, put them back in the drawer, and put the rest in the pocket of my corduroy slacks. I slipped on a cable-knit sweater and my ski parka, which after the destruction of my car coat and my trench coat was my only cold-weather outergear, and went down to my car.

I found her not too far from where I'd discovered her the last time, holding up the side of a wall on Euclid Avenue. I got out of the car and walked over to her. She didn't notice me until I was practically on top of her, so she couldn't run.

"There's nothing to be scared of, Denise," I said. "No one wants to hurt you."

"Whatchoo want, Myron?" she said. She was edging away from me along the wall. The marks on her face from Drago's beating were almost gone.

"I want to give you something."

The suspicion bristled. "What?"

I pulled the roll of bills out of my pocket. "This," I said.

Her eyes widened and shone, but she made no move to reach for the money. "What for?"

"Because I think you're a good kid who needs a break."

"Where you get dis, mon?"

I shrugged. "I'm rich," I said.

Her hand went out toward me, then she pulled it back. "What I got to do for dis?"

"Come with me to the bus station," I said. "Buy a ticket to Cincinnati or someplace. One way. Then get on the bus and don't come back." Puzzlement clouded her features. "Cleveland isn't such a healthy town for you anymore. I think you'll like Cincinnati better." I can't imagine anyone liking Cincinnati better than Cleveland, but in my business you tell lots of lies.

I said, "There's three thousand dollars here, Denise. Don't be a chump. Take it."

She took it, and she took the deal. As I watched the southbound bus pull out, I realized that I probably hadn't done her all that big a favor. She'd be back on the streets screwing for crack as soon as she hit Cincinnati. But Christmas Amboy's sphere of influence wasn't limited to Javier and Ricardo and Bobby and Joan Bennett, and she'd probably stay alive a lot longer in some other venue.

I went to a tavern across the street from the bus station and had a beer. It was noisy and smoky and the TV programs were just as mindless as they'd been at home, but at least there were people here, there was a bit of life.

I drove back toward University Circle on Euclid Avenue, just because it was the quickest route from downtown. I wasn't looking for anyone. It was sheer happenstance that I found him.

It was Drago, and I wasn't particularly surprised to see him. Where better for a vice cop to hang out than the street where most of the hookers ply their trade? His unmarked car was at the curb with its lights off, and he had a young white girl in a pink miniskirt, lemon-colored panty hose, and a fake-rabbit-fur jacket bent over with her palms against the wall, and he was searching her none too gently.

I pulled over. He was too busy feeling the girl up to notice me. I watched, holding my breath, as he turned her around and slammed her against the brick wall, her jacket knotted in his fist. He put his face very close to her and growled something. She couldn't have been more than fifteen years old, slack-jawed and dough-faced, and from where I sat I could read her terror. Even in repose Drago was pretty frightening to look upon, and he wasn't in repose now. His mouth was snarling, his black eyes two glittering dots, and the cruelty on his downturned mouth was enough to turn my stomach.

He yanked her away from the wall and roughly shoved her ahead of him, heading for the entrance to a small dark alleyway at the side of the building. Just before they disappeared from my sight he slammed the heel of his hand into the middle of her back so hard she almost toppled over forward. She staggered, reaching out to the brick wall beside her to keep her feet.

Then they disappeared into the shadows.

I left my car engine running and got out, taking care not to slam the door. My sneakers hardly made a sound against the damp pavement as I rounded the corner of the building and went into the alley, staying close to the wall.

About twenty feet in there was a doorway, probably a delivery entrance. Drago was standing in it, and the little girl was on her knees in front of him, a small puddle soaking her lemon tights, and her blond hair was wrapped around his clenched fist. He'd dropped his pants and his boxer shorts were down around his huge thighs.

I raised my camera, and the flash captured both the surprise and the utter savagery on his face.

"Smile, Dragon," I said. "You're gonna love this picture."

And then I ran like hell. I knew he wouldn't follow me. It's tough to give chase when you're caught with your pants down.

LES ROBERTS

NO ONE writes about the tough streets of Cleveland like Les Roberts. And NO ONE knows those streets as well as Les Roberts' gritty private eye—Milan Jacovich.

PEPPER PIKE
Hours after a wealthy exec hires Milan Jacovich, the man vanishes. Now Jacovich is following a trail through Cleveland's poshest clubs and offices—right to the heart of the Midwest Mob.
_____ 92213-2 $3.95 U.S./$4.95 Can.

FULL CLEVELAND
When a luxury hotel buys ad space in a magazine scam, the Mob gets stung. Now someone's trying to sell Jacovich a bill of goods—and the sales pitch is murder.
_____ 92345-7 $3.95 U.S./$4.95 Can.

DEEP SHAKER
Somewhere between Merle Avenue and Shaker Heights, someone's trying to corner the drug market—and Jacovich will go to the wall to bring him down.
_____ 92795-9 $3.99 U.S./$4.99 Can.

MORE GREAT NEW CRIME NOVELS FROM ST. MARTIN'S PAPERBACKS!